Sugar Spells
J.M. Grosvalet

Sugar Spells

© 2025 by J.M. Grosvalet

All rights reserved.

Paperback ISBN: 979-8-9892880-4-5

Ebook ISBN: 979-8-9892880-3-8

Hardback ISBN: 979-8-9892880-5-2

First Edition: November, 2025

Cover Design by Julsiji Illustrations

Edited by Erin K. Larson-Burnett

*For the weary hearts, the hungry souls,
and anyone who's needed a story to curl up inside of.
May this one feel like home.*

Author's Note

Dear Reader,

Thank you for picking up *Sugar Spells*. This story is a strange little blend of sweetness and sorrow, with laughter and love layered in between. It's about grief and healing, about how two very different people (and one very stubborn cat) stumble their way toward something new—and I hope it gives you both comfort and delight.

In 2020, I lost my sister, Jessica. Her absence left a hollow I didn't know how to fill. But in that darkness, I found my words again. Writing became my way through the grief, a way of reaching for her, of holding on when everything else felt lost. Every book I write will always be because of her—every story shaped by the space she left behind.

You'll see reflections of that in Maude's journey—the guarded walls she hides behind, the way she resists joy even as it finds her, and the way love sneaks in anyway.

While the heart of this story is cozy and magical, it also lingers on themes of grief and mourning. These elements run deeply through the pages and may feel heavy or overwhelming at times. If that weight is too much right now, please be gentle with yourself. Stories will always wait until you're ready for them.

If you carry this book with you, I hope it makes you smile, makes you feel a little less alone, and maybe inspires you to believe in small magics again—whether that's in a perfectly brewed cup of tea, the warmth of bread fresh from the oven, or the simple kindness of someone choosing to stay.

Most of all, I hope that for anyone carrying their own grief, this story feels like a companion rather than a reminder—that it shows healing is rarely tidy, but it can be tender. That laughter, love, and even a little magic can still exist alongside loss.

With all my love and gratitude,

J.M. Grosvalet

Mistwood Hills
Duskmire peaks
Chapel's ruins
Sugar high bakery
Silver thistle pub
Wyvern fountain
Blightbend way
Elixir emporium
The lantern ward
Drift markets
Char&chime
Maude's cottege

One

Maude Harrow hated most things, but above all, she *detested* the perpetually cheerful.

It wasn't just that it was annoying; it felt incredibly insincere. What were people so happy about anyway? Hadn't they ever heard of existential dread?

The early sun filtered through the tree canopy overhead, catching her burnished honey locks and setting them ablaze with light—a beacon she felt only drew more attention. She tugged her hood further over her face, her eyes narrowing to slits as yet another grinning idiot bounced past her on the street.

Unfortunately, every morning, Maude's path to work forced her through the vibrant chaos of Market Square—the beating heart of Mistwood Hills, though Maude thought it more of an ulcer. Dodging people wasn't an option, not with the place swarming like a beehive.

The village of Mistwood echoed with the unwanted sounds of morning greetings and cheerful banter, vendors shouting prices for frost-glazed pears and crystal-bright lanterns. An apprentice witch shouted about spell-steeped tea that *"banished hangovers"* as a copper pipe hissed overhead and a kettle cart belched fragrant steam.

This daily parade of enthusiasm was the worst part of her morning. How anyone could maintain such incessant cheer in a world where coffee sometimes ran out and people insisted on talking before ten a.m. was beyond her. Every overly bright *"Good morning!"* felt like a personal challenge to her commitment to realism—or, as her overly optimistic neighbor, Oliver Hale, liked to call it, *pessimism.*

But really, if expecting the worst and taking grim satisfaction in being right made her a pessimist, then so be it.

Maude continued her march down the street toward her workplace, the comfort of her dark, quiet apothecary awaiting her on Blightbend Way. At twenty-two, most people were chasing apprenticeships or slipping into marriages arranged by parents with too much time and coin. Maude, of course, had instead inherited a crumbling business and a permanent scowl.

Her shop, *The Elixir Emporium*, nestled snugly between an ominously quiet bookstore that sold ancient grimoires and a dimly lit curiosities shop, where jars of pickled dragon toes and phoenix feathers lined the dusty shelves.

She had a soft spot for the crooked street. Blightbend was the underbelly of Mistwood Hills, the shadowy counterpart to the sunnier streets elsewhere. If Market Square was a cheerful smile, Blightbend Way was the sly grin of someone with secrets.

While the rest of Mistwood Hills basked in quaint, postcard-perfect charm with its bustling marts and neatly trimmed hedges, Blightbend Way embraced the darkness. It was a part of town that most people avoided after dark, which made it the best part, in her opinion. It was a place where one could revel in their brooding solitude or explore the darker sides of magic without judgmental stares. The lane embraced her—the chill in the air, the whispers around corners, the sense that anything could be bought or sold for the right price.

Here, smiles were rare and meaningful, and everyone understood the value of a good sneer.

And to Maude, it was perfect.

She sensed him before he spoke, the familiar, annoyingly comfortable energy that meant one thing: Oli was near.

"Coffee," was all he said, his grin cat-like as he fell into step beside her, thrusting a steaming cup into her hands. His green velvet coat swirled dramatically with the movement, the gold stitching at the cuffs probably more costly than Maude's entire rent. He called it flair; she called it *asking to be mugged*.

"You are my favorite today," she admitted begrudgingly, the warmth from the cup seeping into her stiff fingers.

His pout was immediate. "Not every day?"

Maude took a sip to hide a reluctant smile. "Don't get greedy, Oli."

"I thought being greedy was part of the charm you fell for," he quipped, a playful glint in his eyes. His hair, a dark mess of tousled waves, fell carelessly over his forehead, giving him a look of casual disarray that somehow only enhanced his allure. Even now, as he matched Maude's pace, there was an effortless charm about him, the kind that drew people in and made them want to stay.

"No, it was definitely your dubious morals that solidified our friendship."

Oli snorted, leaned in closer, and kissed the top of her head. "And I wouldn't have it any other way."

When they left the square behind, Oliver linked arms with her and steered them onto the shadowy stretch of Blightbend Way. "*So*," he began, his tone too casual to be trusted, "are we ever going to talk about what happened the other night?"

Maude sighed; her gaze fixed ahead as if ignoring him might make the conversation vanish.

It didn't.

"Why are you so insistent that I relive that painful moment?"

"Because it was *hilarious*?"

The memory surfaced before she could shove it back down.

The market had been too loud, too crowded, the kind of place that frayed her nerves on the best of days. She'd been trying to find the rare herb Oliver wanted—*moonleaf*, or *something equally pointless and overpriced*—when the man appeared. Handsome in a way that felt deliberate, like he'd been practicing his smolder in reflective surfaces. She hadn't even registered him until he was in her space, leaning close, his voice dripping with charm as he tried to catch her attention.

She'd taken one step back. Then another. He hadn't taken the hint.

Her pulse had spiked, irritation morphing into something volatile. She hadn't thought twice about the words spilling from her lips. The spell had been small—enough to make his shoes root to the cobblestones, his mouth snapping shut mid-sentence. The shock on his face had been worth it. His polished confidence had cracked, and she hissed, "This is the worst ambush I've *ever* seen. Do better."

The man had sputtered, trying to move, but the spell held. Oliver had walked up right as she'd snapped her fingers, releasing him with a roll of her eyes and a pointed "Learn from this. You're welcome."

Oliver had laughed the entire way home. Maude hadn't realized the man was trying to flirt with her.

She shot Oli a sidelong glance now as he tipped his head back, his mirth echoing down the dark lane. "Maybe if you went out with me more, you'd learn how to interact with people and eventually be able to get someone to toss your—"

"*Don't* finish that sentence."

His mouth twitched, but his eyes stayed earnest. "I'm only trying to help. I know how lonely—and angry—you've been since Bailey died. I just wish you had someone to do the everyday shit with, you know?"

"Isn't that why I have you?" Maude's response was dry, her voice carrying a hint of sarcasm that didn't quite mask the underlying truth.

Oli's smile was quick. "You do. Always."

She looked away, grasping for safer ground. "So, are you going to flash your ridiculous riches with the usual over-the-top show on Samhain?"

Oliver, blessed with a fortune that made kings envious, merely chuckled. His family, after all, owned half of Mistwood Hills. Each year, they transformed the festival into a spectacle of bonfires, lavish decorations, and magical enchantments that lit up the night sky and the faces of the townspeople alike. It was a grand display, yes, but even Maude had to admit, albeit grudgingly, that there was a warmth to it, a generosity that went beyond mere showmanship.

Oli's family didn't just parade their wealth; they poured it back into the town. Crumbling shops and ancient homes were restored to their former glory, not to mention the charities that thrived under their patronage. It was hard to hold a grudge against the opulence when it was wielded with such care.

He watched her closely, his eyes twinkling with amusement. "You know I can't resist making a spectacle on the Day of the Dead. This year, I've got a particular shop in mind to highlight." His eyebrows waggled suggestively.

"Absolutely not. The Emporium has managed perfectly well without your benevolence. Besides, Bailey would have despised it."

"Yes, but Bailey isn't here anymore to charm the customers with his affable nature," he responded gently.

Her eyes narrowed, a dark glint of determination flaring up. "Whatever. It's not like I need a bunch of glitter-obsessed optimists buying pumpkin spice potions, anyway. I'll just find some new customers—ones who actually appreciate the dark, twisted charm of my shop."

"So, what you're saying is, the *entirety* of Mistwood Hills is off the table? Might as well pack up and start pitching your potions overseas, Maude. It's looking pretty grim around here."

She rolled her eyes as they approached the Elixir Emporium, the familiar sign creaking slightly in the breeze. "I do have customers—real ones."

He snorted. "Mrs. Haddingham is your *one* regular, and she's more of a decoration at this point."

As if summoned, Mrs. Haddingham shuffled into view—black shawl, iron keys clinking at her hip, lace cap wilted and flat as ever. She stopped before the shop, her presence eerie as a graveyard fog.

"The woman is practically a part of the inventory, buying her daily thyme. Honestly, why doesn't she just grow it herself?" Oli murmured, half-exasperated, half-amused.

"Shh, let's not inspire self-sufficiency now." She smoothed her skirt before turning. "Mrs. Haddingham." Maude put on her best *I'm barely tolerating you* face, offering a nod that was more obligatory than welcoming.

The old woman mirrored the gesture, her face as stoic and unreadable as a gargoyle's.

Perfect.

No unnecessary pleasantries or painful small talk, just the mutual acknowledgment of existence before ten a.m.

If only Oli could grasp that concept.

Maude pushed open the door, its loud creak like a groan of protest, the bottom scraping against the uneven wooden floor—a reminder of yet another repair she'd put off. Inside, the air smelled of herbs and old spells. Her hand skimmed the doorway, pausing on the shallow grooves Bailey had carved there years ago. *"Runes for protection,"* he'd said. They still thrummed faintly under her fingertips, steady as a pulse. She touched them every time she entered, like muscle memory—half comfort, half punishment.

With a lazy wave of her hand, she conjured a dim glow, coaxing the candles and lanterns to life. The store flickered to a half-hearted warmth, like it was only participating out of obligation. She shuffled over to her worktable, dodging the clutter of her midnight brainstorm—or breakdown, depending on one's perspective. Bottles half-closed, herbs strewn around—this was the mess of someone who'd given up mid-spell. It looked like a pixie had thrown a tantrum. And honestly, she had been a split second away from one.

Tired and sad—*yeah*, she'd admit it, but only to herself and maybe a particularly nosy piece of furniture.

Maude let out a sigh that felt like it had been dredged up from her soul, surveying the mess that was a little too on the nose as a metaphor for her life right now.

She shrugged out of her coat and tossed it onto the nearest chair. Dark wool, practical and heavy with deep pockets—the kind made for stashing herbs, hex slips, and the occasional emergency dagger. Underneath, she wore a black knit sweater over a star-speckled skirt, boots clomping against the floorboards like punctuation.

A soft thud drew her attention to the shelf near the doorway, where Grim, her coal-dark cat, lounged like a self-appointed king. He stretched lazily, his topaz eyes narrowing as he gave Maude an unimpressed look. With a flick of his tail, he leapt down and sauntered toward Maude, weaving through her legs before leaping up onto the worktable.

"So, I'm guessing your attempt at conjuring eternal night over your garden gnome collection didn't go as planned?"

Maude looked up at Oli, a smirk playing at the corners of her mouth. "Why? Did the sun come up today?"

Oli laughed and leaned against the counter. "Speaking of unexpected daylight, there's a new bakery opening across the street. Thought you might want to know, considering it's going to be all sunshine and rainbows over there."

He watched closely for her reaction, and unfortunately, she gave him a rare display of emotion.

"*What?*"

Maude whirled around to peer out the dusty window.

How had she missed it?

The building across the street, which had been nothing more than a shadowed shell for years, was now alive with light and the curling smoke of an early morning start.

"A bakery?" Her tone was incredulous, almost offended.

"Yes, it's a place where people make bread."

Maude's hand shot out, smacking him lightly before she turned back to the window, her expression one of mock horror. "Bread? Like, for eating? What is this, suburbia?"

He rolled his eyes, fighting back a grin. "I guess even Blight-bend Way isn't immune to the charm of a good sourdough. It's the *yeast* we could do."

Maude turned slowly, her gaze lethal. "What did you do?"

Oli leaned in closer. "It's an infiltration, Maude. First, they bring the bread. Next thing you know, there are flower shops and pastel curtains everywhere."

"What. Did. You. Do."

Oli sighed, the playfulness fading as he straightened. "He came to me with a proposal—detailed, organized, the kind of plan you don't see every day. Said he'd only just arrived in town two weeks ago and wanted a chance to establish himself. So I extended him a loan. Fair terms. Enough to get his business off the ground." His tone was half-serious, half-resigned, as if he too was trying to convince himself of the potential upside. "Maybe it'll bring some light to this shadowy street."

Maude glared at him. "I take it back. You're not my favorite today. And maybe not ever again."

He opened his mouth to retort, no doubt something annoyingly witty, but Maude was already turning away, her attention snapping to Mrs. Haddingham, who was shuffling past the window.

"Find everything all right today?"

The old woman nodded silently, clutching her daily sprig of thyme like a lifeline.

"See?" Maude said, turning to Oli with a triumphant smirk. "Loyal customers."

Oli just shook his head. "One sprig of thyme a day. You'll soon be a mogul."

Two

It had been a week since *Sugar High Bakery* opened its aggressively cheerful doors, with its bricks slathered in pastel paint and windows permanently smeared with what looked like fake promises of sugar and starlight.

It was like getting punched in the face with a birthday cake.

Every morning, as Maude flipped the sign on her door to "*Open*," the stench of freshly baked bread and sickly sweet pastries assaulted the street, clashing with the earthy scents of her herbs and potions.

Thankfully, she'd managed to avoid the owner. She usually strolled into work at a leisurely nine a.m., and the overly enthusiastic baker across the street was already buzzing around his shop, doors wide open and looking welcoming, as if he'd been baking and being annoyingly chipper for hours.

She knew little about the man—only that he was blond, male, and unmistakably Oli's type. It was likely the sole reason Oli had betrayed her by granting him a loan.

He was probably the type to do push-ups while baking muffins and flashing a nauseatingly perfect smile. His cutesy shop would've fit better on Market Square, not Blightbend. No way he'd attract customers here.

Maude was practically counting down the minutes until his inevitable crash and burn.

She positioned her chair just right, ensuring a clear view of his shop, the "*Opening Day*" banner waving pathetically in the early autumn breeze.

Slowly, her shoulders sank.

Minutes. That's all it took for a line to appear in front of his shop the second he stepped outside, a tray of free samples in hand like some sort of pastry-pushing Pied Piper.

Where the hell are all these people coming from?

Maude bolted from her chair and dashed to her window, pressing her face against the glass to see crowds spilling over from Market Square. These people never wandered down Blightbend. The sneaky bastard must have put up a sign or something.

Mrs. Haddingham was shuffling down the street, and for a second, Maude felt a wave of relief.

Finally, something predictable.

But then, shockingly, the woman did a sudden about-face, lured by the intoxicating scent of cinnamon and cloves. *No!*

Maude watched in horror as Mrs. Haddingham drifted toward the bakery as if she was under some sort of spell, snagged a free sample, and actually smiled—*smiled!*—before disappearing inside.

Betrayal—thy name is pastry.

She shook her head, refusing to let the circus outside ruin her day. She had more important things to focus on—like the spell Bailey had left half-written on a piece of parchment before he died. It was the one thing she'd thrown herself into, the one thing she allowed herself to obsess over so she didn't have to face the crushing reality of how empty everything felt without him.

Maude turned from the window, shutting out the bustling bakery across the street. She slumped into her chair and unrolled the worn parchment for what felt like the millionth time, each word in Bailey's precise hand twisting her heart a little tighter.

Bailey had been a genius, easily the brightest wizard in all of

Mistwood Hills, and likely the entire realm. Why he'd ever settled in this sleepy village was beyond her, but she was eternally thankful. If he hadn't, he might never have stumbled upon her—might never have rescued her from the Wilds, and who knows who she might've ended up with.

Every few years, a wizard or witchling babe would emerge from the wilderness that surrounded Mistwood Hills, cloaked in moss and mud, speaking the language of the forest.

That was how Bailey found her—shivering and muttering beneath an elder tree like some swamp creature. He watched her for a while, as if to make sure she wasn't a goblin, and then, apparently deciding she was human enough, took her in.

Bailey had become everything to her. In his eyes, she wasn't a wild oddity but a treasure—a continuation of magic as old as the stars. Grumpy and eccentric, he often muttered about the *"good old days"* of magic as if they were lost love letters. He adopted her, and for years it was just the two of them, the quiet of his old house filled with the crackle of firewood and the scent of simmering potions.

But wizards don't live forever, no matter how many rejuvenation potions they down. He had passed, as all must, leaving her the keeper of all his worldly possessions: a crumbling apothecary on the outskirts of town and a house that felt too big without his grumbling echoing through the halls. She supposed she should feel sentimental about inheriting his possessions, but really, she just felt mildly inconvenienced and panicked by the responsibility of it all.

Now, she ran the apothecary, brewing potions that would make Bailey proud—or at least keep him from haunting her for messing it all up.

The shelves still smelled faintly of him, a mix of sandalwood and sage that lingered like a whisper in the air. It was fitting, really, for someone like her—rooted in the solitude of the outskirts, surrounded by relics of a man who had been as much of an oddity as she was.

Maude trailed a finger along the nearest shelf, dust smudging her skin. Her hand shook once before she stilled it, pressing her palm flat against the wood as if she could pin the ache in her chest there instead of letting it spill out. For a moment, it was easier to imagine Bailey stepping back into the room, muttering corrections over her shoulder.

But he wasn't here. And the spell waiting on the worktable didn't care how much she missed him.

It looked simple enough on paper, but she wasn't Bailey. Despite years of shadowing him, picking up his tricks, she hadn't quite mastered his wizard-level knack for wrapping up spells with a wild guess or whipping up antidotes from just a lick of potion.

The spell's runes curved the same way they had in the sabotage spell he'd crafted years ago to short out a magistrate's wards, only bent sideways, twisted toward something else. She felt the echo of it like a bruise in her memory. Sabotage, yes—but turned into...what?

It unsettled her—his last piece of work. Which was exactly why she was hell-bent on cracking it. Even if it bit back.

Maude spread out the ingredients on the counter: ironvine, blackthorn bark, sprigs of rosemary, bloodroot, yarrow, moondust caps—and, most importantly, shadowbell flowers. Bailey had figured out that much before he left the spell unfinished. Disruption, corrosion, collapse. But it was missing some crucial bits—like a couple of ingredients and maybe a line or two to wrap it up.

She spun around, snagged some bloodroot, and tossed in a few ethically sourced fairy wings for good measure, grinding them into her poultice. Just as she was getting into the groove, the door to her shop groaned open, the familiar scrape against the floor yanking her gaze away.

Her breath hitched as a sunny-haired giant strode into her shop, all broad shoulders and annoyingly handsome with an unfairly tan complexion that screamed, *"I spend my weekends at the beach."*

He scanned the room, and his gaze didn't so much as flicker at the shrunken heads dangling in the corner like twisted ornaments —making him either impressively brave or incredibly stupid.

"Can I help you?" Maude asked, drawing his attention from the bubbling cauldron, its fumes reeking of eternal regret—her own invention.

He turned and flashed her a dazzling smile. "Just came in to introduce myself. Name's Wesley Rivers. I opened a bakery across the street."

"Oh wow, I didn't even notice."

The corner of Wesley's lip twitched upwards, and he sauntered closer until only the worktable separated them. "Right. I wanted to say hi to my neighbor and give you a few of these." He set down a box tied with a red ribbon. Even covered, the scent of butter and lemon wafted through, obnoxiously pleasant.

Maude set her mortar down and finally looked up at him, her sea-green eyes locking onto his with an intensity that could wither plants.

"What is *that*?"

He looked momentarily confused, and she couldn't help but enjoy the way his face scrunched up. "Oh, it's what I whipped up for the shop this morning. Cardamom teacakes and lemon-curd shortbread."

"Sounds nauseating."

"Pardon?"

"Great. Sounds just *great*."

He stood there quietly for a moment before laughing outright in her face.

"What is so funny?" she snapped.

"Just—you, you're funny. Though I'm not sure what I expected coming into a shop like this," he said, his laughter subsiding into a chuckle.

"What's that supposed to mean?"

He held his hands up in mock surrender. "I don't mean to be rude. Just that I don't know why I expected anything other than what you're throwing at me from the woman who owns the scariest store in town."

"*My* store is scary? *Your* store is the one scaring away all of my customers!"

He glanced around her empty shop.

Maude bristled. "Well, maybe if your bakery didn't look like a unicorn threw up on it, my customers wouldn't be so distracted." She shot a glare toward the window, where the cheerful *Opening Day* banner fluttered.

Wesley snorted. "You never stopped to think that your lack of business has anything to do with..." He gestured vaguely toward her, his hand sweeping through the air as if to encapsulate her entire being as the issue.

She ground her teeth. "My clients prefer a harder touch."

"Right, because enforcing a *'no smiling'* policy is the key to business success," he quipped, the smirk on his face growing.

Maude's eyes narrowed into dangerous slits. "It sets the mood, *Wesley*. My shop, my rules. If people want glitter and rainbows, they can prance over to your Sunshine Bakery."

"Sugar High Bakery," he corrected, his grin fully formed.

"Whatever," she said, rolling her eyes.

Her boots clicked against the worn wooden floor as she strode toward the door. She flung it open, and the bell above chimed—a low, ghostly sound she'd picked because it reminded her of a horror show. "Run along; I'm sure you have dough to knead or egos to feed."

He took the hint and headed toward the exit, but not without tossing one last jab over his shoulder. "Already did both this morning. Unlike you, I'm productive before noon."

Maude slammed the door so hard the bell gave a startled, angry jangle before it snapped off its hook and clattered to the floor.

"If I have another one of those tonics, I'm going to hurl."

"That's the idea!" Oli sang out, tipping yet another one down Selene's throat.

Maude rolled her eyes. "Nothing says '*healing*' like projectile vomiting."

They were tucked into Maude's bedroom, a small, shadow-softened space. Thick quilts spilled over the narrow bed, their edges brushing a floor scattered with well-thumbed books and a stack of half-melted candles she kept meaning to replace. A chipped teacup sat on the dresser, holding quills instead of tea, and the faint smell of incense clung to the dark-painted walls no matter how often she aired the place out.

Not that Oli and Selene cared. They liked her little cottage on the edge of town and had a habit of inviting themselves over, no matter how many times she warned them about stray curses—or the half-feral house spirit that might live in the walls. Sometimes they stayed for days at a time, and more so in the six months since Bailey died. She thought that might be the reason, but some things were better left buried. Like bodies. *And* conversations about grief.

Selene groaned, fingers drumming weakly against the stool

where she sat slumped. A selkie-turned–healer's apprentice, she'd lived in Mistwood Hills for a year—long enough that her laughter and mischief felt woven into its streets. Her dark hair tumbled in loose, salt-tossed waves, framing a face quick to grin, eyes gleaming like tidepools hiding some secret catch.

She'd left the coastal cliffs of her kind behind, trading seal form and ocean home for legs and what she foolishly thought would be a quieter life. Instead, Oli swept her into his whirlwind —where *"healing"* often meant experimental potions and questionable choices. She had slipped into friendship with Maude and Oli as if it were the most natural thing in the world. Oli, of course, had never given Maude the choice. As children, she'd hexed his hair to his ankles just to shut him up. He'd worn it like a crown, laughing so hard he nearly choked, and paraded it for months until she gave up trying to shake him. He chipped at her walls one joke at a time, until tolerance became something closer to loyalty —to love. Selene's presence had been effortless by comparison, a tide that carried Maude along before she even realized she was drifting.

Maude shoved aside the clutter of bottles on her desk, hunting for a scrap of surface to set down the latest batch of tonics. Crates already lined the wall—tinctures, salves, poultices —most of them bound for the Lantern Ward, where Selene worked. They always needed more. And Maude didn't mind, so long as she could stack the boxes in neat rows and send them off with Selene under the convenient cloak of anonymity. No smiling healers gushing thanks. No forced pleasantries. Just her work, leaving quietly.

Tonight's additions were less noble: an absurd number of headache draughts for the town party Oli was throwing in a few hours.

Ever since Sugar High Bakery opened, her sales had plummeted. Oli's grand solution? A town party. Because nothing says "great marketing strategy" like forcing vendors to mingle under bad lighting with sticky-fingered kids wired on cupcakes.

He'd asked Maude to brew something "*exciting*" to showcase her "*talents*" and win back customers. So she gave the town exactly what it would need after a night of forced merriment: a cure for the splitting migraines they'd all be nursing by morning.

"It's not really healing, though, is it?" Selene managed, grimacing as she fought to keep the potion down. "It's more like… enhancing." She stared, starry-eyed, as her long ebony braid shimmered into a vivid shade of purple, her fingers twining through it in awe.

Oli threw his head back, laughter echoing through the bedroom as Maude's eyes widened in shock.

"*Seriously*, stop screwing with my potions!" Maude jabbed an elbow into his side, shoving him back. She bent over the cauldron meant for a simple headache remedy—yet instead of lavender and chamomile, a bizarre and decidedly unsuitable mix of firethorn berry and ghost orchid—and was that a hint of *moonleaf?*—assaulted her nose.

"Oli, you didn't."

His grin was wicked. "Oh, but I did."

Maude ran to the mirror, half-expecting some hideous transformation. But no—everything looked the same, except for one horrifying detail: she was *smiling*.

Smiling like a deranged peddler hawking miracle elixirs at a village fair.

She whirled on Oli, fury tangled with involuntary glee. "You son of a bitch!" she yelled, the words at odds with the wide, ridiculous grin splitting her face.

Oli and Selene tumbled off their stools into a heap on the floor as they clutched their sides, laughing uncontrollably.

"That really is *so* unnerving," he managed between bouts of laughter, wiping away tears.

"You look like a serial killer, Maude. It's cute," Selene said, pushing herself up off the floor.

"Please, narrate my downfall louder." Maude dug through her bag as if it were a matter of life and death, her hands aggressively searching for any ingredients that might reverse this, all while plotting a dark and fitting revenge on Oli.

"No, you don't," Oli said, catching her wrist. "You want more customers? Then listen—headache tonics won't cut it. You need fun, flash. What better draw than potions that change people's looks while they're smashed on Willerby's spirits and Daphne's herb-laced cookies?"

Maude yanked her wrist free. "No one's going to be doing that tonight except *you*, Oli. Some of us have jobs—and reputations. Standards. Not high ones, but still."

"You said you wanted my help, so let me help you." Oli cocked a brow. "If this isn't the massive, world-changing success I *know* it's going to be, we'll pivot. But for now, just trust me. Trust that I have your best interests at heart."

Maude stared at him, resisting the urge to roll her eyes so hard they'd exit her skull. He wasn't wrong—she needed help, and fast. But this felt like selling her soul, and not even for something worthwhile, like a pact with a shadow demon.

Times were changing. People didn't want to hex their neighbors anymore; they wanted selfie-worthy potions and novelty spells. If she didn't adapt, her shop would vanish into obscurity, just another relic of the past.

Bailey's legacy would wither with it.

Maude would rather walk into the sun than sell out. She just wished Bailey were here. At least he'd know how to make this garbage fire of a plan feel less soul-crushing.

Evening settled cool around them as Maude walked with Oli and Selene, the last threads of daylight fading while lanterns blinked awake along the lane. The town rose ahead, windows glowing like scattered embers, and the cottages they passed, with moss-covered roofs and ivy-draped walls, looked as though they'd been lifted from a fairy tale. Each had a brightly painted door—cobalt, emerald, or an aggressively cheerful sunset orange—often left ajar, as if to invite in neighbors or the occasional wandering charm.

The streets hummed with life: enchanted scarecrows kept watch over gardens, while self-stirring cauldrons clattered in kitchens. Idyllic at first glance. But Maude knew better. Magic wasn't charming. It was messy, chaotic, and almost always ended with someone begging her to fix their catastrophic mistakes for free.

As they neared Market Square, the cobblestones grew more uneven, and the sounds of merchants setting up stalls drifted toward them. Oli, as usual, was vibrating with the kind of over-caffeinated energy Maude could only describe as deeply suspicious. He was rambling about his "*big plans*" and "*turning everything around*," his voice bouncing off the ancient stone buildings.

Selene trailed beside them, her violet hair catching the lantern light like a crystal ball.

"Look, Maude!"

Maude squinted. At least fifty stalls crowded Market Square, but of course Oli's stood out like a peacock in a flock of pigeons.

He had gone completely over the top. The booth's shimmering fabrics practically screamed, *"Look at me!"* Twinkling enchanted lights framed the edges, and a gaudy spinning sign hung overhead, blaring *"Maude's Mystical Makeovers!"* in bold, glowing letters. Bottles of her potions and spellwork lined the counter in neat little rows, though only the mildest ones had made the cut—tonics for clear skin, potions for minor aches, a charm for slightly shinier hair.

Front and center, though, was the star attraction: a huge, glittering cauldron surrounded by golden jars of her newest concoction, proudly labeled *Shifter's Delight: Change Your Look, Change Your Luck!*

Maude didn't need to get closer to see the chaos—it was already in full swing. A line of customers snaked around the stall, coins clattering into the tin like a wishing well as people clutched their potions with giddy delight.

Oli ran behind the stall, beaming like he'd just invented magic itself. "It's not just a potion—it's a *lifestyle*," he announced dramatically, handing a bottle to a grinning customer.

Maude's cheeks ached, the muscles pulled taut in a grin that refused to budge. "Oh, perfect. My life's work reduced to a sideshow for impulsive drunks."

Selene tilted her head, studying the crowd with a serene smile. "I think they're quite enchanted. It's like watching a shoal of silverfish."

"You mean the silverfish living in my attic?"

Selene giggled. "Not *those* silverfish. Sea-silverfish. But look at them..." She gestured toward the growing line of customers, many already laughing and marveling at their magically altered appearances. "People are drawn to transformation—it's in their nature." Her gaze flicked to Maude. "Except you, of course. You'd rather haunt your apothecary than let anyone see you smile."

Maude shrugged. "Once you stop showing up, people stop expecting you to." She glanced at the crowd and sighed. "I'll admit, it's...something. They're happy, I guess. And Oli..." Her voice trailed off as she watched him chatting animatedly with another customer, his enthusiasm boundless and infectious.

"Sometimes people just need a little magic to remind them of who they might be," Selene said, her smile never faltering. "Even if it's just their eyebrows turning green for a night."

Maude rubbed at her temples. He had gone out of his way to help her, turning what could have been a humiliating disaster into something that actually seemed...fun. Not her kind of fun, but still. She'd been so wary of his endless schemes that she'd never stopped to consider the why. He didn't have to do any of this.

She glanced at Selene, her tone softer this time. "You're starting to sound like him."

Selene gave her a knowing smile. "Maybe he knows something we don't."

Maude turned back to the booth, watching as he poured his heart into every interaction. She didn't know if she'd ever match his energy—or his optimism—but for the first time, she allowed herself to wonder if maybe he was right.

"Man the stall, would you?" Maude said to Selene, though her eyes were fixed on Oli, who was already collecting money like a gremlin hoarding gold. "And keep an eye on him. If he starts making promises he can't keep, I am *not* cleaning up the fallout."

Selene blinked, her expression briefly flickering with what might have been exasperation. "Fine. But if he juggles potions, I'm letting him deal with the consequences. He could use the lesson."

"Fair," Maude muttered, tugging the strap of her bag higher on her shoulder.

Without waiting for more commentary, she turned on her heel and slipped away, heading for the woods. The cobblestones gave way to dirt, the cool evening air brushing against her face as the noise of the crowd faded behind her. Her cheeks burned, muscles aching from the relentless smile plastered on her face.

She needed this curse off *now*.

These woods were hers. Every twist in the path and every shadowed glade felt like an old friend, familiar from years of foraging for the rare ingredients that kept her shop alive. Not everything she ever needed grew here, but what she needed tonight was close at hand.

Her boots crunched over fallen leaves as she moved with purpose, scanning the underbrush until she spotted it—starlight thistle, its dusky purple petals curling like tiny fists.

Perfect.

Maude snapped a few off, careful to avoid the sap that could make her fingers numb for hours. Next, she found a patch of weeping sage nestled under a jagged rock. She crushed them between her fingers, releasing their sharp, almost metallic scent. The last piece was trickier—she needed water touched by moonlight.

She scoured the underbrush for ten minutes before she found a tiny, glistening spring. Maude dipped her hand into the cool water, scooping enough to fill the small flask she always carried.

With her supplies gathered, she found a flat clearing and grabbed a large rock. She closed her eyes and muttered a low incantation, her breath steady as she channeled her magic. The rock shimmered, its rough surface softening and reshaping until it became a small, lopsided cauldron.

Maude placed it on the ground, drew a circle of salt from her pouch around it, and snapped her fingers. A faint blue flame flickered to life beneath it, heating the water until it bubbled. One by one, she added the ingredients. The mixture hissed and spat, releasing a faint mist. She stirred it with a stick, muttering under her breath about Oli's idiocy.

When the potion turned a pale green, she reached out to dip her finger into the concoction, but the rustling of bushes nearby made her freeze.

A tall, broad man burst into the clearing, his jet-black hair sticking out at odd angles, a thick beard swallowing half his face. His wild eyes locked on hers, and for a split second they just stared. Then the bushes behind him rustled again, and his face drained of all color.

Before Maude could even process it, he *lunged* toward her.

She raised her stick in defense. "Listen, Bigfoot, I've had a *day*—"

"Quick," he blurted, panic dripping from every word. "I need you to pretend to be my girlfriend."

Maude froze, one eyebrow shooting skyward. "I'm sorry, what?"

"My girlfriend," he repeated, dragging a massive hand through his equally massive beard. "You're my girlfriend. Right now. Please."

Her eyes widened, the cursed grin still plastered on her face as a middle-aged woman stepped out of the bushes, her sharp gaze locking onto the stranger like a hawk on prey.

"There you are," the woman said, her tone as sweet as poisoned honey.

Maude turned, her stick still raised.

The man let out a casual laugh, though the strain in his voice exposed him. "Ah, you found me!" he said, sliding an arm around Maude's waist and yanking her to his side. She let out an indignant squeak as he pulled her closer. "My lady here summoned me—very urgent business."

The woman narrowed her eyes, clearly unimpressed. "This is your...lady?"

He dipped his head solemnly. "Yes. Like I told you, I am very much spoken for. Extremely. Happily so."

Maude sighed. "Oh, yes. Overjoyed." She jabbed his ribs with her elbow. "Couldn't be luckier."

His grip only tightened, and Maude turned her head to glare at him—just as he leaned down, aiming for her cheek. Their lips collided.

Maude's breath caught as his eyes widened in shock. He jerked back so fast it was a wonder he didn't snap his neck, then cleared his throat hard, as if that could erase the moment.

The older woman's shoulders sagged, reluctant acceptance settling over her. But as she turned to leave, she shot the man a sly, lingering smile. "Well," she drawled, voice low and suggestive. "If you ever tire of...that one, you know where to find me. I'll even let you call me mommy."

"Wow." Maude blinked, her grin somehow stretching wider. "That's horrifying."

The man coughed into his fist, gaze fixed anywhere but the woman. "Uh...noted."

He stayed rooted to the spot, stiff as a board, while she sashayed back into the bushes.

Maude patted his chest. "Congrats, lover boy. You survived."

His shoulders sagged, arm dropping from her like dead weight. "Saints, what the hell was that?"

"It's the beard," Maude said, not even looking at him. "Ladies go wild for it."

He laughed, running a hand through the offending facial hair. "Apparently, it didn't work on you."

Maude rolled her eyes as she turned back to her potion. "It takes a lot more than a beard to hold my attention."

With a quick spell, she conjured a small cup out of a fallen leaf, dipped it into her potion, and drank more than she probably should have. Warmth spread through her cheeks, and she felt her face finally relax, the cursed grin falling away into her preferred neutral, deadpan expression.

"Oh," the man said, gesturing toward the cup. "Let me get some of that."

Maude arched a brow but handed it over. He gulped down the serving without hesitation. Within seconds, his jet-black hair faded to blond, and his beard vanished completely.

Maude stared at him, horrified, as realization dawned. It was *him*.

The bakery bastard.

She shoved Wesley so hard he almost stumbled into the cauldron. "Why didn't you tell me it was you?!"

He grinned sheepishly, scratching at his now-bare jawline. "I dunno. Thought the beard might buy me some time."

Maude groaned, burying her face in her hands. "I cannot believe the guy who sells sugar-coated death traps to children kissed me."

"Well, technically, *you* kissed me, so."

Maude reached for her stick. "Start running."

He tilted his head, that infuriating grin still in place. "You seemed unusually pleasant tonight. I thought maybe that smile meant you'd finally warmed up to me."

"You *lying snake*. You knew I didn't know who you were."

His brows shot up. "Why the hostility? What have I ever done to you?"

Maude jabbed a finger at his chest. "You ruined my life!"

He blinked, incredulous. "I ruined your life by opening a bakery? Next to your shop? Do you *hear* yourself?"

She stormed off, stomping through the underbrush toward Market Square. "Leave me alone before I curse you."

Behind her, Wesley sighed but didn't follow.

"Enjoy being miserable!" he called after her, his voice thick with exasperation.

She flipped him off without breaking stride.

Four

Maude's cottage came into view at the end of a narrow road, its slanted roof and snarl of brambles giving it a lopsided, haphazard charm. The windows were dark, and the faint scent of damp earth hung in the air as she trudged up the uneven path.

The door creaked when it swung open, then slammed shut with a thud that echoed through the heavy stillness. Maude leaned back, chest tight, breath shallow.

She didn't know how to do this—how to be *normal*. How to act like she wasn't a walking disaster, barely holding it together since Bailey died. Not that she'd ever been good at normal; she wasn't the "smile and roll with it" type. But before, at least, she'd been functional.

Now it felt like every decent part of her—the parts that kept Oli and Selene in her life, that kept Bailey's shop running—was being buried alive beneath the suffocating weight of grief and rage.

Because she *was* angry. Angry that Bailey had the nerve to die. Angry that he'd left her to deal with the flaming wreckage of their life. Angry that every morning she had to drag herself out of bed and pretend she wasn't gutted—pretend she wasn't stitched together from the wrong pieces, trying to pass as the person she used to be.

But she wasn't. Not anymore.

That person was gone. Just like him.

And all these changes...it was too much. Too fast.

Her gaze drifted across the house, catching on the faint glow of the protective lines carved into the walls.

More of Bailey's runes.

He'd left them everywhere she might linger—etched into the beams above her bed, tucked into the doorframe at Oli's house, scattered in quiet corners in town—as if he could still watch over her when he wasn't there, guarding with the same steady care he'd once given her.

After Bailey had died, somehow the world had just...kept spinning. Shifting. It was almost like his death had been the catalyst, setting off a chain reaction of chaos. Part of her wondered if he was behind it somehow—like this was his big cosmic joke. *"Change, Maude. Grow, Maude."*

But she wasn't growing. She was drowning.

Maude scrubbed a hand down her face, muttering a curse under her breath.

"This is your fault, isn't it?" she said, glancing toward the ceiling like Bailey might hang out there, waiting for her to notice. "All these upheavals, all this...nonsense. You think this is what I needed? Because it's *not*." Her voice cracked on the last word, and she hated herself for it. With a shake of her head, she pushed off the door and trudged toward her bedroom.

Maude talked to Bailey a lot these days. Too much, probably. It made her look mad—but she didn't care. The quiet got to her otherwise, and sometimes it felt like he could actually hear her. Like if she said the right thing, he'd walk in from the back room, wipe his hands on his apron, and give her one of those looks that always felt like equal parts exasperation and fondness.

But he never did.

She flopped onto the bed with a groan, staring at the cracked ceiling above. "If you're up there, Bailey, I hope you're laughing. Because this? This is hell."

The cottage creaked again, but this time, it almost felt like an answer.

She turned her head on the pillow, her gaze snagging on the stack of overdue bills teetering at the edge of her desk. The sight made her stomach twist. With a long, slow sigh, she closed her eyes. Maybe tonight's madness would put a dent in some of those. But even if it did, how was she supposed to cover next month's bills on top of everything else she already owed?

A dull ache bloomed behind her eyes, and she cursed Oli under her breath for tampering with her headache potion. She could really use it right now.

Her teeth pressed into her bottom lip. Maybe he was right. Maybe if she wanted to keep Bailey's shop—and his house—she'd have to adapt, bend with the times. But even the thought felt suffocating, like burying another piece of herself.

Like another death.

A tear slipped down her cheek, and she didn't bother to wipe it away. When the groan of her bedroom door echoed softly, she kept her eyes shut. She didn't need to open them. The runes carved into the cottage made sure only one other soul besides hers could enter uninvited.

Oli slid beneath the blanket without ceremony, his warmth pressing against her side. She hated how instantly it calmed her, as if his very existence were a weighted blanket draped over her frayed nerves.

"I'm sorry, Maude," he said, voice softer than she was used to hearing. "I went overboard."

She sighed, letting her head fall against his shoulder. "You're just trying to help."

He pulled her closer, tucking her under his arm and resting his chin on the top of her head. "You made a boatload of money tonight. If this keeps up, I'm going to start expecting you to buy my coffee every morning."

Maude snorted. "Fine, but only if I get to hex anyone who cuts in line."

"Done," Oli said, squeezing her shoulder. "But if you do, at least make it something funny."

Maude shook her head, the tension in her chest easing just a little more.

"You're keeping the shop," Oli said firmly. "Whatever it takes, we'll figure it out."

Oliver had offered more times than Maude could count to help pay off her bills or fix up the house, but she refused every time. Too proud to accept his charity, just like Bailey had been. It was a stubborn streak she'd inherited, and if anything, she clung to it tighter now than ever.

"What about the bakery boy?"

"*What about* the bakery bastard?"

Oli burst out laughing. "He's nice, Maude. And his business is booming. Maybe do a Blightbend Way collaboration? You know, join forces, pool your talents. I'm sure he'd be up for it."

Maude turned her head to glare at him. "I see right through you, Oliver Hale. You *want* him. Let me guess—granting him that loan and loitering around my shop, hoping to catch his eye, hasn't worked yet?"

Oli gasped. "Excuse me, I do not *want* him. He's just nice. Full stop. Besides, he's clearly not my type."

"Yeah, sure. Whatever you say."

Oli settled back into the pillows. "Just think about it."

Maude didn't respond, only stared at the ceiling, listening to his breathing slow until he started snoring. Her mind raced. Oli *was* right about one thing—the bakery bastard's business was booming. His frosted monstrosities were scaring away her customers and turning Blightbend Way into a twee tourist trap. Maude didn't need to "evolve" or "adapt to the times." No, what she needed to do was destroy him. Wipe that smug, flour-dusted grin off his stupid, perfect face.

She smiled to herself, nudging closer to Oli as a calm settled over her. For the first time in weeks, she drifted off peacefully, dreaming of all the ways she could ruin him.

By the time the first light of dawn filtered through the crooked blinds of the Elixir Emporium, Maude's plan had crystallized into something deliciously wicked. As she wiped down the counters and rearranged jars of herbs, she turned the details over in her mind like a well-rehearsed script.

A spell—small, subtle, unassuming.

It wouldn't hurt anyone. Not *permanently*, at least. Just enough to nudge Wesley's bakery toward sabotage. The kind that would make customers wrinkle their noses and second-guess every bite.

She smirked, reaching for a bundle of dried mugwort and twisting the brittle stems in her hands. Slow and steady—that was the beauty of it. His business would crumble bit by bit until he had no choice but to pack up and leave Blightbend Way for good.

On the worktable before her, Bailey's old parchment lay pinned beneath a pestle, the half-finished scrawl catching the lanternlight. She traced the final, broken sigil with the edge of her nail, humming under her breath.

"Well," she muttered, "you won't mind if I finish it for you."

She'd seen him cast something similar once—a curse disguised as decay. A whisper of entropy, nothing more. Maude spread the ingredients across the counter, lining them up in neat little rows: ironvine, blackthorn bark, sprigs of rosemary, bloodroot, yarrow, moondust caps—and the shadowbell flowers, their petals still dark with dew. Those were his. The foundation.

The bones of the spell.

Then came her touches: a touch of nightshade to lure in the rats, belladonna to soften the wood, and just a drop of myrrh oil for that lingering note of decay. It was the kind of thing Bailey would have called "quiet sabotage."

Steam rose in thin, silvery ribbons as Maude measured each ingredient with a practiced hand. She crushed the yarrow between her palms, the scent sharp and clean, then scattered the shadow-bell petals across the surface. The potion caught instantly, shimmering like liquid dusk. Leaning over the parchment, she copied Bailey's runes along the rim of the cauldron, her chalk strokes clean but impatient. The last line—unfinished in his hand—she filled herself, twisting the rune just slightly, the way she imagined he would've. Her own flourish. Her own proof that she could do this too.

Maude could already picture the bakery bastard trying to fix the "mysterious" problems, blissfully unaware of the spell weaving itself into his walls. The thought made her lips curl into a smile—one that grew wider as she ground a handful of herbs into powder.

She paused, glancing out the window as the square stirred, the faint sounds of carts creaking and vendors setting up for the day reaching her ears. Her smile didn't falter as she muttered to herself, "Good luck baking your way out of *this*, Wesley."

Revenge, she decided, smelled faintly of smoke and resin, with just a hint of malicious glee.

She reached for a moondust cap, grinding the gnarled piece into powder between her fingers. The fine dust shimmered in the air before falling into the cauldron, where the liquid darkened to a murky gray. The cauldron began to hum. Softly at first, a low vibration she felt in her fingertips. Maude frowned and gave the mixture another slow stir. The color deepened from gray to violet, then to a shimmering gold that caught the light like sunlight on oil.

"That's... different," she muttered.

The hum grew louder. The parchment quivered against the counter, the ink glowing faintly. Her stomach turned cold.

"Wait—"

The potion flared and the brew boiled over, spilling across the counter and onto the floor.

"Shit." Maude staggered back as the light intensified. The hum split into a crack, and before she could move, a pulse of magic burst outward, rippling through the shop like a wave.

The floor pitched beneath her. Shelves rattled violently, jars shattered, and books tumbled in a chaotic cascade. Maude lost her footing and hit the ground hard, the breath jolted from her lungs. The walls shimmered like water around her, bending and warping as if the entire shop were being rewritten.

Then, the surge stopped.

Silence pressed in, broken only by the faint hiss of the cauldron, its contents collapsed into an iridescent sludge. Maude stayed sprawled on the floor, chest heaving, palms stinging where she'd caught herself.

That's when the smell hit her.

Sugar.

Overwhelmingly sweet, cloying—so thick in the air it made her stomach turn. Her eyes widened, and she scrambled upright, heart hammering.

The shop had changed.

Her dark, brooding sanctuary of potions had been horrifically fused into something unholy—neither hers nor his, but both. Shadowed shelves gave way to pastel trim. Her jars of herbs sat beside trays of glittering cupcakes.

The Elixir Emporium and Sugar High Bakery had become one.

Maude's breath quickened as her gaze darted around the room. The smell of lavender and damp wood fought desperately against the saccharine aroma of cinnamon rolls. The air felt... confused, like it didn't know what it was supposed to be.

The counter she'd been leaning on had transformed, the rustic wood of her workspace now clashing violently with the polished marble of his. Her cauldron had somehow fused with his massive mixer, the two machines grotesquely intertwined, gears and enchanted runes spinning together in a chaotic union. Even the walls had changed. Where her shelves had once displayed neat rows of tonics, tinctures, and bottled charms, they now curved into racks of baked goods—tarts stacked in pastel towers, truffles dusted in edible gold, and bread loaves piled high. Her small, cracked window was gone, replaced with his massive display case, now stuffed with a horrifying blend of cursed trinkets and cheerful, frosted madness.

And then she spotted him.

Wesley stood beneath the row of shrunken heads that used to dangle ominously from her rafters. Now they were strung together with pastel ribbons, swaying gently like some grotesque parody of party décor. His mouth hung open as he surveyed the shop.

"What did you do?" Wesley's voice broke through the suffocating silence.

"This is not real," Maude muttered, dragging a hand down her face.

"Unfortunately for both of us, it looks very real," he said as his eyes flicked to the cauldron-mixer hybrid.

Curiosity—or stupidity—drove him closer. He peered inside the warped contraption, his brow furrowing as he noticed the sheen on the potion. It had an almost living quality, the same shimmering film that now coated the walls, the counters, and every horrifyingly fused object in what used to be their separate stores.

Realization flickered across his face, and he spun toward her, his expression a mix of disbelief and exasperation. "What exactly were you trying to do here? Open a portal to hell?"

Maude rolled her eyes. "Don't be ridiculous. Hell is more organized than this."

He looked at her like she had grown two heads.

She sighed. "It's just a miscast spell. I can fix it."

"Fix it?" Wesley snapped. "Do you know how long it takes to laminate dough? Of course you don't." His muttering picked up as his gaze swept the carnage. "Weeks of work—profit margins shot to hell..." He cut himself off with another exhale, shaking his head.

After a beat, he turned and walked out, jaw tight. Maude hesitated, then followed—only to have her breath catch in her throat the moment she stepped outside.

She looked across the street to where Wesley's shop used to be. An empty lot. Not a single trace of *Sugar High Bakery* remained —no pink awning, no sign, not even a crumb. Just vacant air, as if the place had never existed at all.

Her stomach twisted. *How in the hell did this happen?*

She turned back to the building behind her. The fusion she'd seen inside hadn't been an illusion. It was an abomination. Half Sugar High Bakery, half Elixir Emporium—the left side gleamed with his obnoxious pastel colors and giant, swirling lollipops in the window, while the right side stayed dark and familiar, jars of dried herbs and faintly glowing vials still intact. The dividing line wasn't even clean—it was jagged and haphazard, as if the building itself couldn't decide which identity to commit to.

"Must've been a powerful spell," Wesley said, his tone clipped as he stared at the monstrosity.

Maude sighed, pinching the bridge of her nose. "Or a stupid one. I must've botched one of Bailey's runes."

"Bailey?" Wesley turned to her, his brow furrowed. "Does he work for you? Maybe he can help us out."

"*Bailey* is dead."

He flinched, his face paling. "Shit. Sorry."

The reaction was everything she'd wanted—to unnerve him, to make him feel bad. And it worked. But the way his expression twisted with genuine shame hit harder than she expected, knocking the satisfaction clean out of her.

"It's fine," she muttered, looking away. "Forget it."

For once, Wesley didn't argue. He just nodded, then turned suddenly and strode for the narrow stairway that climbed the building's side. Maude stiffened, realizing with a start what he was doing—checking his apartment. His *home*. The thought struck her sideways. She'd never thought of it that way before, and the realization unsettled something deep in her.

A window screeched open above. "Still intact!" Wesley called down. "Well... mostly. Pantry's sprouting loaves like weeds, and one of your potion jars has claimed my nightstand, but the bed survived."

Her breath left her in a shaky rush. Saints, she really had gone too far. She hadn't meant to ruin his life—just rattle it a little—maybe drive his business off Blightbend Way and into Market Square where he belonged—not wreck the place he lived. Watching him lean out that window, hair rumpled, voice still light despite everything, guilt pooled low in her chest.

She folded her arms, forcing her expression into something neutral until he disappeared back inside. Moments later he came down the steps, jaw set tighter than before, hands shoved into his pockets as he took his place beside her again, surveying the cursed storefront.

"So, what do we do?" he asked, glancing at her out of the corner of his eye.

"*We* do nothing. You sit there, look pretty, and in an hour, you'll be back to clogging arteries and handing out early-onset diabetes like it's your life's purpose."

Wesley cocked a brow. "You think I'm pretty?"

"Shut up and let me work."

Five

It did not take an hour.

In fact, several had passed, and all Maude had to show for it was a sheen of sweat dripping down her forehead.

She leaned over the cauldron-mixer abomination, her jaw clenched as she stirred furiously. Why wasn't this working? She'd tried everything—isolating the original hex's core signature and identifying the threads of intent laced within it. But when she tried to reverse the flow of energy, the spell simply absorbed her counter-charm, reinforcing itself instead of breaking down.

And to make matters worse, behind her, Wesley hummed. Some nameless little tune, probably one of those tavern songs. She ground her teeth, ignored him, and moved on to Bailey's potion. Forcing back panic, she began carefully deconstructing its properties, mapping how they might have interacted with the shadowbell.

The shadowbell, she discovered, functioned as a catalyst—amplifying and blending the magical frequencies of her hex with Bailey's lingering intent. Even after she introduced stabilizers—dried ironwood bark and a few drops of binding solvent—the merged energies refused to hold, lurching unpredictably whenever she applied counter-magic.

Finally, she resorted to a neutralizing charm, meticulously layering opposing elements: iron shavings for warding, ground yarrow root for purification, and distilled moonlight to weaken the binding threads. Yet, instead of dissipating, the spell seemed to adapt, spreading its influence further into the shop with each attempt, as if it were feeding on her efforts.

Maude's grip on the stirrer tightened as she peered into the cauldron. The liquid churned in unnatural patterns, its surface rippling—a clear sign of a spell caught in self-perpetuating stasis. The logic of it infuriated her. A spell, even a hybrid one, shouldn't be this impervious to countermeasures.

The walls bore faint traces of enchanted residue—magic actively reinforcing itself. Worst of all, her ingredients were now nearly all compromised. Herbs that should smell earthy and bitter reeked faintly of buttercream.

Her chest tightened as she gripped the stirrer harder, her eyes burning with frustration. Finally, she snapped, slamming it down on the counter with a loud crack.

"Fuck!" Maude screamed, her voice echoing through the warped shop as her chest heaved.

Movement outside caught her eye, and she glanced up to find Wesley standing by the window.

"There's more of them," he said, his voice caught between amusement and alarm as he gestured to the street.

Maude shoved the sweat-soaked hair off her forehead. "Well, shoo them away again!"

"I *tried*," Wesley shot back, throwing up his hands. "Apparently, telling people to leave just makes them more curious."

She growled, rubbing her eyes. "That's it. I can't work here anymore."

Without a second thought, she waved her hand over the cauldron-mixer, banishing hours of effort with a flick. She stomped into the back room, shoving aside a dried frog leg inexplicably coated in fondant as she snatched up her gathering bag and headed for the back door.

"Where are you going?" Wesley's voice called from behind her.

She didn't bother slowing down. "Out, obviously."

"You can't just leave my store like this!" he said, catching up to her as she reached for the door handle. "I have hours of prep to do! There's a catered party tomorrow night that I need to—"

Maude snorted, turning to glare at him. "Yeah, that's not happening." She gestured wildly at the shop. "Look around, bakery bastard. Unless you're planning to serve cursed croissants, you're out of luck."

She shoved the door open, but Wesley stepped in front of her, blocking her path.

"Get out of my way."

He took a step back, running a hand through his hair in frustration. "What is wrong with you? *You* did this. And instead of owning it, you've been acting like it's *my* fault. Promises to fix it have gone nowhere, and it's obvious nothing's working. I need this resolved, or—"

"Or what, Wesley?" Maude cut in, her voice dripping with venom as she stepped closer. "You'll cry? Post an angry little note in your window about how the big bad witch ruined your perfect frosting factory?"

Wesley's mouth opened, then closed, his expression torn between outrage and incredulity.

Maude smirked, pushing past him with a dramatic flick of her hair. "Thought so," she said, letting the door slam shut behind her.

Maude was halfway to Oliver's stables when the sound of footsteps behind her broke through the quiet. The night air clung damp and cool, carrying the sour tang of hay and horse musk.

Lanterns swung lazily from posts along the fence line, their glow carving crooked shadows across the path.

Her heart spiked, a cold twinge of irritation shooting through her chest. She didn't need to look back; she already knew who it was. Grinding her teeth, she quickened her pace, the rhythmic crunch of her boots against the gravel matching her rising frustration.

The footsteps followed, closing the distance.

Reaching the gate at the edge of Oli's property—a broad, wrought-iron thing with decorative scrollwork and a gleaming brass latch—Maude didn't hesitate. She spun, gripped the cold metal with both hands, and shoved it shut with a loud crack—just as Wesley's face appeared on the other side.

The gate slammed into him with a satisfying thud. He stumbled back, clutching his nose.

"Really?" he bit out, glaring over the top.

"This is private property." Maude crossed her arms.

Wesley straightened on the other side, cheeks flushed from the chase, ash-blond hair a windswept mess. His chest still heaved as he stepped closer, eyes locking on hers. The insufferable man was at least three heads taller than her. She did not appreciate the way he loomed.

"Look," he said, his words low, clipped, and cold, "I get it. You don't care about my shop, my life, or the royal fuckery you've dumped on me. But I want to help. This mess is just as much my problem as it is yours, and I need it fixed. Stop fighting me. It's a simple request, and frankly, not a crazy one."

Maude's jaw tightened, a sudden stab of pain shooting down her neck from grinding her teeth so hard. She didn't want his help. She didn't *need* his help. She'd never worked with anyone besides Bailey, and she wasn't about to start now.

But...he wasn't wrong.

As much as she hated to admit it, this was her fault. She'd set out to sabotage his shop, and she'd succeeded—spectacularly. Still, she hesitated, eyes narrowing as she studied him. *He hadn't ruined her life. He'd just walked into it and upended the quiet, predictable misery she'd made peace with.* She didn't hate him for what he'd done. She hated him for what he'd stirred awake.

She crossed her arms. *Fine. Let him help.* If that's what he wanted, allowing him to "*help*" would only remind him how much he should hate her—and everyone else on Blightbend Way.

"Fine, but if you get in my way—"

"I won't," he said, grabbing the gate and pushing it open with more force than necessary. "Contrary to what you might think, I'm not an idiot."

"Wow. Inspiring."

She didn't bother looking back as she stalked away.

Oli's stables came into view, and from the nearest stall a familiar head poked out—a gray braid thick as rope. Sylvie leaned against the door, sleeves rolled up, bits of straw clinging to her skirt. Her face was lined but not unkind, her eyes gleaming with the mischief of someone who collected gossip the way others hoarded coins.

"Well, if it isn't Maudie Harrow," Sylvie drawled, "taking Pickles out again?" Her gaze slid to Wesley, lingering, and she arched one bushy brow. A smirk followed. "And who's this? Don't tell me you've finally brought me a suitor to inspect."

Maude bit back a sigh. The woman had made a sport of teasing her for the better part of two decades. "I'll need two horses today, Sylvie," Maude said, jerking a thumb toward Wesley without looking at him. "And make sure this one's mount is extra sturdy. I don't want one of Oli's precious mares throwing a hip carrying this giant."

The corner of Wesley's mouth twitched. "Pickles?"

Sylvie's grin split wide, teeth flashing. "Ah, yes. That's Maudie's first beast. She named him when she was still knee-high and barely speaking the common tongue. Ate pickles every day 'til her belly ached, so of course she named her horse the same. Bailey nearly choked laughing when she first declared it."

Maude's cheeks warmed despite herself. "Why are you *still*

telling that story?" She shook her head. "You already have half the town thinking I peaked at five."

Sylvie laughed before turning to Wesley. "Pleasure," she said, wiping her hands on her apron before offering him a firm handshake.

"Charmed," Wesley said, giving her one of those dazzling smiles that probably had the entire market's wives buying bread they didn't need.

Sylvie cackled. "Careful, boy. That grin's wasted on me. But keep flashing it at this one—" she jerked her head toward Maude, "—and I might actually die happy."

Maude's groan was loud enough to spook the horses as she stalked past, heading to the stall she knew well. The familiar sight of Pickles—a sleek black horse with a temper as bad as hers—was the first thing all day that didn't make her want to scream.

"Hey there," Maude said softly, running her fingers through Pickles's mane. The massive horse nuzzled her hand before nibbling on her fingers, his usual greeting. She felt the sting in her eyes—the one that always crept up when she least wanted it—and clenched them shut until the feeling passed.

"I'm sorry I haven't been to see you in a while," she muttered, her voice low. "I've been... It's been hard to do the normal things."

Pickles kept nibbling, blissfully unaware—or entirely indifferent—to her words. Still, his ears flicked in contentment, and the sight hit her with a wave of guilt. He had been her gathering partner, carrying her through the wilds around Mistwood Hills while she foraged for rare ingredients. They'd spent days in the mountains, sometimes camping beneath the stars for nights on end just to track down a single elusive herb.

Those trips were some of her favorite memories—and she'd been avoiding them.

Bailey had taken her out since she was little, teaching her how to find everything she might ever need in the wilderness so she wouldn't have to rely on the overpriced, half-dead stock from the town shops. He had a way of making it all feel like an adventure, pointing out the smallest details—a patch of moss that meant water was nearby, the faint glimmer of moonseed hidden in a cluster of vines.

He taught her to trust herself, to read the land and understand it. Those journeys weren't just about gathering ingredients; they were about being together. Riding side by side, Pickles carrying their gear while Bailey told her stories, laughed at her jokes, and treated her like she was capable of anything.

She hadn't gone back out since he died. The thought of doing it alone left her chest hollow. Instead, she'd been spending money she didn't have, buying weak, overharvested ingredients in town just to avoid stepping into the woods without him.

Maude sighed and rested her forehead against Pickles's neck. "I know I've been a terrible friend. But I'm here now."

The horse huffed, warm breath brushing her cheek. A small comfort—but enough to remind her why she needed to keep going.

Bailey had spent years teaching her to be self-sufficient.

He wouldn't want her to give that up.

Maude and Wesley barreled out of Oli's property and into the Wilds, where fences and gardens gave way to untamed green. Trees rose tall and dense, branches arching overhead like a cathedral. Pickles's hooves pounded against the ground, sending sprays of dirt and leaves flying like shrapnel. Maude leaned forward as the wind clawed at her hair and whipped it across her freckled face.

Behind her, Wesley's horse thundered close, each breath a hot snort at her heels. She risked a glance back. He was annoyingly composed—reins steady, posture clean—and smug as a portrait. Like he'd just waltzed out of some nobleman's hunting scene.

She snorted. "Show-off."

Maude dug her heels in. Pickles surged forward with a burst of speed.

That should've been the end of it. But Wesley let out a low laugh—half amusement, half dare—and urged his mount forward, the beast matching Pickles's pace with insulting ease.

And just like that, it was war.

No declaration, no challenge—just two stubborn morons driving their horses faster, dirt flying, neither willing to yield.

The path blurred around them: moss-slick stones, skeletal branches arching overhead, the world spinning into a tunnel of speed and breath and pounding hooves. Her coat snapped back, her dress riding up past her thighs as the air tore at it.

She dared a glance. Wesley was right there, his horse's stride eating the distance until they were neck and neck. He threw her a smirk—all infuriating teeth and golden-boy confidence—then his gaze flicked, brief but unmistakable, to her exposed thigh before darting back to the path.

Heat climbed her neck.

They tore across the last rise, neither of them giving ground until the first clearing opened before them, ringed by whispering pines. Only then did they slow, both horses lathered with sweat, steam rising in the cool air. Maude's lungs burned, her curls plastered to her face, and still she straightened with as much dignity as she could muster.

Wesley was grinning like a lunatic.

"Congratulations. You beat a girl on a horse named Pickles. Truly a heroic victory."

He snorted, wiping his brow with a sleeve. "Don't be sore, Harrow. You almost had me."

She scowled, though her pulse still thrummed from more than the ride.

At the top of the hill, Maude stopped, her mind running through her mental list. She'd need to refill her entire stock—an ambitious goal, but not impossible. Some ingredients would have to wait: the ones that needed harvesting under a full moon or at specific times of the day. But most of what she needed to undo the spell should be within reach this afternoon.

She swung off Pickles and looped his reins around a sturdy oak. A quick pat to his flank earned her a snort, which she pretended was gratitude.

Wesley dismounted and tied his horse beside hers. "So," he said, "what exactly are we hunting for?"

Maude dug into her satchel. "Ironvine. Blackthorn bark. Rosemary. Bloodroot. Yarrow. Moondust caps if we're lucky. And —" she pulled out a small knife, the glint sharp as her tone, "— shadowbell flowers. The spell doesn't break without them."

"Shadowbell flowers," Wesley repeated, nodding like he understood. "Got it. Let's split up. I'll look for the rosemary, yarrow, and moondust caps."

Maude's head snapped up. She stared at him, brow knitting. "You...know how to forage?"

Wesley tugged at his sleeves. "Don't look so shocked. Just because I sell tarts doesn't mean I don't know what a yarrow root looks like."

She kept staring, fingers locked tight on her bag strap. Foraging wasn't exactly common anymore—most people just paid the apothecaries and made do with limp, overpriced herbs. That he knew how to find things himself was...unexpected. Impressive, even. Not that she'd ever admit that.

Her silence stretched too long. Wesley's smirk faltered, his posture shifting. His fingers drummed once against his thigh, then stilled.

"What?"

Maude blinked. "Nothing. Just be quick—we're losing light, and I'm not waiting while you figure out which end of a plant is which." She turned away, but his gaze clung like a burr snagged on her sleeve.

Over an hour bled by as she combed through the Wilds, circling her usual foraging spots. The late September air bit cool against her skin, crisp enough to make her breath visible. Fallen leaves carpeted the ground in gold and crimson, disguising the herbs she hunted. She crouched low, gloved hands brushing through damp foliage, scanning for familiar shapes and textures.

Ironvine grew in abundance. She ducked near a shaded patch beneath a cluster of elder trees and brushed away leaves to reveal it. Its dark, twisting tendrils clung to the base of the tree like they were hanging on for dear life. Maude pulled a knife from her belt and carefully sliced a few lengths free, rolling them into a tight coil and stuffing them into her bag.

Farther into the forest, she came across a gnarled shrub of blackthorn, its thin, spiked branches jutting like warning signs. Maude pressed her knife to the bark, scraping it clean in careful strokes, mindful not to cut too deep and harm the plant.

Bloodroot demanded more from her. Its red-veined leaves could be mistaken for half a dozen useless weeds, but Maude knew the signs: the faint copper tang that lingered when she brushed the stalks and the way they bowed ever so slightly toward the ground. Eventually, she spotted a patch and dug carefully around the base, easing a small cluster free before shaking the dirt loose.

Shadowbell flowers, though, left no trace. She hadn't expected them to. Elusive, dusky things, they bloomed where the light forgot to reach. So Maude pressed deeper into the woods, the air cooling around her.

At last, the hillside appeared: steep, jagged, the kind of place where shadowbell sometimes clung in narrow cracks of stone. She eyed it warily. The climb wasn't one she wanted to make, but desperation weighed heavier than caution.

Maude dug the toe of her boot into the slope, skidding as loose stone rattled down. She caught herself on a sharp inhale, fingers latching onto a jut of rock that scraped her palms raw. Breathless, she hauled herself upward, dirt crumbling beneath her weight and smearing across her skirt in gritty streaks.

At the top, she steadied herself on her knees, scanning the

terrain. Deep fissures in the stone. Shadows thick enough to cradle something rare. Her fingers brushed aside tufts of grass, peeled back moss.

And then—

Dusky petals. *Shadowbell.*

Relief punched through her chest as she reached for the bloom. But the stem bristled with near-invisible thorns, and when her wrist brushed against one, the sting was immediate, sharp as glass. She hissed, jerking back, but not before a long, clean slice opened along the skin.

Blood welled instantly. She pressed her hand to it, muttering the beginnings of a healing charm. The wound stayed open.

Maude froze, her stomach dropping. *Not* shadowbell. Tricker's bane. A parasite plant that mimicked whatever you most wanted to see. Bailey had told her once it "liked the taste of stupid," and she'd sworn she'd never fall for it.

The bloom pulsed faintly, like it was breathing her in, and the cut burned cold, spreading like frost up her arm. She gritted her teeth and tore a strip of fabric from her skirt's hem, binding the wound tight.

"Fantastic," she muttered, more irritated than afraid.

She backed down the slope carefully, her legs unsteady, the satchel heavy at her hip. Fury churned under her ribs, hot enough to outpace the pain. She should've known better. She *did* know better. And still she'd let herself hope.

By the time she reached level ground again, her wrist throbbed in time with her heartbeat, and she wanted to throw herself into the nearest ditch from embarrassment.

She grimaced, stalking back toward Pickles.

As she broke through the tree line, Wesley came into view by the horses, arms full of plants. He had rosemary tucked under one elbow, yarrow sprouting from his fist, and a little clutch of moon-dust caps dangling like trophies. He looked like a walking farmers' market.

The smugness vanished the moment his gaze dropped to her

wrist. The badly wrapped cloth was already soaked, blood dripping sluggishly down her fingers. He strode toward her.

"What happened?"

"I'm fine." Maude waved him off. "Don't get all worked up. I can handle it."

"You're bleeding."

"I said I'm fine." She shoved the bundle of herbs into Pickles's saddlebag.

He didn't move, just stood there with his ridiculous armful of plants. "What did you hurt yourself on?"

Maude exhaled hard, like dragging the words out of her throat was physical labor. "Tricker's bane."

That shut him up for a second. His brow pulled, but not in disbelief—more like calculation. "You should pack it with witch hazel. Or comfrey, if you've got it. Pressure won't hold otherwise. And burn the wrap before the fibers turn."

Her head snapped around. "How do *you* know that?"

He shrugged as if it was nothing. "My mother was a healer."

Was.

The word lodged under her ribs. She snapped her mouth shut on the dozen questions that clawed to the surface. Something in the way he said it—matter-of-fact, without elaboration—made her hesitate.

Maude turned away, suddenly feeling uncomfortably warm and slightly dizzy, and she did not know why. She shook it off, gripping the saddle carefully before using her good arm to hoist herself onto Pickles's back. She let out a small sigh of relief when it didn't hurt as much as she'd expected.

"Did you find everything you needed?" Wesley asked, handing her the bundle of herbs he'd gathered.

"Everything except shadowbell."

He frowned, his nose scrunching. "So, what do we do?"

"Nothing for now. The spell will have to wait until tomorrow. I've got a few other spots in mind that might have it, but we're losing light fast, and I'm not about to sacrifice my other arm."

He nodded, swinging onto his horse with an ease that still annoyed her. "So—one more day of our nightmare mash-up, then?"

She bit her lip, her mind already sketching out the tangled lines of a counter-curse in which she wasn't entirely confident. They'd be lucky if she could untangle the mess in a single day. But she didn't admit that. Just nodded, quick and curt.

Wesley seemed satisfied—or at least didn't push. But on the ride back, Maude couldn't shake the sensation of his curious gaze on her.

Six

The ride back to the stables was mercifully quiet, the sun sinking low on the horizon and casting the sky in shades of orange and blush pink.

Oli's manor came into view at the crest of a gently sloping hill, its silhouette elegant and imposing against the glowing sky. The sprawling estate was a patchwork of ivy-covered stone and towering chimneys, with tall windows that reflected the last light of day like molten gold. The slanted slate roof had peaks crowned with decorative ironwork, and the chimneys puffed faint wisps of smoke into the cool evening air.

As Maude and Wesley approached, Oli bounded across the gardens like an overly enthusiastic puppy.

"Well, well, if it isn't my two favorite shopkeepers!" he called out.

Maude narrowed her eyes as Wesley dismounted, handing the reins to Sylvie, who had just emerged from the stalls. "Oliver, always a pleasure," he said with practiced politeness, turning to offer a hand to Maude.

She ignored him at first, shifting and resettling to find a position that didn't send fresh pain shooting up her arm. After a few awkward tries, she huffed and grudgingly accepted his help. Her scowl deepened when his other hand went straight to her waist, steadying her as she swung her leg over the saddle.

Oli's brow shot up. "Careful there—how bad is the arm?" She waved him off, and only then did his grin return. "Maude, when I suggested you two collaborate to boost your sales, I didn't realize you'd take it so literally."

"Ha-ha," she deadpanned, slinging her bag over her shoulder. "So, you saw the shops?"

Oli let out a laugh. "Impossible to miss. Looks like an alchemist and a confectioner had a drunken love child." His gaze flicked to Wesley. "Now, I know *you* had nothing to do with this. Maude's the brightest witch in all of Mistwood Hills, but even she's going to have her hands full fixing that before the party. Did you want to use my kitchen to prep?"

Wesley's relief was visible. "Saints, yes. My flat's a glorified closet with a sink."

"Perfect." Oli clapped his hands together, beaming.

Maude shifted her weight to one hip "Wait—you're throwing a party? Since when?"

"It's not really a party, per se," he said, scratching the back of his neck. "More like...a business meeting. With a couple of sponsors and vendors. For a new project." Maude narrowed her eyes, but before she could speak, Oli raised a hand, words spilling out. "It's still very much an idea— barely brewing. I was going to tell you when I had an actual plan."

He didn't owe her an explanation, technically, but Maude was so used to Oli oversharing—down to the details of his skincare routine and bowel movements—that this felt borderline treasonous. Keeping something this big from her? Strange didn't even begin to cover it. She bit her lip, debating whether to push him, but let it slide.

For now.

Oli turned his full attention back to Wesley, all charm and enthusiasm. "Tell me what you need, and I'll have it ready at the house. Feel free to set up and work as you please—and, of course, I'm happy to help if you like."

Oli's warm, mischievous smile practically lit up the clearing, and Maude fought the urge to roll her eyes. Yeah, he wasn't acting like Wesley wasn't his type *at all*.

"In fact," Oli continued, "Maude was just telling me how much she's been wanting to get into baking. What do you think about a pair of sous-chefs to help you make up for lost time?"

Wesley's gaze slid to Maude like he could smell the lie from across the yard. "Sure...that sounds great."

"Yeah," Maude ground out, her teeth clicking on the word. "*Great.*"

Oli's grin widened, and Maude swore she could see the matchmaking gears turning in his head. She shot him a glare, silently promising payback—something involving permanent glitter or a hex that made him hiccup every time he said her name.

Still, she didn't argue. Not because she wanted to play house in Oli's kitchen, but because technically...*technically* it was her fault. She'd blown up Wesley's shop. If the wreck bled over into Oli's party, she'd never hear the end of it. No, better to grit her teeth, suck it up, and pretend to cooperate.

She adjusted her bag with a tug and stalked toward the house.

"I'll need whole wheat flour, almond meal, caster sugar, unsalted butter, heavy cream, fresh vanilla pods, cocoa powder, baking chocolate—good stuff, not that waxy crap—yeast, sourdough starter..." Wesley paused, glancing at Oli's raised brow. "What? Artisan baking isn't exactly low-maintenance."

"And the baked goods?" Oli asked, grinning like he was ready to eat half the list on the spot.

"Lemon curd tarts, almond croissants, sourdough boules,

chocolate ganache eclairs...maybe some rosemary focaccia if there's time."

Maude half-listened as she unloaded the foraged ingredients onto the oversized island in Oli's absurdly pristine kitchen. Iron-vine, bloodroot, blackthorn bark—all lined up in neat little rows, her hands moving on autopilot. Every piece of the spell was here. Every piece but one. Shadowbell. Always elusive. Always late-season fickle. If she wanted it, she'd have to climb into the mountains.

Her gaze snagged on the window, twilight spilling across the fields. Her fingers twitched restlessly. The Duskmire Peaks weren't exactly close, and shadowbell wasn't the kind of thing she'd usually settle for buying. It had to be fresh, and no vendor in town would touch it—too finicky, too much trouble to stock. Besides, the Peaks carried their own warnings: hunters who never came back, voices echoing in the stone that didn't belong to anyone living. People didn't wander there unless desperation drove them.

With a sigh, Maude categorized the day's findings, neatly sorting and tucking them back into her pack. Her wrist throbbed under the half-assed wrap she'd tied. The rosemary tincture she'd slapped on earlier was doing exactly nothing, and the blood had soaked through again, streaking down her palm. She flexed her hand once, hissed, and decided she'd pushed it long enough.

"I need to get back," she said, tightening the strap on her pack. "Fix my arm. Check on Grim. Wish I could stay."

Oli paused mid-conversation, glancing at her. "Need help?"

Maude snorted. "*Please*. Stick to pastries."

"Hey," Oli said, hand to his chest. "I'd be excellent moral support."

That earned him a ghost of a smile. She couldn't help it. The last time Oli had offered "*moral support*," he'd ended up sprawled on the floor himself, white as milk, after watching her stitch up a split knuckle. He'd muttered something about "*sympathy pain*" while she'd finished the job one-handed and called him pathetic until he finally staggered back upright.

Not exactly the résumé of a battlefield medic.

She shook her head, the corner of her mouth still twitching. "Yeah. Sure. I'll call you next time I need someone to pass out dramatically and make the situation all about them."

Oli laughed and strolled over, dropping a kiss on the crown of her head. "There's my Maudie girl. Where have you been all my life?"

She slouched in exaggerated sulk-mode, arms folded.

"None of that," Oli scolded, bopping her on the head.

It startled a laugh out of her—quick, unwilling—and she shoved him back with both hands. When she glanced up, Wesley was watching, his expression unreadable.

Oli turned to him with all the theatrical flourish of a man stepping onto a stage. "*Wesley...*" He leaned in conspiratorially. "Have you ever seen a copper-clad, temperature-controlled proving cabinet imported from Avenshire?"

Wesley's eyes lit up. "No. Never. You have one?"

"Oh, I *do*. Come on, I'll show you."

Before Maude could ask when he had purchased a proving cabinet, Oli wagged a finger at her. "See you later—and don't forget to check in every hour with the scry-stone. If I don't hear from you in the twenty minutes it takes to get to the shop, I'm going to assume you're dead and send out the brigade."

Wesley shot her a sidelong look, brows lifted in silent commentary.

She ignored him. "You don't have a brigade."

"Details," Oli said breezily, already walking away. He flapped a hand over his shoulder. "Love you, bye."

Wesley stuttered, opened his mouth, then shut it again before turning and stalking after him.

The last smear of daylight bled into the horizon by the time Blightbend Way curled into view. The street was drowning in dusk—muted gold dripping into gray, lanterns humming faintly with starlight.

Normally, she'd have welcomed it. Shadows suited her.

But tonight, something was...off.

Halfway to her shop, she stopped dead. Her eyes snagged on the patch of green a few feet ahead, and her brain immediately began filing complaints.

The grass looked wrong. Too perfect. Too glossy. Suspicion prickled down her spine. Maude crouched, pushing her sleeve up with a muttered curse, and brushed her fingers over the blades.

Her stomach dropped.

Not blades. Not grass at all.

Her hand sank into the ground like a sponge, sweet stickiness clinging to her skin.

"Marshmallow," she muttered, her voice shaking with disbelief. "The grass is marshmallow."

Her heart stumbled, then kicked into double-time. She shot to her feet and bolted down the road, sprinting toward her shop. By the time she barreled onto Blightbend Way, she stopped so abruptly her teeth clicked hard enough to sting.

Oh. *Fuck*.

Her stupid curse—her spectacular disaster of a curse—was spreading. And it was so much worse than the nightmare reels her brain had been running.

On Wesley's half, everything was turning edible. Cobblestones gleamed like sugar cubes. A wheelbarrow slouched against the bookshop wall, now pure chocolate, already sagging. Even the streetlamps glowed in candied amber, their poles glossy like hard caramel.

Her half? Worse.

Where her curse touched, things died. Grass shriveled to brittle gray husks. Trees twisted in on themselves, branches clawing as if they wanted to crawl out of the soil. The cobbles cracked and crumbled, rotting as if centuries had passed in hours.

Half candy-land, half graveyard. Entirely her fault.

Grim.

She shoved through her shop door, wood groaning as the half-rotted frame scraped against its new chocolate trim. She didn't stop to take in the grotesque disaster—her focus was singular.

"Grim!"

The silence was deafening.

Then—paw prints. Tiny. Leading across the dusty floor, faintly sparkling like someone had powdered them with confectioner's sugar. They trailed straight toward the backroom. Her chest tightened. She followed, pushed the door open—and there he was.

Sitting like a smug gargoyle in the middle of frosting carnage, calmly licking his paw.

Maude sagged against the doorframe, a long, shaky breath tearing out of her.

But then he looked up at her. His ears glowed. His nose was bright candy pink.

"Saints."

She scooped him up, heart clawing at her throat. His fur was hot against her hands, his nose twitching like nothing was wrong while she fell apart.

"I'm sorry," she whispered into his fur, guilt hitting like a gut punch. She carried him outside, crouched low, and set him carefully in the grass. "Stay," she said firmly, even though Grim had never once in his life listened to her.

Maude dropped to her knees beside him, fingers shaking as she yanked her pack open. Yarrow. Bloodroot. Anything that might buy time.

She should've done this before she left. She knew better.

Bailey would've hexed her ears off for forgetting containment. She grabbed a rock, muttered a low incantation, and twisted it into a crude cauldron. Herbs crushed under her palms, bitter smoke rising as she worked. The mixture glowed faintly; the light swirled like tiny embers caught in a breeze.

This spell was an old one. Bailey had taught it to her back when she'd been a walking disaster of magical accidents, and it had saved her more times than she could count. She hadn't needed it in years, but her hands moved instinctively, the motions etched into her muscle memory.

When the glow brightened and the spell felt stable, Maude stood and cast it toward the shop. A shimmering dome of energy sprang to life, enclosing the building in a protective barrier. The sickly, decaying air within seemed to pause, the creeping curse halting in its tracks.

Maude stared at it for a long moment, waiting for any sign of failure. When none came, she let out a shaky breath, wiping her damp hands on her skirt. For once, something worked.

Grim sprawled beside her, tail flicking, ears still faintly pink. She ran her fingers through his fur, murmuring a detection charm. No deeper curse. Just surface level.

Maude lay back beside him, the ground cool beneath her, the dome humming faintly over her shop like a heartbeat she didn't trust.

This wouldn't hold forever. She knew it. The curse was a bomb, ticking louder every second. If she didn't find shadowbell —soon—half of Mistwood Hills would go down with her mistake.

And when it did, they'd all remember. They'd mutter about it for decades. *Remember Maude Harrow? Turned the square into a candy graveyard. Really brightened the place up. Until it killed us all.*

She scowled up at the sky. "Yeah, no. Not giving them that story."

Grim sniffed like he didn't believe her for a second.

Seven

Sleep had been a mercy Maude didn't deserve. The containment dome still shimmered faintly in her mind's eye, even when she shut her lids tight and buried her face in Grim's fur. He had purred like nothing had happened, like his ears hadn't glowed neon pink hours before, like the world wasn't two bad spells away from collapsing into either a rotting mausoleum or a bakery from hell.

Cats.

Unbothered, immortal, *smug* little gods who looked at you like your breakdowns were merely background noise.

But Maude wasn't a cat. She didn't get to stretch, yawn, and move on. No—her failures followed her into sleep, curled up at the base of her ribs, heavy as stone.

She woke with a headache, of course. A splitting one. Bailey would've called it poetic justice.

The ceiling beams blurred above her until she blinked them into focus, every rune Bailey had carved staring down like they were judging her life choices. Which, *fair.*

Dragging herself upright felt like swimming through mud. Every muscle ached, but her wrist—the one she'd finally given in and treated exactly as Wesley had suggested—burned with that prickly, half-healed sting. The comfrey poultice was already doing its work, the spell threaded through it settling into her skin with a dull throb. Annoyingly, it should feel better in a few hours. Infuriatingly, he'd been right.

Maude muttered a curse at the universe on principle before shoving herself to her feet.

She bathed, the water already tepid and biting at her cut wrist, a petty punishment she probably deserved. When she finally dragged herself out, she dressed in something that matched her mood: a black wool skirt, a gray blouse with cuffs sharp enough to cut, and a belt that could double as a weapon if she felt inspired.

The cat yawned, unimpressed.

Maude pulled on her boots, the leather creaking, and pinned her curls back with more irritation than care. She caught her reflection again in the mirror—the strawberry-blonde that refused to stay tamed, freckles standing out even harsher against her pale skin after the bath.

Twenty-two and already done with humanity.

She flipped the mirror off and shrugged into her heavy coat, its deep pockets clinking with vials. She cinched the belt tight—like maybe it could hold her together too.

The air slapped her cheeks the moment she opened the door, cool and biting, the kind of cold that crept into bone if you let it. She pulled her hood low and started down the lane.

Grim came with her, of course—launching onto her shoulder like a demon familiar who'd lost a bet and been forced into housecat form. Maude kept her injured arm tucked close, every jolt a reminder of her spectacular failure.

The streets smelled of frost-glazed pears and woodsmoke, sweet and acrid all at once. The market had already shaken itself awake, merchants hollering prices, neighbors chirping greetings. She let it all slide past, eyes fixed straight ahead, Grim thumping his tail against her back like a metronome mocking her solemn stride.

But the further she pushed into town, the thinner the cheer

grew. Laughter gave way to murmurs. Smiles shrank into whispers. By the time Blightbend's crooked archway came into view, the sound had curdled into something worse.

A crowd.

Of course.

A knot of townsfolk clustered outside her shop—*the abomination*, as she'd started calling it in her head. Her stomach sank.

The containment spell still glimmered faintly, but it wasn't enough to hide the wrongness—to hide the creeping curse that slithered down the street. People gawked openly, whispering behind gloved hands, some with expressions of horrified fascination, others with the gleam of opportunity in their eyes.

A baker's dozen children pressed sticky palms to the glass, squealing about cupcakes that shimmered faintly on the shelves. Behind them, a woman crossed herself as if she were warding off spirits. A man muttered loudly enough for Maude to hear: "Told you she'd snap one day. Bailey kept her steady. Without him, well..."

Her jaw clenched.

Grim hissed, tail puffing as if he'd understood the insult.

And then, of course, there was *him.*

Wesley Rivers, in all his golden-haired, disgustingly approachable glory, already working the crowd. He leaned casually against the shopfront, smiling. "Good morning!" he called, handing out what looked like cinnamon twists wrapped in parchment. "Yes, yes, free samples—still perfectly edible. No curses included, *I promise.*"

The audacity.

The crowd chuckled, tension dissolving. Some even clapped him on the shoulder as though he'd saved their children from a burning building instead of actively participating in a magical crime scene.

Maude stalked closer, Grim digging his claws into her shoulder like he knew she needed restraining.

"Is this a joke to you?" she said when she reached him, low

enough that only he could hear.

Wesley's smile didn't falter. He leaned closer, lowering his voice. "Leftovers from the party last night," he said lightly. "It went well, in case you were wondering."

Her mouth pressed into a line.

"If you do not want them to panic," he went on, still smiling for the crowd, "you have to act like everything's fine."

"It's not fine."

"Of course it's not," he murmured, flashing another grin at a passing couple who blushed under his attention. "But they don't need to know that."

Before she could retort, the crowd shifted. Someone else had arrived.

Two figures in dull gray coats, marked with the sigil of the town magistrates, strode toward the shop with the air of bureaucrats who thought a clipboard could solve anything. One of them, a sharp-nosed alderman she vaguely recognized from Bailey's old disputes about licensing fees—*Veyne*, possibly—squinted at the fused building.

"What in the Saints' names is this?" he demanded, pulling a ledger from his satchel. His companion scribbled furiously beside him. "Unregistered alterations? Structural instability? A hazard to public safety." His gaze snapped to Maude. "Miss Harrow, this wouldn't be your doing, would it?"

Wesley beat her to it. "Not at all," he said smoothly, "just a minor magical hiccup. Contained, as you can see. Nothing unsafe —our customers are as happy and healthy as ever."

The inspector's brow furrowed. "Still, it's highly irregular—"

"Absolutely," Wesley cut in, nodding sympathetically, as if the man's words pained him. "We'll file the proper reports today. Safety's our priority, I assure you. In the meantime, we're keeping everything under strict control."

Maude bristled, heat flooding her chest.

We?

The alderman hesitated, visibly soothed by Wesley's easy

cadence, before harrumphing and snapping his ledger shut. "Very well. But mark me—if the building isn't stabilized by Samhain, we condemn it. Both of you. Shops shuttered, goods seized, property razed if necessary." His hawk's gaze flicked between them, settling a heartbeat longer on Maude. "One month. Not a day more."

The words landed like a curse, final and cold.

"Of course," Wesley said warmly, shaking his hand like they'd just sealed a lucrative deal.

Maude wanted to hex them both into oblivion.

Of course the magistrates would listen to him. Men like Wesley were made for this kind of thing—charming, steady-voiced. Men like Bailey.

She used to try to be that sort of person too—smiling at festivals, pouring cider at market fairs, pretending the chatter didn't make her skin itch. Bailey had always made it look easy; people wanted to love him. When he died, she stopped pretending, and the town had stopped pretending with her. They'd let her drift to the edges, easier to pity than to include, easier still to dislike. Every town needed someone to whisper about, and she'd made the mistake of being convenient.

When the inspectors departed, the crowd dispersed in fits and starts—still buzzing, but calmer now, the sting of panic dulled. Some chuckled as they wandered off, already spinning the story for neighbors: The fused shop. The witch and the baker. Condemned by Samhain if they don't fix it.

Brilliant. Exactly the kind of notoriety she'd spent her entire life avoiding.

The door groaned like a dying man as Maude shoved it open. Inside, the scent hit her immediately: lavender and sage locked in a death match with buttercream and yeast, the air thick enough to choke on. The shelves sagged under their mismatched burdens, like even the wood knew it wasn't built for this kind of nonsense.

She didn't know why it still surprised her. Every time she walked in, some stubborn corner of her brain seemed to expect order—as if the universe might have tidied itself up overnight out of pity. Ridiculous. Nothing in here was getting fixed without her. Still, she couldn't quite believe it. Couldn't quite accept that this catastrophe was hers now.

Her abomination.

Grim hopped down from her shoulder, tail lashing as he stalked across the fused counter, pausing to sniff a frosted cupcake that had sprouted beside her jar of powdered bone ash.

With a disdainful hiss, he leapt down and disappeared into the shadows. *Sensible.*

Wesley stepped in behind her, brushing dust from his sleeves. "Well," he said mildly, "that went better than expected."

Maude stalked behind the counter, snatched a blank sheet of parchment, and flattened it against the scarred wood. The quill jar rattled as she grabbed one, dipping it into ink with more force than necessary.

Wesley leaned against the counter, arms folded. "What are you doing?"

"Writing."

"I can see that. Why?"

"Because it helps me think straight." She scrawled the first words in her angular script: *Terms of Truce.*

"Truce?" His voice held a laugh.

She shot him a lethal look. "You want your precious ovens back, don't you?"

He spread his hands. "Lead the way, General."

She bent over the parchment, scribbling furiously. "Number one: All potion brewing and spell casting is my jurisdiction. You don't touch a cauldron, stir a vial, or so much as sneeze near the herb jars without permission."

"Noted," Wesley said. "And all ovens, mixers, and dough

belong to me. You don't stick a single witchy finger into my frosting."

She arched a brow. "Fine. Two: Customers with magical ailments are directed to me. Customers with a sweet tooth to you. No poaching."

He tapped a finger against the counter. "And what about customers who want both? Someone could, hypothetically, crave a lemon tart *and* a migraine cure."

"They'll get whichever is least likely to kill them."

"So, *me*."

Her quill dug into the parchment so hard that the nib nearly split.

"*Three*," she bit out, "you clean up your own mess. Sprinkles, flour, sticky fingerprints—your problem. My shop doesn't tolerate glitter."

"Sprinkles aren't glitter."

"They're weaponized sugar. Close enough."

He snorted, leaning closer, the light catching in his hair. "You're very particular, aren't you?"

She ignored him, writing harder. "Four: Personal boundaries. You stay on your side, I stay on mine. If our paths cross, we make it quick, clean, and silent."

"Silent?" His brows lifted. "What about necessary communication?"

She jabbed the quill in his direction. "Then keep it brief. I don't need your constant chatter infecting my concentration."

His lips twitched. "Noted. No chatter. Just smoldering glares."

"Five—"

"How many of these are you planning?"

Her hand flew across the parchment, ink blotting at the edges: *Five: No unauthorized tampering with experiments. Six: If the building collapses, you're responsible for digging me out. Seven: If the building kills customers, you're responsible for explaining it to the magistrates.*

By the time the list was complete, the parchment was filled top to bottom with Maude's cramped handwriting. She shoved it across the counter like a declaration of battle.

Wesley glanced at it, eyes skimming over her script. His mouth spread wider with each line. "'If late to meetings, forfeits first claim on counter space.' ... 'No humming while working.' ... 'Absolutely no unauthorized smiling.'"

"That one's non-negotiable."

His chuckle rumbled low. "Saints, you really hate me, don't you?"

Maude stiffened, quill poised above the inkwell. "Don't flatter yourself. I hate everyone. You're just...particularly offensive."

"Particularly." He nodded as if honored. "I'll take it."

She turned, grabbing a jar from the shelf just to give her hands something to do. But the words on the parchment glowed faintly in her periphery, a fragile order in the chaos. Her rules. Her control.

Wesley signed at the bottom with a flourish, his script annoyingly elegant. "All right," he said, setting the quill down. "We have our truce. Now what?"

Maude exhaled slowly, staring at the grotesque cauldron-mixer hybrid across the room. "Now," she said, voice flat, "we fix this. Before Samhain. Or we both go down together."

His smile tilted, softer this time. "Guess I'd better get used to your charming company."

Market Square was loud.

The kind of noise that made Maude want to hex her own ears shut just so she wouldn't have to hear another vendor screeching about *"fresh butter!"* or *"mystic charms guaranteed to attract true love!"* It was late enough in the morning that the whole village had spilled into the square, and early enough that the dew hadn't burned off the cobblestones yet. Her boots slapped against them anyway, damp soaking into the leather, as she wound her way past stalls of candied nuts, steaming cider, and twinkling crystal lamps.

The whole place smelled like roasted chestnuts and too many perfumes fighting to be the loudest in her nose.

And none of it was what she needed.

Shadowbell.

It was the one thing she couldn't fake, couldn't replace, couldn't substitute with clever runes or Bailey's scribbled notes.

She stopped at a stall where a red-faced man sold jars of powdered roots and dried leaves. The labels were hand-scrawled, half-legible, and the kind of dubious that usually meant *"exactly what you want if you don't ask too many questions."* Maude leaned an elbow on the counter.

"Shadowbell," she said flatly. "Do you have it?"

The man blinked at her as though she'd asked for unicorn marrow. "That's a dangerous thing to say out loud."

"It's also a yes-or-no question."

His face screwed up. "No."

Ugh.

She pushed off the counter and stalked away, already irritated.

The next was a woman with a tray of dried mushrooms, all different shades of brown and black, the kind that made people believe they'd seen the future after chewing on them. Maude leaned down, voice low.

"Shadowbell."

The woman barked a laugh. "Do I look suicidal to you? Try the grave robbers by the east wall. If anyone's stupid enough, it's them."

Excellent.

The grave robbers—three men with missing teeth and the odor of people who lived closer to corpses than soap—looked at her like she'd grown horns when she asked.

"We sell bones, miss," the tallest one said. "We don't sell

curses."

"It's a flower," Maude snapped.

"Exactly."

They shuffled her off with nervous glances, like her even speaking the word out loud might taint their stock.

By the time she'd burned through every contact, her mood had frayed to a brittle, snapping edge. She'd gone through the obvious vendors, then the back-alley sellers, then the people who were technically "farmers" but definitely weren't farming anything legal. Each time, the same reaction: wide eyes, nervous laughter, sudden silence.

She was used to being looked at like she was dangerous, but today they looked at her like she was insane.

By midday, she leaned against the stone fountain in the center of the square, her coat heavy on her shoulders, her bag cutting into her side. The cold spray from the fountain misted her face, and she shut her eyes against it.

It wasn't supposed to be this hard.

Still, she wasn't ready to give up. Not yet.

She made her way to the farthest corner of the square, where the cobbles started to buckle and the market stalls thinned. The vendors here weren't official. Most didn't have permits. Some didn't even have names, just reputations. And the woman Maude was looking at now? She had both.

Madam Quill.

Not her real name. No one knew her real name. The "*Madam*" was sarcastic; the "*Quill*" came from the handful of porcupine spines always sticking out of her tangled bun like she'd fought one and lost. She sat behind a stall piled high with boxes, cloth bundles, and tiny locked chests, none labeled. Her clothes were bright in a way that looked almost aggressive—orange skirts layered over purple ones, a shawl patterned with stars. She had the smile of someone who'd steal your shoes and charge you for the privilege.

Maude squared her shoulders, stepped up, and didn't bother

with pleasantries. "I need shadowbell."

Madam Quill's grin widened, showing teeth too sharp for comfort. "Well, well. You've got gall, asking for that."

"Do you have it?"

"Not today." She wagged a finger, her bangles clinking together. "But I could put you on my list."

"What kind of list?" Maude asked warily.

"The kind where you get what you want, eventually. Two weeks, maybe three." Maude's gut sank. Two weeks was two weeks too long. Still, she clenched her jaw. "What's the price?"

Madam Quill leaned forward, eyes glittering. "For you, sweetheart? Costly. Dangerous flowers bring dangerous prices. Half now, half on delivery."

Maude's fingers tightened around her coin pouch. It wasn't heavy to begin with. She'd already spent most of her savings shoring up the shop, patching mistakes, and bribing inspectors. All she had left clinked softly when she opened the pouch: a sad collection of coins that wouldn't buy her a decent coat, let alone survival.

She dropped it on the counter anyway. "That's everything. Consider it a down payment."

Madam Quill swept it up with a hand quick as a crow's beak. "Done."

"It better be fresh."

"Fresh as your fury, darling."

Maude didn't like the sound of that at all.

She turned on her heel before she could say something biting enough to raise the price further and stalked down the lane, coat snapping at her ankles, something prickling against her skin.

It wasn't relief. Not even close.

It was worse than nothing—because now she'd pinned her hopes on someone else.

Someone with questionable ethics and a porcupine hairdo.

Her gut told her she'd regret it.

Her gut was usually right.

Eight

The first week of their so-called partnership could only be described as a carnival of disasters.

It began, inevitably, with salt. Maude had carefully drawn protective lines across the warped floorboards, a ring of containment charms precise enough that Bailey himself might've nodded in approval. Wesley, all broad shoulders and incessant humming, wandered through with a tray of rolls, sneezed, and scattered flour across the salt. The magic bled instantly, merging protection with yeast. The result? Loaves that sang.

Not quaint little ditties, either—*dirges*. Funeral hymns that rattled through the room with such mournful intensity that Mrs. Haddingham bought three, cradling them like she'd just secured the soundtrack for her own burial.

"Most exciting breakfast I've had in years," the old woman crowed, tottering away with her purchase.

Then Oli decided to help.

He arrived midmorning, as if summoned by Maude's rage, sweeping through the door with the smug energy of a man who had never once in his life been told to leave. He carried a basket of suspiciously expensive wine and was dressed like a romance-novel hero—loose shirt, boots that gleamed, hair swept back artfully.

"I thought the newlyweds might be thirsty," he announced, ignoring the fact that Maude looked one tantrum away from setting the curtains ablaze.

"Perfect timing," Wesley said, grinning. "Grab an apron."

Maude nearly hexed them both. "Absolutely not."

"Absolutely *yes*," Oli countered, already tying the strings around his waist.

The next hour was hell.

Oli had the attention span of a magpie and the chaos of a hurricane. He stole spells and enchanted piping bags to refill endlessly—"So efficient!"—and within minutes frosting geysers erupted, coating the ceiling in pink swirls and dripping onto Maude's tonics. Wesley doubled over laughing as Grim launched himself onto the counter, skidding through the icing like a sled, and knocked two bottles straight into Wesley's rising dough.

The dough promptly sprouted legs.

Six sticky muffins leapt off the counter and began marching toward the door like a buttered army. Oli clapped like a delighted child. "It's a parade!"

Maude shouted herself hoarse while Grim pounced on each muffin, growling with such ferocity that frosting splattered across the walls.

And the worst part? Somewhere in the frosting storm, Maude realized they were laughing together. *Her* Oliver—her greedy, chaotic, loyal Oli—was actually bonding with the bakery bastard.

The horror nearly felled her on the spot.

After that, things blurred together into a week-long nightmare. Cupcakes that oozed shadows. A pie that wouldn't stop screaming every time someone cut into it—high-pitched, dramatic, eventually punted into the alley. Sugar mice sank their teeth into Wesley's hand and scattered into the flour bins, tails whipping like banners. Jam jars whispered petty secrets Maude never wanted to know ("Your neighbor steals spoons"), while a broom tried to unionize with the rolling pins, demanding *"fair sweeping hours."* A child who ate a cursed eclair floated to the ceiling and refused to come down until Maude reversed it—while her parents applauded like it was theater.

The shop filled daily with gawkers. The Elixir Emporium, once comfortably desolate, now teemed with tourists who laughed at the *"Haunted Bakery."* Some bought pastries. Others demanded potions with candied pearls. Against her better judgment, Maude let a few coin purses lighten her shelves.

Maude's terms of truce—the painstakingly written list she'd taped behind the counter—proved worse than useless. *"No humming,"* it said. Wesley hummed anyway, and every time he did, the dough rose higher. One morning he whistled an entire ballad, and the bread inflated so violently the oven door snapped off. *"No tampering with experiments."* He tampered constantly, sneaking spoonfuls of frosting into her cauldrons *"for science."*

By the seventh day, she was ready to commit homicide. And then Wesley stopped laughing. It was subtle at first. One evening, when Oli tried to charm her into letting him host "themed evenings" in the shop—*"Haunted Tea Tuesdays!"* complete with an interpretive dance she refused to dignify by describing—Wesley's voice cut in.

"That's enough, Oliver."

Maude stilled mid-glare. Oli blinked like someone had just slapped him with a trout.

"She's not a spectacle." Wesley's voice wasn't raised, but it carried, firm enough to cut through the clutter of shelves and half-baked curses. "She's holding this place together with blood and string, and you're treating it like a game."

Oli's easy grin faltered, guilt flashing across his face. "I was only—"

"No." Wesley scrubbed a hand over his face, exhaling. "I know you mean well. And I've been an ass too." His eyes flicked toward Maude, and the quiet there made her stomach dip. "Sorry." He didn't look away from her.

Maude swallowed, fingers tightening on the edge of the counter.

Wesley finally turned back to Oli, pointing toward the door. "Out. Let her breathe."

Oli stared at him for a beat too long, then glanced at Maude like maybe she'd swoop in and rescue him. She didn't. She just arched a brow, daring him to test it.

With an exaggerated sigh, Oli raised his hands in surrender. "Fine. But for the record, Haunted Tea Tuesdays would've been legendary." He left without another word. The door shut, and silence crashed down.

Maude turned on Wesley. "You don't get to—"

"I wasn't defending you," he interrupted, wiping his flour-dusted hands. "I was defending the shop." Then he shrugged, rolling his sleeves higher as he turned back to the ruined counter. "And you looked like you were about to break. Didn't seem fair."

Her chin lifted a fraction but the fight slipped out of her. It was a small thing, what he'd said, but it was more than she'd expected.

"Don't go getting all noble on me, baker."

His mouth curved, slow and infuriating. "Still a bastard where it counts."

She hated that her lips twitched. Hated worse that he saw it.

Wesley lingered a moment, still looking at the door. "You and he…" He trailed off, voice casual, almost careless. "Are you—?"

Maude huffed. "Oli's family. Closest thing I've got to one, anyway."

"Right," he said quickly, tone smoothing itself out. "Didn't mean to pry. He just seems… close to you." A beat. "Which is good. Everyone needs someone like that."

Maude's brow arched. "Didn't realize you cared so much about my emotional well-being, Rivers."

He smiled faintly. "Don't. Just making conversation."

She tilted her head, studying him for a heartbeat too long before letting it drop.

The shop had slipped into that hour where even the ghosts got bored.

Lanterns outside sank to patient embers; the gutters whispered with runoff; Blightbend's clamor dwindled to the clack of a distant cart and the soft hiss of starlight orbs dimming along the lane. Inside, the Elixir Emporium—currently the *Haunted Bakery*, as Mistwood Hills had christened it—breathed a wary, sugar-and-sage quiet. The yeasty warmth from the cauldron-mixer on Wesley's side seeped over the chalk line that divided their *"domains,"* meeting Maude's lingering nettle and nightshade like two strangers stuck sharing a pew.

She should've gone home hours ago. Grim would be perched in the window, a furry gargoyle judging her life choices. Her cut wrist tugged whenever she flexed her fingers, a low, irritated throb beneath the bandage. She'd told herself she would lock up after decanting the blackthorn steep.

Then Wesley started working.

He had his sleeves rolled to the elbow and a clean apron tied carelessly at his hips. The flour-dusted world made a frame around him: scales, scrapers, a brass timer, a small bowl of water for smoothing stubborn edges. He moved as if he was counting in some internal rhythm—four-beat measures, the same tempo he kept when he built dough from nothing: weigh, whisk, fold, rest. He always made it look easy, which was vexing, because nothing was easy anymore. Not for her.

She found herself leaning on her own counter, pretending to organize tincture labels while actually watching him. The curse had left everything jittery—jars buzzed on their shelves; the chandelier tinkled as if impatient. But the longer he repeated the sequence—roll, fold, quarter-turn, pat—the calmer the room felt.

The magic that usually prowled the eaves like a hungry thing seemed to curl up and breathe with him.

Huh.

She scoffed at herself for even noticing and pretended she'd only wandered over because she needed the mortar he wasn't using. "You always do it exactly like that?"

He glanced up, a curled lock of hair stuck to his forehead. "Like what?"

"The ritual," she said. "The obsession. The sacrament of butter."

A smile curved at the corner of his mouth. "It's lamination. Not a cult."

"Hm. Looks cultish."

He tipped his chin at the slab in front of him. "Want to see?"

Her first instinct—say no, bite, retreat—flared and went out. A different impulse rose, smaller and far more dangerous: *curiosity.* She was too tired to fight it. "Fine," she said. "Enlighten me."

He wiped his hands, then slid the dough toward the center of his bench. "This is détrempe—the base dough. Not sweet. Just flour, water, salt, a little yeast. It's chilled so the butter won't melt when we fold."

She approached warily, as if the dough might bare fangs. It was cool and obedient under her fingertips, lightly floured, pale as bone. He nodded toward the square of butter on parchment—softened, then rolled thin. "That's the block. We're going to marry them."

"Romantic," she said, because she couldn't help herself.

"Practical," he returned, unoffended. He set the butter in the center of the rolled dough. "You wrap the détrempe around the block like a present, then you roll it out to a long rectangle. Here."

He handed her the pin. Their fingers grazed. It was nothing—except her skin apparently hadn't gotten the memo, because heat chased along her knuckles. She pretended to be fascinated by the grain of the rolling pin.

"Even pressure," he said. "Don't smash it. Coax it."

The dough yielded with a faint sigh. She could feel the butter as a cool, pliant layer beneath the surface—resistant, then giving, the way grief sometimes let you out for errands before dragging you back inside. She rolled it into a long rectangle. Wesley watched her hands, not correcting, merely tracking.

"Good," he said. "Now, fold: bottom third up, top third down. That's a letter fold."

She folded it; he turned it a quarter. "Then rest," he said, lifting the packet onto a sheet tray, setting it aside. "The gluten relaxes; the butter chills."

"Like naps."

"*Exactly* like naps," he said, dead serious, which she did not need to find charming. He pulled forward another chilled packet and slid it to her. "Again."

"Repetition," she said. "How thrilling."

"Order," he said, matching her tone. "How scandalous."

She pressed the pin again. The room felt oddly patient, the nerves she'd grown accustomed to—hers and the shop's—smoothed by the rhythm. Roll. Fold. Turn. Rest. When she worked magic these days, everything inside her buzzed and spiked and came out feral. This? This was a meditative insult. She might even like it, which was unacceptable.

"Do you do everything like this?" she asked, because silence made her fidget.

"Like what?"

"In steps," she said. "Exact. Measured. If someone moved your scales an inch to the left, would you riot?"

He huffed a laugh. "I might sulk. But...yeah. To an extent. The shop's better if I build the day the same way—mix at dawn, first prove by the time the kettle whistles, laminations by second bell." He shrugged, eyes on the dough. "When there's noise, you can either wave at it or give yourself a railing to hold."

A railing. She pictured the night Bailey didn't come home and the weeks after, when she'd worked by muscle memory because thinking hurt and not thinking was worse. It had felt like drowning in a room with windows. No railing. No anything. Just water.

"Mm," she said, which was less a word and more a noncommittal grunt with emotions she refused to unpack tied to it like baggage.

He slid a third packet her way. "Last turn for this set. Then we chill the stack, start a fresh slab, and give the first one a chance to settle."

"Fine," she said, like she was put-upon. She wasn't. It was almost...soothing.

She rolled. The pin whispered. He asked for the scraper; she handed it to him without looking. The small transactions stacked up into something that felt suspiciously like ease.

When the dough had been turned and rested, he tapped the bench. "You want to try something?"

"I am trying something," she said, but he shook his head, amused.

"I mean...try weaving your magic through the fold."

A hundred responses presented themselves, all with teeth. She chose the least defensive one that still sounded like her. "That's a terrible idea."

"Probably," he agreed, "but this room stops buzzing when we do this. You noticed."

Of course he'd noticed that she'd noticed. *Annoying.* She lifted her hands, then dropped them. "If I blow up the bakery again, you're explaining it to Veyne."

"Deal."

"And Mrs. Haddingham."

"Absolutely not. She scares me."

Against all better judgment, she bent over the cool slab. "You're going to be insufferable if this works."

"I'm already insufferable," he said, eyes kind, voice easy.

She exhaled a slow, thin breath. The rune she chose was minor —binding, basic, something safe enough to test on a cowardly day. She shaped it with two fingers over the dough's surface, not speaking aloud, just forming the lines in thought, the angles she'd traced since she was small enough to stand on a stool to watch Bailey draw them in salt.

The air at the edge of the bench hummed.

She pressed the rune into the fold—not on top, but between the layers. Butter, flour, bind. The magic spread like melted wax, slipping through the seams, coaxing the layers to cling where they should have torn apart. It took a breath, and held.

No lurch. No crackle-back. No flaring jars or offended runes —a hum, then quiet.

Her throat went tight. She blinked suspiciously. "Again."

He didn't say *I told you so*. He didn't say anything at all, which might have been the smartest thing he'd done all day. He turned the dough. She drew the rune and fed it into the next fold. The glow softened into the layers, steady as tidewater, and nested.

"Oh," he said softly. Not triumph. Not surprise. Awe.

She snorted because she was constitutionally opposed to sincere moments. "Don't get poetic."

"Too late," he murmured. "You found the groove."

"It's your groove," she said, hating the way the words warmed something under her breastbone. "The shop listens when you count."

He tipped his head, thinking it over. "Maybe it's not listening to me," he said. "Maybe it's listening to the metronome."

"Now you're insufferable *and* mystical," she muttered.

He grinned, small and a little shy, which was unfair. "Roll."

She rolled. They folded. With each repetition, she fed a thin line of her magic into the seam—keeping it low, disciplined, like leading a wolf on a short leash. The wolf...behaved. It flowed where she pointed, settling into butter and flour alike, tightening each fold until the layers felt locked, resilient. It liked the warmth of the butter, the compression of flour, the predictability of the turn. Saints help her—her grief wanted rules.

They stacked the packet on its tray. He slid it onto the chill shelf over his proving drawers. The glass fogged briefly, then cleared. The room felt like it...exhaled.

"Again," she said, already reaching for the next slab.

His mouth quirked. "Bossy."

They fell into a rhythm that felt perilously close to comfort. He dusted; she rolled. He turned; she folded. When the parchment stuck, he nudged it free with the scraper; when the butter threatened to break through, she patched it with a cold fingertip and a muttered line. She could feel the shop tracking them the way deer track the wind—ears flicking, then settling. Several times the chandelier tinkled, as if startled to find itself un-startled.

By the second chill, her shoulders had loosened. Not relaxed. Never that. But less tautly strung. She flexed her fingers and felt the absence of ache, which startled her: normally magic left her humming with residual voltage, as if she'd swallowed a storm. This left her...centered.

"If you tell anyone that my magic plays well with butter, I'll hex your eyebrows into retirement."

"Never," he said solemnly. "Your fearsome reputation is safe."

Maude gave him a sidelong glance. Maybe he wasn't a bastard after all. Maybe '*idiot*' was the promotion he deserved.

Wesley pulled down the first tray to begin shaping. Lamination flashed in delicate strata along the cut edge—thin, precise layers like pages in a book. The rune was invisible now, but she felt it inside the fold.

He cut a long strip; she watched his hands. When he handed her a piece to shape, he stepped back to give her space, which she noticed and pretended not to.

She shaped the pastry and set it on the tray. The tiny rune nested inside the layer clicked into place with its neighbors, as if they recognized one another, and the dough sighed again. Together they built a tray of crescents and layered squares, nothing too fussy, then slid it into the proving drawer where low warmth and a whisper of steam would wake them.

"Now we wait," he said.

She hated waiting. She propped a hip against the counter and pretended she wasn't vibrating—then realized she, in fact, wasn't. The usual itch to control every atom had been replaced by a cautious quiet.

"You're scowling," he observed, leaning beside her.

"I'm thinking," she said. "It looks the same from the outside."

"You could patent that. Weaponized contemplation."

She let the corner of her mouth move half a millimeter, which for her was hysterical laughter. "Bai—" *Bailey used to say.* The sentence almost stepped into the room without knocking. She froze, nostrils flaring. "I've heard that magic needs a container," she said at last. "Body to hold mind. Intention to hold force. That it frays if you let it go unshaped." She cleared her throat. "I hated that. I wanted it to do what I told it because *I told it.*"

"How old were you when you decided that?"

"Six," she said. "I was short and furious. Still am."

He made a small sound that wasn't quite a laugh and wasn't pity either. "Maybe he was right."

"Don't you dare," she said, but there wasn't any heat in it.

They watched the drawer. Dough lifted from itself, layers taking breath. The shop's temperature eased into a sweeter place; the chandelier's tiny prisms went still. On the shelf behind them, a jar that had been vibrating imperceptibly since the curse abruptly settled, as if grudgingly convinced to behave.

"You're doing it again," he said, not unkindly.

"What? Being excellent?"

"Counting all the ways it could go wrong."

"Useful habit."

"Sometimes," he allowed. "Sometimes it keeps you from seeing when it's going right."

She turned to say something biting and discovered he was closer than she'd clocked. Not looming, not crowding, but warm in that annoying way he specialized in. Lantern light drew copper from her hair and gold from his. For a second, the whole room felt paused, like the space between inhale and exhale when you're about to laugh or cry and haven't chosen yet.

The timer chimed.

They both exhaled and moved at once, grateful for motion. He slid the tray from the proving drawer; she held the oven door like a priestess holding a portal. Heat breathed out—clean, good, carrying a faint mint of rosemary from her side and the butter-fat prayer from his. He slid the tray in. They stepped back, shoulder to shoulder, bathing in warmth like cats.

They didn't talk for the first few minutes. It felt sacrilegious, somehow, to put words on top of the visible chemistry: the water flashing to steam, lifting layers; the butter basting from within; the delicate brown drawing like dawn across each ridge. The faint line of the rune moved—no, that wasn't right. It didn't move. It persisted. It held quiet in the middle of unfolding.

When the crescents were done, he pulled the tray. The room filled with the most unfair smell on earth: warm butter and proof that she had done at least one thing correctly. He set the tray down; she leaned in to inspect: laminated layers, clean lift, no butter bleed, no curse shimmer. She could feel her rune under her teeth, a hum that said *here, here, we're holding.*

He tore one in half to check the interior. The layers parted with a sigh, steam brandishing the scent in her face like a dare. He held half out to her. "Taste."

She took it, bit down, and the outside shattered. The center was honey-laced and tender. The magic didn't spark on her tongue; it sank. Carefully. Gentle as a hand over a frantic heart. She hadn't realized how bitter everything had tasted for months until it didn't.

"Well?" he said.

She chewed and swallowed and considered. "It's...fine," she said, and then, because the joke felt too small for what was happening in her chest, she added quietly, "It's steady."

He let out a breath that landed like a laugh that hadn't found voice yet. "Yeah," he said. "It is."

She stared down at the half in her palm, at the clean line of layers. A scandalous thought arrived uninvited and sat down: maybe she couldn't force her magic to stop mourning. Maybe she couldn't un-grief her grief. But she could give it steps. She could hand it to a process that knew how to repeat itself until the noise became muscle memory.

She knew this should make her furious. That it made her relieved felt like betrayal.

Silence stretched again, but it had changed shape—less the echo of a crypt, more the hush of a sanctuary. He looked at her hands—flour-grazed now, rune-warm—and then at her mouth, probably debating whether he had earned the right to say the thing forming behind his teeth.

"Say it," she said. She hated dithering.

"I think...your magic likes the way mine counts."

She should have bitten him for that. Instead, she set her half-crescent on the tray, pressed her palm to the cool bench, and gave a single nod. "Maybe. Don't let it go to your head."

"It already lives there," he deadpanned. That made her snort, which made him grin—like someone she could accidentally trust.

They made another tray.

Nine

The cold had finally arrived. It wasn't the soft kind that nipped playfully, but the sort that clawed at skin and tried to bore into bone.

Maude had stitched extra warming charms into her coat that morning, just to make it from her door to Market Square without turning into a freckled icicle. They worked well enough, humming faintly against the seams as she tugged the collar higher, breath misting in the air.

Strange, though. People were looking at her. Not in the usual way—like she carried a sickness everyone feared catching—but directly. A butcher gave her a nod as she passed. A young couple, arms tangled together, offered tentative smiles. One woman even lifted a hand as if to wave, then thought better of it and pretended to adjust her shawl.

The *"Haunted Bakery"* had changed something. The whole cursed, ridiculous abomination that had once been her private humiliation was suddenly...theirs. A story the whole town had claimed ownership of.

It was unsettling. They'd always loved Bailey. *Always.* She'd just been the quiet accessory trailing behind him—the grumpy punctuation to his practiced smile. A man could brood and be called thoughtful; a woman did it and became unlovable.

The town had tolerated her out of affection for him, not for anything she'd done. And when he was gone, she'd assumed whatever tiny margin of grace she'd inherited went with him.

It had never mattered what they thought. Not really. She had her shop, her friends, her cat. *Enough.* But now, as a few people nodded her way, her throat tightened against the unfamiliar weight in her chest. Strange. That's all it was. Strange.

"Excuse me!" A woman's voice cut through the square, bright and a little frantic.

Maude turned, already regretting it, but the woman—harried hair, smudges under her eyes, and three toddlers clinging to her skirts like leeches—looked desperate. The kids babbled nonsense words, their hands tugging at her dress, one of them waving a wooden spoon like it was a sword.

Maude exhaled slowly, then followed her inside. The house smelled of milk and exhaustion. The toddlers immediately circled her like small, chaos-wielding familiars, speaking in their own language of shrieks and squeaks. She startled herself by...smiling. Just a little.

The mother wrung her hands. "It's the hearth. The fire won't hold."

"Of course it won't," Maude muttered, brushing past. The runes carved into the fireplace were shoddy at best—done by some hack who thought chalk was an acceptable substitute for ash.

She pulled a small vial from her coat, flicked a sprinkle of yarrow ash across the carvings, and whispered the proper words. The flames leapt obediently to life, steady and warm.

The mother sagged with relief, murmuring thanks. Maude waved it off. "No charge. Just...keep them from licking the walls or whatever."

The toddlers giggled so hard their little shoulders shook, eyes shining like she'd just revealed their grand scheme.

Back into the chill, her boots slowed when she spotted him. Wesley. Striding down the lane like the cold bent around him, hair mussed like he'd been up since before dawn baking, steam still curling faintly off him.

Maude's stomach did something unpleasant—flipped, then settled in the wrong place. Last night flickered back into her mind. The rhythm of it, the folding, the way her magic had held steady for once when it ran through his careful process. It hadn't blown up, hadn't warped into ruin, hadn't turned the entire counter into licorice rope.

It had...worked.

Some kind of truce had slipped between them without her permission, unsteady and unsigned, but binding all the same. She felt weird about it. And yet...

Her fingers tightened on her coat strap. She forced her gaze away before she stared too long. Idiot or not, he wasn't terrible to look at. Not that she'd ever admit it out loud.

"Morning," he called, as if the word didn't taste like gravel. In his hands, two steaming cups. When he reached her, he held one out—ceramic glazed dark, a small star etched near the rim. "Peace offering?"

She eyed it like he'd just handed her a snake.

Wesley smirked. "Don't worry, if anyone here should be afraid of being poisoned, it's me. I wouldn't even know where to start with you."

The corner of her mouth twitched. She lifted the cup, sniffed. The scent hit like a punch—warm cinnamon, nutmeg, a whisper of clove. Autumn in a cup.

She took a cautious sip. The flavor bloomed rich and deep, comfort layered on comfort, and for one fleeting moment she let herself close her eyes.

"Good?" he asked.

She grunted.

"Was that a thank you?"

Maude ignored him, focusing on the path ahead.

They fell into step together, their strides mismatched but oddly companionable.

It didn't last.

The moment she turned onto Blightbend Way, her stomach dropped. The shop still pulsed with the faint glow of her containment spell—flickering, fragile, but holding. Yet the curse kept crawling outward, creeping down the street like ivy gone feral. Slow, yes, but undeniable.

And next in line was the floral shop.

Lydia Dross, the owner, was already outside, broom in hand as if she might sweep the rot away by sheer force of will. Her shrill voice cut through the street the second she saw Maude.

"This is *unacceptable*!" Lydia snapped, jabbing her broom. "You've ruined my begonias! My *begonias*! And if this...this nonsense touches a single petal of my orchids, I'll have the magistrates fine you into the ground."

Maude pinched the bridge of her nose. Of course Lydia Dross would be the one to make this worse. The woman had built her reputation on overpriced peonies and tactical customer complaints.

Beside her, Wesley gave a low whistle. "She's...spirited."

Maude shot him a glare. *Spirited* was not the word. Lydia Dross was a banshee with a license to sell daisies. And if Maude didn't do something soon, Lydia's shrieking would be the least of her problems.

Her mind turned fast, calculating. They didn't have time to test another patchwork spell. Waiting for Madam Quill to bring in shadowbell was laughable. No, this was outpacing them already. If she wanted to save her shop, her street, maybe even the entire block, she'd have to go to the source.

The Duskmire Peaks.

Maude sighed, the decision solidifying like iron in her chest. Dangerous. Far. Exactly the kind of thing Bailey had once warned her against attempting alone. But Bailey wasn't here, and she wasn't alone, was she?

She turned to Wesley, who was still sipping his coffee as if none of this was catastrophic. "We don't have time for tinkering."

His brow furrowed. "Meaning?"

"Meaning," she said flatly, "we're going after shadowbell. *Today.*"

Lists.

Maude trusted lists more than she trusted people.

So, naturally, Wesley got one.

It was scrawled in her quick, angular handwriting, folded twice, and shoved unceremoniously into his palm before he could argue. "You'll need all of this. Don't improvise."

He unfolded it and read aloud with mock solemnity. "'One: rope. Two: salt. Three: dried meat. Four: boots that won't fall apart at the first patch of mud. Five: more rope. And six: don't be an idiot.'"

"It says water flasks before that," she muttered as she searched for her gathering bag.

"Oh, it's there," Wesley said, grinning. "Just written in such tiny letters I nearly missed it. But don't worry, your little *'don't be an idiot'* note is bolded and underlined. Priorities."

"Exactly." She ducked behind the counter for her bag, fussing with the buckles. "Saints know, someone has to keep that face humble."

For once, his grin faltered—then came back twice as bright. "Careful there, Harrow. Keep talking to me like that and I'll have no choice but to fall for you."

Mischief flickered through his expression, a spark she'd come to recognize as trouble. Maude plucked a quill from the counter and pressed it into his chest.

"Start making your own packing list."

The shop's shelves clattered as she moved briskly through them, pulling jars and bundles down. Dried nightshade for warding, bloodroot for protection, powdered iron to throw down in case the Wilds grew teeth. A small vial of Bailey's old fire-starting tincture went into her satchel, tucked beside her rune stones. Another flask—this one filled with a potion for warding off frostbite—was stoppered tight and slipped into her coat pocket.

The space was chaos, as always, but it was her chaos, and every object had its place. Her hand lingered on the jar of shadowbell seeds Bailey had once harvested himself. Seeds wouldn't help; they needed the flower in bloom. Still, she brushed her thumb across the glass, then shoved it back into place before her chest tightened too much.

"Closed," she murmured, flicking her hand at the hanging sign on the door. The letters shimmered, shifting from **OPEN** to a more pointed **CLOSED. IF YOU TOUCH THE DOOR, I CURSE YOUR PETUNIAS**.

Satisfied enough with the decision, Maude scrawled a quick note on a scrap of parchment. *Cancel my order. Keep the coin. I don't care.* She folded it once, sealed it with wax that smelled faintly of rosemary, and slipped it under Grim's collar. He gave her a withering look, but she scratched between his ears anyway. "Drop it at Madam Quill's stall, then come back. Don't let her talk you into anything. And if she tries to pet you, bite her."

Grim blinked, unimpressed, and padded off toward the window, clearly weighing whether her request was worth the effort.

Maude didn't wait to see if he'd follow through. She swung her bag over her shoulder, pulled her hood low, and marched toward her cottage. Inside, she packed quickly: two clean tunics, one wool coat, leggings thick enough for mountain air, and boots already scarred from years of foraging. Her knife slid into its sheath. She bound her hair back in a braid so tight it made her scalp ache—better than loose strands whipping in her face when she needed her wits.

When she stepped out, her street buzzed with its usual strangeness. A brass weathervane spun in circles though the air was still, and Mrs. Calloway's mailbox was already growling at a delivery boy.

She hurried, her bag heavy, her mind heavier. At Oli's stables, Wesley was already waiting, leaning against the fence with a bundle of supplies slung over his back. To her faint surprise, he'd followed the list exactly: rope, flasks, rations. Even the boots looked decent. He caught her assessing glance and smirked.

"See? Not an idiot." He waggled the folded list between his fingers.

She rolled her eyes.

They didn't linger. Oli's manor rose behind the stables, lamplight glowing in every tall window. But today, the place was crawling. Carriages lined the gravel path, coats and polished boots shuffled up the steps, and a low hum of conversation spilled from the open doors. The kind of company Maude had no interest in ever keeping.

Oliver's family hosting officials wasn't unusual. But Oliver always told her. Always. Yet again, he was keeping something from her.

Her brow furrowed. "What's this?"

Wesley adjusted his bag. "Charity, from what I've heard. He catered one of their dinners last month—something about an endowment, funds for restoration, maybe. He was vague, but..." Wesley's shoulders lifted in a shrug. "Sounded like more than just a vanity project."

Maude narrowed her eyes at the sight of Oli, dashing in his emerald coat, laughing too easily with a cluster of aldermen. "He would."

"Would what?"

"Play both sides," she muttered. "Host the magistrates, play benefactor, keep everyone guessing which way his loyalties fall."

Wesley glanced at her, curious, but didn't press. She was glad.

Sylvie emerged, leading two saddled horses. Pickles for Maude and a sturdy bay gelding for Wesley.

"Your chariots, as requested," Sylvie said with a grin, passing the reins. "And if you come back with half the forest following you again, I'm quitting."

"Noted," Maude said, swinging onto Pickles. Wesley mounted beside her just as Oliver appeared inside the barn doors, gilded in early light, grin wide enough to split his face.

"Going somewhere, my darlings?"

Maude clicked her tongue. "If you don't start talking, I'm testing poisons in your wine cellar."

Oliver only laughed, waving them off. "Safe travels! Bring me back something scandalous!"

Maude gritted her teeth, spurred Pickles forward, and let the manor fall behind.

They passed the outer farms first, cottages crouched in mist, smoke curling from crooked chimneys. Farmers paused their chores to watch—pitchforks idle, wary eyes following.

The road soon narrowed to a dirt vein, swallowed by forest within minutes. Branches clawed at her coat, skeletal fingers snagging for want of purpose. Leaves whispered overhead, mottling the path in green-gold shadows that shifted with every gust.

Maude tugged her hood lower, fabric brushing her lashes, her pack a dull weight against her shoulders. Wesley rode beside her, posture infuriatingly straight, reins loose in his hands.

For a few hours, the only sound was hooves against the forest floor and the occasional snap of a twig—that was, until, the Peaks came into view.

Pickles's stride was steady, comforting in the way only an old, slightly bitter horse could be. Even so, unease scraped along her spine. The deeper they went, the stranger the air felt.

It started small. A crow perched on a branch, silent. A squirrel frozen mid-scamper, eyes too wide. Even the wind seemed reluctant, brushing the branches in half-hearted sighs. Pickles shifted uneasily beneath her.

Maude's fingers tightened on the reins. Something about this stretch of woods was wrong. Not dangerous in the obvious sense —no wolves, no bandits—but wrong the way milk turned overnight.

Untamed. Liminal. The kind of place that ate people whole and left their bones moss-coated in the underbrush.

Her throat closed like a trap. She shoved the thought down where all the sharp ones lived and risked a glance sideways. Wesley sat tall in the saddle, jaw tight, eyes forward. No grin. No infuriating smirk. Just silence and that furrow between his brows he probably didn't know he had.

So he felt it too. The sough of wrongness that clung to the bark, to the stones, to the air itself.

For a second, just one, she almost asked him. Almost. The words gathered in her throat, heavy as iron, but she couldn't force them past her teeth. Vulnerability wasn't her language.

Instead, she said, "If you get yourself killed, I'm not hauling your body back."

His mouth twitched, just enough to be irritating. "All right. But if you get yourself killed, I'm selling your cat to Lydia Dross."

A startled laugh cracked out of her before she could strangle it. The sound felt foreign in this place, a flare of light in all the shadow. She tried to turn it into a scoff, narrowing her eyes at him, but the edges softened anyway.

"Idiot."

"Pot, kettle."

Ten

The Peaks did not hurry to greet them.

They loomed on the horizon, jagged and spectral, their crowns pale with snow despite the season. The closer the road bent toward them, the quieter the world became. Birds abandoned the branches. Even the air thinned, edged with a steely tang that tasted like old coins.

Maude rode in silence, her chin tugged low against the rising chill. Her focus stayed on the path. On the way the shadows deepened in the underbrush, stretching into strange, too-long shapes.

Bailey had taken her this way once. Years ago, before his hair had gone entirely silver, before her sarcasm had hardened into a weapon. He'd pointed out the signs—the way moss clung heavier on one side of the trees, how the wind carried wrong in the hollows. Places where magic lay thin as parchment, easy to rip.

The Duskmire had always been hungry.

Now she felt its hunger pressing against her skin.

Ahead, Wesley rode straight-backed, easy, one hand loose on the reins. She hated that he hadn't cracked a joke for miles. The absence of his usual chatter left her unsettled.

Idiot, she reminded herself. *Not a bastard.*

Idiot was safer. Bastards could wound. Idiots you could dismiss.

Still, when his head tilted slightly, sunlight catching on the line of his jaw, she felt something traitorous stir in her chest. Not attraction, she told herself firmly. Just nerves. Just the strangeness of being here, of not being alone.

Pickles snorted, and Maude muttered, "Traitor," under her breath.

The road dwindled to little more than deer tracks, trees knit close together, branches clawing across the sky to blot out the last of the light. The horses stepped carefully, their hoofbeats muffled by packed needles. The Duskmire Peaks didn't welcome strangers. That was Bailey's first lesson, and Maude felt it keenly now.

"Charming place for a stroll," Wesley murmured at last, his voice pitched low.

"Don't get cocky—it's not impressed with you either."

He glanced over, and there it was—the twitch of his mouth, that smirk she'd been waiting for. But it didn't land the way it usually did. It looked like armor, not amusement.

They pressed deeper until the first sign emerged from the mist. It rose pale from the earth, tendrils coiling around tree trunks like restless spirits. And then it moved. Fast.

A shape coalesced in the fog, lupine, with eyes like lantern coals. Another followed. Wolves, their bodies half air, half shadow, their teeth bared and glinting wet though nothing solid moored them.

Maude's hand flew to the pouch at her belt. "Spectral beasts," she hissed. "Don't let them surround us."

Wesley's horse danced nervously under him, but his hands stayed steady. "Tell me what to do."

The words did something unhelpful to her chest. The immediate trust.

"Salt," she said, digging in her satchel. She tossed him a small pouch. "Circle wide. They can't cross it."

They split without another word, riding opposite arcs through the ferns and damp bracken. Maude leaned, scattering a pale ribbon that hissed where it touched the ground. The mist wolves stalked sideways, testing for gaps. One lunged and struck the white line. The impact rippled the fog that made its chest, then recoiled as if shocked. It snarled, a sound like breath dragged over glass.

"Left!" Wesley called.

She adjusted, closing the loop between a jut of stone and a fallen birch. He mirrored her on the right, salt streaming steady from his fist. Then he wheeled his horse inside the incomplete circle and cut hard left.

Two wolves overshot, momentum carrying them straight into the not-quite-visible mesh. They hit the ring and howled—an awful, splitting sound—as their forms fizzed against the salt like fat on a griddle.

Wesley glanced at her—hair wild, eyes burning green, salt flashing from her hand like lightning in a storm. His mouth curved, breath ragged. "Pretty."

"Bite me."

"*Later*," he shot back, reckless grin flashing as he skidded past —and she would have hexed him for that if three more wolves hadn't paced closer, eyes burning, jaws parting in silent howls. One tried again; the line hissed brighter. The beast wavered, tore apart like smoke in the wind, and reformed outside the ring.

"Hold," Maude said, breathless, more to herself than to him. "Just hold."

They waited. The mist thinned by a measure, the air relaxing its grip on her lungs. The wolves' eyes guttered to embers and then—finally—faded. The last of them bled back into fog and was gone. Silence fell so quickly it rang.

Wesley guided his horse back toward her. His grip on the reins was white-knuckled.

"Don't get comfortable," she said, pulse still banging at her ribs. "Those weren't wanderers—they were scouts. The Peaks always send scouts."

"Of course they do," he said dryly.

She urged Pickles forward. The salt circle would lose its charge in minutes. They needed distance. They needed high ground, rock to break the mist's hold. She scanned ahead, mapping the rise between twisted pines and black spruce.

They didn't make it far.

Wind sighed through the canopy with no leaves to justify the sound. The moss at their horses' feet shivered. A curling motion began at the edges of the world, so subtle at first that Maude thought it was just her vision adjusting to the gloom. Then it thickened, coalescing into a river of fog flowing downhill to meet them.

"Move," she snapped. "Now."

Wesley didn't ask a single foolish question. He dug his heels inward; his bay surged. Pickles lunged after him. They pounded up the slope, the ground slick with a skin of wet needles. Mist wheeled at their sides and swept forward to cut them off. Three wolves formed ahead in the span of a heartbeat, more solid than the scouts, sinew of fog twined tight over lanes of emptiness, the suggestion of ribs. An alpha pushed its head through the air, muzzle sharpened out of nothing, and bared spectral teeth.

"Right!" Wesley called.

"Left!" she countered at the same time.

They split again on instinct, a living pair of parentheses around the threat. Maude yanked her horse hard and spat a quick ward, flicking two iron shavings from the vial in her palm. The shavings burned with a dim red spark where they landed. One wolf swiped a paw over them and lost half its foreleg for a second; it reformed with a shuddering ripple, slowed.

Wesley's bay bunched its haunches and leapt a fallen tree. For a breath he hung in the air with the animal, coat flaring, and Maude had a stupid, ill-timed thought: *Beautiful.* The moment broke, and the mist crashed against the bark, spilling in a hiss around his horse's legs.

"Don't let it wrap the fetlocks!" she yelled. "It leaches heat first."

"How comforting," he called back. He slammed his boots to ground on the far side, reined in, and—*saints*—tore free the iron buckle from his saddlebags. He dragged it along the earth in a half-circle, sparks biting from stone, the line smoking where iron met soil.

"Clever," Maude muttered, and didn't hate him for a full second.

Her side was worse. The alpha tracked her, reading intention like a book. Pickles's ears flattened; the horse surged, sure-footed and furious. They crested a lip of land—and the ground dropped away. A sinkhole masked by debris yawned under the horse's forefeet.

Pickles threw himself sideways in a move that would have sent a lesser rider flying. Maude clung with knees and breath and every ugly fear she owned. The horse found purchase, skidding, and she felt the hole's cold breath on her ankle. The alpha took the chance and lunged.

She didn't think. She flung a hand and spoke a word Bailey never let her use unless it was truly bad. Power cracked in the air like a snapped bone. The wolf's muzzle struck an invisible pane and split apart, reforming with a wet sound on the far side. Its eyes burned brighter.

"Here!" Wesley's voice—too close, too fast.

He barreled in, swinging out of the saddle before the bay had even stopped. Hitting the ground in a low crouch, he yanked the salt pouch straight off her hip, caught it in one smooth motion, and slashed a white line across the mouth of the sinkhole. Then he planted himself squarely between Maude and the alpha.

"Move, Wesley!" she snapped. "It'll—"

The alpha struck the new line; the salt flared. The thing's head blew wide in soundless fury, then re-knit, slower this time. She used the beat. Pickles scrambled up enough to step away from the hole. Maude swung a leg over and dropped to the ground, ankle shrieking. She didn't listen.

"Give me the iron shavings," Wesley said, not looking at her, palm open.

She tipped a measured heap into his hand. He flung them low, wide, shallow. They landed like a scattering of dark stars across the moss. The mist thickened there, unhappy with the field of bite.

The alpha paced, testing for a gap. The fog at their backs bunched into another wolf, and another, flank to flank, hemming them to the lip of earth. Above, the canopy shivered like it had remembered wind.

"We hold here," Maude said. "Anchor. Fire if you can."

He didn't argue. He glanced once at the slope, measuring. "You have anything fast?"

"Not elegant," she said, already digging. "But fast, yes."

She pulled a squat jar from her satchel, wax-sealed and smudged with soot. She cracked the seal with a thumbnail, whispered a string of ugly little syllables, and slammed the jar down. Flames crawled out like a curious animal, then roared. The wolves recoiled with a hiss.

Wesley had flint out and a bundle of twigs gathered in seconds. He fed the jar's blaze, coaxing it along the iron-salted arc he'd scratched, turning the firewall into scalloped teeth. The air heated so fast, Maude's face stung.

The wolves shifted tactics.

They bled upward into the smoke—then dropped, raining down like shredded cloth. One hit just beyond the salt line, shoulders driving through, jaws snapping for Wesley's throat.

Maude didn't have the angle or time for a pretty spell. She threw her body into his, shoving him sideways. The wolf's teeth scissored shut on empty air.

He rolled with her, came up on one knee, and—damn him—

laughed once, short and unbelieving. "You're very strong for someone I could carry with one arm."

"*Saints*, you never shut up. Hand me the branch."

He did. She plunged the end into the flame; it came out a screaming brand. She slashed it through the wolf's face. Fog peeled back, soot-blackened and unsteady. It snarled and leaked away.

They moved together after that because there wasn't any other option. She handled heat and iron; he handled speed and angles and the blunt mechanics of staying alive. Twice he dragged her coat out of the snapping mist. Twice she scorched beasts off his boots.

And through it, the alpha waited. That was the worst of it. It paced beyond the fire's tongue, eyes two careful coals, letting the underlings tire themselves. Trying to read the seams in their defense. And Maude knew, with the part of her mind that still calculated under panic, that they couldn't hold a wall forever. The jar would give; the salt would dampen; the iron would cool.

"We need rock," she panted. "Stone holds wards. This—" She gestured at the slab of moss under their feet. "—is soup."

"Up there," Wesley said, chin jerking at a shoulder of granite showing through the green thirty paces left. "We sprint. On three."

"You'll never make thirty paces."

"We'll make it together."

"I hate that you sound so certain."

"One," he said, because of course he would.

"Wesley—"

"Two."

"Fine," she snarled, and grabbed his wrist.

"Three."

Maude slashed the air, and the wall of fire split open, a jagged wound of light. They ran. Pickles—long accustomed to her madness—swerved to flank them, ears pinned, head low and snaking. Wesley's bay plunged once, then surged forward, hooves tearing clumps of soil loose. The wolves poured after them, fog breaking like foam around their legs. At last, the alpha moved—uncoiling into a long, black ribbon of killing intent.

She threw the last of the iron shavings in a fan and felt the pouch go light. She lost a step swearing. Wesley took that half-stumble on his own body. His arm came around her waist without asking and hauled her forward. They hit rock and skidded. The granite was slick with a skin of fern, but it was stone, and that mattered. She slapped both palms to it and spat a ward so old she tasted blood.

Lines burned outward beneath her palms, etching a spiderweb of fire into the lichen—knot after knot, the net weaving itself bright and unyielding. The first wolves struck it and dissolved, collapsing into water for a single offended heartbeat before misting back together on the far side. But the far side wasn't inside. They prowled just beyond the barrier, reforming with low growls, their shapes circling, testing. The alpha only watched, eyes narrowing to slits, hunger sharpening in the dark.

"Keep them busy," she said through her teeth. "I'm going to anchor it. It'll hold better if it's fed."

"Fed with what?"

She looked at him, breaths quick. "Me."

"Absolutely not."

"Move, baker."

He didn't move. "Let me do it with you."

Her laugh ripped out, ragged as her breathing. "Left of me. The seam." She pointed. "Press your palms down. Even pressure. Don't let your pulse race."

"My pulse is—never mind." His palm found granite, fingers spreading. Heat rolled off him; it steadied, like laying a heavy book on a restless page. The ward's flicker evened.

She pressed her brow to the rock. It was slick, cold, braced with the memory of mountains. She gave it the thing the Peaks always understood: grief. Not the immaculate version she offered polite company—*oh yes, he passed in his sleep, he was old, it was time*—but the feral thing. The stubborn, ugly anger that he had left her with a shop that creaked and a town that judged and a heart full of knives. She didn't shape it; she let it be. And the stone took it like dry earth drinking rain.

The ward-web flared. Light spidered outward in furious lines, humming against her bones.

Maude's body shook with the effort. Her stomach hollowed as if she'd bled half her insides into the stone. But it was working. The wolves reeled back, hackles snapping flat. The air changed— the scent of snow and ash blowing through the glade, as though she'd opened a door to somewhere older, colder. A few shadows shredded outright, dissolving like paper in a storm. The rest skulked back a pace, repelled by that raw, ancient thing grief became when someone reckless enough—or desperate enough— let it out.

She tried to push herself up, but her legs trembled uselessly beneath her. Her vision stuttered at the edges.

Wesley's hand closed over hers. He didn't crowd her, just fitted his palm so their fingers wrapped the little curve together. "Breathe on the count," he said softly, not looking at her face. "In —two—three. Out—two—three."

She wanted to snarl. She breathed.

"In—two—three."

She hated him. She followed his count.

Her lungs steadied. The web held.

"Now," he murmured, and together they shoved the last of her magic into the ward.

The ground jolted beneath them. The alpha flattened, black shadow pressed razor-thin, eyes gleaming red as hot coals. It surged forward anyway, aiming for the seam where ward met stone.

"Hold," Maude rasped, throat raw.

"I'm not letting go."

The alpha hit the seam and punched through with its muzzle. Cold slammed into the circle. Maude's teeth clattered. Wesley dropped her hand, flung himself forward, and—idiot, absolute *idiot*—caught the alpha's jaws with his forearm.

The world went white.

He didn't make a sound. His body bowed, every muscle pulled taut in protest. Frost bloomed across his skin in a lacework sleeve where the mist touched—instant rime, glittering and lethal. Still, he held the creature's head in a wrestler's lock, using the sheer solidity of his body to keep the nightmare from pushing farther in.

"Finish it," he grated out.

Maude couldn't let herself think about the frost gnawing at his arm, the way his skin was blooming with crystalline lace.

There was almost nothing left. No iron. No salt. She dragged a nail across her palm, hissed, and smeared a bright, human line over the place the alpha's muzzle wanted to be.

Blood recognized truth. The web surged toward it like a tide.

The ward caught, edges gleaming like broken glass, locking the wolf's head in a vise of old magic. The alpha convulsed violently, shuddering between ribbon and beast, shadow and flesh. Every shift poured more winter into Wesley's arm. The ice climbed higher, flowering up his veins, every tendon strung in frozen fire, starbursts glittering under his skin.

"Let go!" she shouted, the command tearing from her throat.

"If I let go, it comes through," he ground out, jaw clenched, every word bitten between his teeth. "Do it."

Maude slammed her bloodied palm against the wolf's not-there skull, shoving her magic deep, up to the wrist, reckless and feral. The alpha shrieked in silence, soundless and terrible, as the web blazed brighter than fire. It didn't break—it cut.

The wolf sheared in two, split clean down some line only magic could see, and evaporated, sucked backward through the world like smoke through a keyhole. The glade roared empty. The rest of the pack broke like mist in wind, unraveling into nothing.

"Ha," she said, baring her teeth, pleased and vicious and only slightly unhinged.

Silence fell. Not the listening kind, but the kind that comes after a miracle or a catastrophe, when the world takes a breath and decides which way to tilt.

Wesley's laugh came out like something broken, then repaired. "Well," he said hoarsely, "that was terrible."

"Agreed," she said, equally hoarse.

He staggered. From wrist to elbow, his forearm was the sick gray of frostbite, ice etched into his veins in branching patterns like a shattered window. He cradled the arm tight against his chest, eyes pinched shut, breath pulled steady by sheer force of will.

Maude caught him by the shoulders and hauled him down to the rock. "Stupid," she said, voice shaking. "Stupid, heroic—*suicidal maniac*."

"Says the witch bleeding all over the mountainside."

"Hush."

She ripped open her satchel, hands moving faster than her heart. Comfrey salve—no good. Thawing tincture—yes. Warming draught—not for drinking; for skin. She uncorked a vial with her teeth and poured it over the ice-tattoo. Steam ribboned. He hissed finally, the sound she'd been waiting for and dreading, and clamped his jaw shut on the rest.

"It'll burn," she said, softer. "Better to burn than be dead."

"Convenient motto for your shop."

"Don't speak." She rubbed the tincture in with brisk, careful circles. The frost receded grudgingly, inch by inch, color creeping back. The branching pattern remained—faint white threads under the skin, a memory of having been almost not-alive.

She wrapped the arm in wool and laced the bandage with a whisper of heat that would hold for an hour. Then she just...sat back on her heels and looked at him. Looked at what he'd done. At the ward-web glowing like old starlight over their heads. At the cooling line of her blood.

She heard herself say the unthinkable. "Thank you."

His eyes flicked up to hers, surprised into something unguarded. "You're welcome," he said, equally unadorned.

She looked away first and bent to rearrange her vials, which did not need rearranging. Her hands wouldn't stop shaking.

"We make an excellent team," he said after a moment, voice rough but returning to its usual shape.

"We make a functional catastrophe."

"Semantics."

She wanted to laugh. She did not. The ward web dimmed a fraction and steadied; the air lost its blade-edge. The forest exhaled, a little resentful, a little impressed.

Maude wiped the blood from her palm on the moss and hissed when it stung. Wesley caught her wrist gently, with his good hand, and turned it to examine the shallow slice. He didn't comment, didn't tease. He tore the clean strip from his own sleeve with his teeth and bound her hand like he'd done it a thousand times—because he had—an apprentice, a baker—burned on hot trays, taught plants and pain by a mother who knew both well.

She waited for the pull to hate him again. It didn't come right away.

"We move when you can stand," she said—logistics were safer than truth. "The ward will hold an hour, maybe two. After that, the wolves will be back. They always come back."

He rolled his shoulder, tested his fingers under the wool. "My arm will work. Maybe not for pastry."

"Tragedy."

"Unspeakable."

The corner of her mouth betrayed her by moving, and she scowled at the trees to punish it. The light had shifted. That was the worst of it—how the Peaks bent time into useless shapes. Afternoon had become evening without consulting her.

She rose. The world swayed once, briefly. Wesley stood too, even slower. For a moment they simply stood there, close as they had been at the mixer, closer maybe, heat and breath finding a rhythm that had everything to do with not dying.

"Wesley," she said, which was stupid because she had nothing ready to follow his name.

"Yes, Maude."

She swallowed. "If you ever throw your arm into a monster's mouth again, I will turn your hair into bubble-wrap."

Lines bracketed his eyes. "Understood."

She picked up what was left of the salt. He gathered the reins. They didn't talk about how hard he shook when he thought she wasn't looking. They didn't talk about how she had to press a fist to her sternum like she could shove the heart back in through the bone.

The forest closed behind them, the web of light receding until it was only a rumor hung in branches.

They walked in step without trying. Not because they liked each other; not because fate or magic or the Peaks had decided it, but because sometimes surviving meant matching your breath to the person beside you. Even if he was an idiot. Even if she was impossible. Even if the mountains listened and reached and wanted.

Maude kept her eyes forward.

The quiet crouched, attentive. But it listened to something new now, something the wolves couldn't quite translate: two heartbeats, stubborn as iron filings, ringing like a bell through the trees.

Eleven

By nightfall, they made camp in a small glade where stone jutted through the earth in crooked slabs.

The Peaks loomed closer now, their ridges serrated against the crescent moon. The forest had thinned into a clearing where fern fronds glowed faintly silver under starlight, and the air carried the clean bite of pine and cold stone. Even the horses seemed relieved to stop, stamping and snorting in the shadows.

While Wesley built the fire, Maude walked the perimeter, pressing her palm to rock whenever she found it. She let her nails bite into her scab and offered blood to the cracks, a bead here, a smear there, weaving protection line by line until the glade pulsed with it. She worked quietly, careful not to draw Wesley's attention. She wasn't sure why she hid it. Instinct, maybe. Or because she knew exactly what he'd say—that she was reckless, bleeding herself thin; that there were likely smarter ways. He'd give her lip for it, and she didn't have the energy. Easier to keep it to herself.

By the time she finished, her head swam faintly, but the air around them felt lighter, clearer. The wards pulsed steadily in the stone. Maybe, with luck, the wolves would leave them alone for the night.

She returned to the fire, settling cross-legged across from

Wesley as he coaxed the flames higher—kindling, tinder, logs stacked like he'd done it a hundred times. Maude tried not to watch him. Instead, she unpacked her satchel, laying out herbs and vials in tidy rows, as though neatness might stitch the frayed seams of her mind back together.

The firelight licked over Wesley's face as he sat back on his heels, and for once, his expression wasn't smug. It was careful. Quiet. His eyes, usually bright as frost, softened in the glow, blue deepening to dusk.

"You've done this before," Maude said at last, if only to fill the silence. Her voice was low, scratchy. She gestured at the fire, the pan he balanced over it. "Camping. Roughing it. Not exactly bakery skills."

Wesley stirred whatever he had in the skillet, shoulders shifting. "I grew up on it. My mother...plants were her language." He paused long enough that Maude almost thought he'd stop there. But then he added, softer, "I picked up a little."

The fire popped. She should've left it there, let the silence fall back into place. But something in his tone—the gentleness in it—slipped under her armor.

"I haven't been out here since Bailey died."

She bit the inside of her cheek hard enough to taste copper. Six months of choking silence, and she'd handed a piece of herself to Wesley of all people?

But he didn't sneer. Didn't laugh. Didn't offer the empty platitudes people still tried to press on her like useless poultices. He only stirred the pan once, then set it aside, the firelight catching in his eyes.

"I figured," he said, his voice quiet. "The way you looked at the woods. Like they'd stolen something from you."

Her throat burned. She glanced away, focusing on the flames chewing logs into glowing coals. Anger, the only thing that ever seemed to come easily anymore, swelled in her chest.

For a long stretch, the fire was the only sound, pine sap hissing as it cracked into sparks.

Then Wesley said, softer still, "Bailey taught you, didn't he?"

She swallowed. "Everything I know."

"My mother was the same," he said. The firelight danced, mirrored in his eyes like glints off a frozen lake. "Not spells, exactly. She wasn't much for words of power. But she knew plants —how they healed, how they harmed. People came to her more than they went to the physicians. She could look at you and know if your lungs were wrong or if your blood was thinning. Could put the right leaf in your tea and you'd breathe easier by morning."

"What happened to her?" she asked before she could stop herself.

The pause was long. His gaze had shifted past her, somewhere into the trees where shadows bent crooked. "She died. Fever. Even knowing every herb in the forest, she couldn't cure herself."

The flames popped again.

Her hands clenched on her knees. "He left me with all of this." She gestured at the satchel, the herbs, encompassing in the motion the cursed shop that was waiting for her back home. Her throat went tight. "And I don't know if I'm angry at him for leaving or at myself for being the one left."

"I was angry too."

She lifted her gaze, and he was already watching her.

"After my mother. I thought if I worked long enough, hard enough, I could shut it out. But anger was all I had left for a while. Anger's easy. It feels clean. Like you're doing something, even when you're just...burning."

Her heart gave a traitorous twist. "And now?"

His voice was so low, quiet enough that she almost missed it. "Now I'm still angry. But it's not *all* I am anymore. That's the trick. It doesn't leave you. It just...stops being the only thing in the room. Eventually, I realized anger wasn't keeping her with me. It was only keeping me from living without her."

The words landed like a stone in Maude's chest, reverberating through the hollow space she tried so hard to keep locked. Her throat tightened. She looked away, but the fire blurred. *Damn him*, she thought fiercely. *Trust him to ruin a perfectly good sulk with logic.*

The silence stretched again, but it felt different now—less like suffocation, more like shared weight. He offered her food after a while: bread crisped over the fire, sprinkled with herbs. When she bit into it, the warmth spread down her chest, steadying.

"Not bad," she muttered.

His brows shot up. "From you, that's practically a standing ovation."

"Don't get used to it."

He grinned, quick, then let it fade back into the quiet.

When the pan was scraped clean, Wesley lay back on the ground, folding his arms under his head. Maude hesitated, then unrolled her coat and stretched out beside him, far enough that their elbows wouldn't touch. The sky opened above them—ink-black, spattered with stars like shards of glass. For a long time, they only listened to the crackle of the fire and the sigh of wind through the trees.

Then Wesley asked, "What did you love most about it?"

She blinked at him. "About what?"

"Working with Bailey. The thing that made you keep going after he was gone."

Her chest tightened, air catching on the question. She turned away so she wouldn't have to see him watching her, fixing her gaze on the star-pierced sky instead. Easier to speak to the night than to his face.

"I loved..." Her voice snagged, and she swallowed. "I loved the way he turned everything into a lesson without making it feel like one. How he'd drag me out to the Wilds in the middle of the night just because he'd spotted glowcaps blooming and thought I should see them before they burned out." A brittle laugh caught in her throat. "Or how he insisted every festival needed a prank— once, he hexed the mayor's wig to scream obscenities until sunrise. Claimed it was '*for morale.*'"

Her lips curved, then flattened. "He taught me how to climb cliffs without breaking my neck, how to haggle until merchants cried uncle, how to dance badly enough no one could accuse me of trying." She exhaled shakily. "He gave me all these pieces of a life I didn't think I'd get to have. But most of all... he never made me feel like I was in the way. He made space for me in everything. Even when I got it wrong, he'd laugh and make it part of the lesson. He made me feel like I wasn't just...some stray he'd dragged out of the woods. Like I mattered."

The last word cracked, and she bit it back, furious with herself.

Wesley adjusted himself, leaning on his side to face her. "That doesn't die just because he did. The way someone sees you—that's the piece that stays."

Her vision blurred again, traitorous, and she shut her eyes tight like a lock on a door. "And you?" she asked, forcing the words out. "What do you love most about baking?"

His chuckle was low, almost self-conscious. "The way that it's the opposite of healing."

She frowned, peeking at him. "That's a strange way to say it."

Firelight carved shadows along his jaw. "Everyone thought I'd become a healer. Maybe I could've. But healing's about fixing what's already broken. Baking's about making something that didn't exist five minutes ago. Both take care of people. One's just...sweeter."

His gaze tracked the stars, distant, thoughtful. "I like how a meal slows down time. A bite forces a pause. People sit. They breathe. For a moment, they're just...there." He glanced at her then, eyes catching firelight. "No one cheers when you balance the town books. No one sings when you mend a roof. But a tray of fresh rolls?" His mouth curved faintly. "Suddenly the whole street's smiling. I like that. That joy you don't have to bargain for."

The embers spit sparks, lifting like fireflies into the night. He leaned back on his elbows, eyes closing briefly. "Maybe someday

I'll open a stall at the docks—give free bread to the night workers. Or teach kids to bake. Something small, something good." He exhaled, long and even, and the sound carried like a promise into the cold air.

Maude's throat worked, words pushing up and tangling before they could form. She opened her mouth—closed it again. All that came out was a thin breath, frayed, as if her chest had forgotten how to hold anything gentler.

The night pressed close, cold and vast, but for the first time in six months, the ache in her chest didn't feel unbearable.

Not gone—she wasn't naïve enough to think it ever would be. Grief wasn't something you misplaced and forgot about. It was bone-deep, a permanent tenant. But, after speaking of him— Bailey—the good parts, the stupid little memories that had stitched their days together...it felt different. Different than saying the words to Oli or Selene, no matter how much they loved her, no matter how desperately they wanted to help.

Wesley hadn't pitied her. He hadn't hurried to soothe or fix. He'd just...listened. And somehow, that left her lighter.

Sleep crept in like fog off the Peaks. Her body yielded inch by inch, her breath falling into step with Wesley's, both moving to the quiet crackle of the fire.

Twelve

Morning came soft and silver, the Peaks veiled in mist as though the mountains had drawn curtains around themselves. The glade was still, dew clinging to every blade of grass, the fire a faint bed of embers pulsing in the half-light.

Maude stirred first, blinking against the pale dawn. Her ward shimmered faintly along the perimeter. She pressed her palm against the earth, testing. The weave held. No unraveling, no fractures. Pride sparked in her chest.

She rose stiffly, pulling her coat around her shoulders, and only then realized how close Wesley was. Sometime in the night, they must have drifted together, bodies hunting warmth the way roots seek water. His shoulder brushed hers, his breath a slow fog in the cold air. His face, slack in sleep, looked nothing like the man who needled her in waking hours with endless teasing. His cheeks were flushed red from the chill, his nose pink at the tip, his ash-blond hair a tousled snarl that refused to be tamed. She found herself caught by the stillness of him—the softened mouth, the faint crease at the corner of his eye that hinted at laughter even in rest.

Her gaze lingered a moment longer before she pushed to her feet, pulling her coat close as she turned toward the waiting work.

The horses stood at the edge of the clearing, their breaths steaming white in the cold. Pickles flicked his ears as she approached, nuzzling her hand with a familiarity that made her smile. She busied herself with the practical: checking hooves, rubbing down damp coats, doling out oats from the leather pouch tied to her saddlebag. Wesley's gelding muscled in for his share, snorting against her palm. Maude shoved his nose back, muttering, "Greedy brute," even as she measured out an extra handful for him too.

By the time she returned, Wesley was crouched by the fire, coaxing flame from ash. A pan already sat warming, strips of dried meat laid across it. "Breakfast," he said without looking up.

Maude sank onto her haunches beside him, pulling a small cloth bundle from her satchel. She unwrapped it slowly, revealing a handful of dried figs, their skins wrinkled and dusky, seeds glinting faintly in the firelight. She'd tucked them away more out of habit than intent—a forager's instinct to hoard small comforts when she found them—and promptly forgotten until now.

She held one out wordlessly.

Wesley glanced over, brow lifting, then took it without hesitation. With a quick twist of his thumb, he split the skin, revealing sticky, seedy flesh. He smeared the dark sweetness over a flatbread warming on the fire, then added a few thin slices of cured meat, pressing them down until the fat began to melt into the heat.

The scent rose immediately—smoke and salt, sweetness and spice—curling through the air until Maude's stomach tightened in response.

He broke the flatbread in half and held one piece out to her.

She didn't thank him, just tore a bite with her teeth. The tang of fig hit first, rich and honeyed, followed by the salt of the meat and the soft warmth of the bread. A sound slipped out of her before she could stop it.

Wesley didn't comment. He didn't even look at her. He only smiled faintly down at the fire.

When they finished breakfast, Maude brushed the crumbs

from her lap and pulled the map from her satchel. The parchment was creased from years of folding, its ink smudged in places by damp fingers and spilled potions. She traced the ridges and winding trails until she found what she wanted.

"We'll follow the ridge trail," she said at last, her voice steady. "If the weather doesn't turn, we'll make the ruins by midday."

"Ruins?"

Maude didn't look at him. She folded the map along its worn seams and tucked it back into her satchel. "Bailey and I used to gather shadowbell there. They like places that remember what's been lost. Leavings of death, decay, battles...memory clings to the soil, and shadowbell thrives in it."

His brow arched higher, but—for once—he didn't comment. She was almost disappointed.

They broke down the campsite in silence. Wesley doused the fire, scattering the embers with a stick before tipping the last of their water over the coals. Maude gathered the bedrolls, folding hers with neat, exacting corners while his was shoved into a bundle that still somehow looked tidy. She tucked her satchel shut, herbs and vials clinking faintly inside, then tugged her coat back over her shoulders, fastening the clasp at her throat.

Once everything was in order, Maude swung up into the saddle, ignoring the pull in her arm as Wesley fell in just behind, his horse's hooves crunching steadily against the frost-hardened earth. The sun was pale overhead, weak and washed out. Maude kept the map in her mind, following landmarks burned into memory—old oaks split by lightning, a crooked boulder shaped like a crouching beast, the faint ridge trail winding toward the Peaks.

Pickles's ears flicked nervously. Wesley's bay huffed, restless, its muscles bunching under the saddle.

And then Maude felt it.

It wasn't mist this time—it was memory. The air grew heavy, the way a room feels when someone has just left it forever. Sound dulled around them. The wind stilled. Even the horses' steps seemed muffled.

Her skin prickled. She knew this place. Knew it in her bones, though she hadn't been here in years. Bailey's laugh ghosted through her head, echoing against stones long since fallen. She shoved the thought away before it could lodge too deeply.

The path bent once more, and the ruins came into view.

They were neither grand nor close, just a broken skeleton of a chapel. Moss clung to cracked pillars, and the altar lay in shards, half-buried under ivy. Yet the place throbbed with presence. With sorrow soaked into the stones.

And in the center of the ruin, a shimmer of light congealed into form.

The guardian.

It rose taller than a man, its body a shifting weave of smoke and memory. Its face was featureless, yet Maude felt its gaze pierce her, cold as moonlight. When it spoke, the sound pressed inside her skull, hollow and resonant, like bells tolling under water.

"All bloom is bought in pain. All grief must pay its tithe.
Lay bare the wound that bleeds the loudest—
surrender the memory that chains your soul.
One truth for one truth.
One loss for one flower."

The words shivered through her bones, and her pulse slammed.

It wanted a tithe. A memory—a memory so raw it ached in the moment of offering. And once given, it would be gone. Forever.

The specter turned toward her, its shape wavering like water disturbed by a breath. *"What do you offer, child of the Wilds?"*

Her stomach clenched. Bailey's face rose in her mind, silver hair falling loose as he bent over parchment, his muttering voice in her ear, his warm hand steadying hers when she fumbled a sigil.

She couldn't—not him. Not even a piece.

"No," she whispered. Louder, she said, "I won't."

The guardian tilted its head, formless face unreadable. The air thickened, pressing like stone against her lungs.

Beside her, Wesley dismounted slowly. His boots whispered against the cracked stones as he stepped forward. "I'll do it."

Maude spun toward him, heat spiking through her chest. "What?"

He didn't look at her. His gaze stayed fixed on the guardian. "Take mine."

The guardian's voice pressed harder. *Truth for truth. What memory do you yield?*

Wesley's jaw flexed. His hand closed at his side, knuckles whitening, but his voice stayed even. "My mother...she used to sing while she worked. Nothing grand—just simple things. Humming under her breath while she mixed salves. When I was a boy, I thought it was the sound of safety. The sound of home."

Maude's breath caught as the air stilled. The guardian drifted forward, and for a moment the ruins filled with the scent of rosemary and smoke. Then it surged, rushing through Wesley as if his body were nothing but a doorway.

He convulsed, breath tearing from him. The guardian's quivering outline shuddered once, then dissolved into the stones, gone as though it had never been.

The ground trembled.

Between the cracked bones of the altar, buds unfurled, pushing up through dust and ruin. Dusky blossoms curled open, their petals dark as twilight, their shimmer tinged with sorrow. Shadowbell.

A sour twist knotted Maude's gut. "What is wrong with you?" she said, fury spilling from every word. "Why would you— why would you give that up? Something that *precious*?"

Wesley turned, his face pale but composed. His eyes, when they met hers, were unflinching. "What's the point of holding it," he said quietly, "if it doesn't help someone else?"

The words punched through her anger, striking deep. She opened her mouth, but nothing came. She wanted to scream at him.

She wanted to shake him until his teeth rattled. Instead, she stood frozen, breath ragged, staring at him as the shadowbell shimmered in the ruin's gloom. For the first time, Maude didn't see a rival, a thorn in her side, the bakery idiot who ruined everything. She saw a man who gave of himself freely. Who lost and still chose to offer what remained.

And it shook her more than any curse.

Her knees went soft, her breath hitching sharp and shallow. Fury surged hot under her skin, tangled with devastation so serrated she thought it would split her open. She shook—hands, chest, every bone trembling as though her body couldn't decide whether to collapse or combust. Her throat burned, bile rising. She pressed a hand to her mouth, convinced she was going to throw up.

And then, in two quick strides, Wesley was in front of her. Pulling her into him like it was the most natural thing in the world. Her face pressed hard against the solid breadth of his chest. Heat radiated through his shirt, carrying the faint, grounding scents of flour and smoke, yeast and spice, a touch of pine from the woods still clinging to him.

It was jarring. Lovely. Warm.

She hated it.

Saints, she *hated it*.

Him.

For giving something so sacred. For making her feel like she was the selfish one, clinging to grief like a dragon hoarding bones.

Maude fought the urge to shove him away, to spit every venomous word she had saved for him since the day his bakery doors had opened. But her arms betrayed her. They lifted, hesitated, then clutched him tight, fingers curling in the fabric at his back. She buried herself deeper into his chest and let the tears fall.

They came hard, hot, and endless, streaking down her cheeks until the ruins blurred into nothing. She didn't sob—there was no sound, just the violent shake of her shoulders, her chest heaving like it couldn't contain the heartache anymore.

And he held her.

One broad hand cradled the back of her head, the other firm at her spine as though she might shatter if he let go. His chest rose and fell beneath her cheek, slow, steady. When she finally forced herself to lift her head, her face worn and damp, she found his eyes waiting. They were glassy, rimmed faintly red. His cheeks flushed as though he'd stood too long by the fire. He blinked hard, but it didn't mask the truth of it—what he'd given up. It had scraped him raw, too.

Maude thought of him humming in the mornings, tuneless, infuriatingly cheerful, as if mocking her gloom. How she'd resented it. How she'd muttered curses under her breath each time he did it. All this time, he had been humming his mother's song. Carrying her with him into every loaf, every roll, every cake while Maude steeped in her fury, crafting spells and potions with Bailey's voice in her head.

And now that song—its sound, the shape of it—was gone. Surrendered to the ruin. Did he still know the tune? Could he still feel it in his bones, or had the guardian truly stripped it clean away?

The thought gutted her. It was too much.

With a ragged sound, Maude shoved back—broke free of his arms, turning hard so he wouldn't see the tears that still hadn't stopped. She wiped at her face furiously, scraping her skin until it burned, until it felt like something she could control.

She dropped to her knees before the newly blooming shadow-bell, the flowers glowing faintly in the hush of the ruins. Her hands shook as she reached for them, but she forced her breathing even, steady enough to cut the stems clean and tuck each bloom carefully into the pouch at her belt.

Behind her, Wesley didn't move. Didn't speak. She could feel his presence, though—warm and watchful, like the hearth-fire she wanted to ignore but couldn't.

Eventually, his shadow fell beside hers. He knelt without a

word, his long fingers moving with surprising gentleness as he helped gather the blossoms.

Neither spoke.

And though she wanted to hate him, wanted to shove him back into the mist and pretend he hadn't given something up so she didn't have to, she couldn't.

Not with him kneeling in the dirt beside her.

Thirteen

The ride home blurred into one long, bone-deep ache. Hooves struck the soil in a dull rhythm, leather groaned, breath rasped. Wesley rode a little ahead, shoulders squared, the moon catching the line of his coat and the rigid set of his back.

Maude kept her eyes there. She told herself it was something to follow, something solid. But the truth sat heavier: he steadied her.

They didn't talk. Not after the ruins. The silence clung, thick as damp wool, not empty at all but swollen with everything they'd lost.

The mist wolves didn't return. Maude couldn't say whether the tithe frightened off or appeased them. She only knew the absence of them felt like borrowed grace, a reprieve she hadn't earned.

The Peaks fell away behind them, craggy silhouettes shrinking into gentler hills. Trees thinned and the path widened, but neither of them suggested stopping. They rode hard, letting distance eat up the night. By the time Mistwood's lanterns winked faintly across the valley, Maude's bones buzzed with exhaustion, every muscle hollowed out and humming.

It was well past midnight when they clattered into Oliver's

stables. The horses came in heaving, hides lathered and steaming, but grateful to be done. Maude and Wesley worked in silence, moving by habit—slipping bridles off, offering water, dragging brushes through their coats. Maude's hands shook against Pickles's mane, the tremor running all the way to her shoulders. The gelding pressed his great head into her chest with a weary huff, solid and warm, and she bent low, whispering thanks into the soft curve of his ear.

When she finally turned, Wesley was standing there with his hands shoved into his pockets, eyes shadowed. His hair was mussed, his shirt smeared with dust and travel, and he looked— well, he looked human in a way she hadn't quite seen before.

He shut Pickles's stall door, then straightened. "I'll walk you home."

She let out a dry laugh. "Home? No."

His brow furrowed.

"I'm going to the shop."

His mouth dropped open slightly, incredulous. "Now? You can barely stand."

She squared her shoulders, though her legs trembled under the effort. "I have to end this, Wesley."

Something in her tone made his expression shift. His gaze lingered on her a beat too long, heavy enough that she felt it. As if he were searching her face for something she hadn't said aloud. His jaw tightened. Then he gave a single nod—curt, resigned. Whatever he thought he'd found in her words, it wasn't what he'd wanted.

"Fine," he said, "lead the way."

Blightbend lay hushed under the moon, its crooked row of shops sleeping like old dogs in the dark. Only theirs was awake. The fused façade pulsed faintly, pastel sweets and creeping rot locked in their uneasy stalemate. From a distance, it looked less like a shop and more like a beast—breathing shallowly, waiting.

Maude's hand hovered on the latch. Every part of her wanted bed, silence, five hours of being no one. But pride stitched her spine into something resembling upright, and she pushed inside.

The air slapped her. Sugar clogged the back of her throat; damp rot crept like mold under the floorboards. It smelled like a wedding and a funeral shoved into the same church and told to get along.

Grim appeared from behind a tower of boxes, tail flicking, yellow eyes gleaming with that eternal feline expression: *I've been in charge since forever, and everything you've done is wrong.*

Maude dropped her satchel and crouched, fingers twitching into sigils. "Hold still," she ordered.

He didn't. He never did. He arched his back into the spell like it was a back rub he'd been waiting for all night.

The wards skimmed his fur—nose, ears, paws—glowing briefly. No new spread. Still just the faint pink shimmer, stubbornly contained.

Relief pooled in her chest. "Of course you'd fight off a curse out of spite," she muttered, pressing her forehead to his.

That should've been the end of it. But Grim, contrary menace that he was, did something almost alien—he butted his head against her chin once, twice, hard enough to sting. Then he purred. A real, rolling purr, deep and even.

Maude went very still. Grim did not dole out affection. He tolerated. He suffered. He sometimes refrained from murder. But this—this was love, plain and uncamouflaged.

Her throat tightened around words she didn't know how to say, so she just held him there, one hand curled in his fur, letting the vibration shake through her bones until it almost felt like they belonged to her again.

Eventually, Grim tired of her sentimentality and hopped down like he hadn't just shattered her heart in the gentlest way possible. The warmth went with him, and in its place came the colder, heavier truth waiting on the counter.

She spread Bailey's parchment across the scarred wood and pinned the corners with jars. The shadowbell flowers waited beside it, the price of them still lodged in her chest. One by one, she set out what they'd dragged from the Wilds—less a list on paper than something carved into her bones:

Ironvine, coiled tight as tempered wire.

Blackthorn bark, bitter to the tongue.

Rosemary, biting clean, its scent cutting through the mix.

Bloodroot, damp, still smelling faintly of copper.

Yarrow, pale and stubborn as weeds between stones.

Moondust caps, fragile spheres that powdered to silver at the touch.

"Salt and iron filings," she said at last, her voice steady for once. "Circles. Wide. Runes at the quarters."

Wesley moved without question, sifting the mixture into careful arcs. Pale dust drifted in the lamplight. It powdered his hair, softened him, made him look like he'd been standing under falling snow.

Grim hopped onto a stool like a disapproving overseer, tail giving a single thump when Wesley finished the circle and dusted his palms clean, waiting for her next move. Maude ground the shadowbell flowers into powder, the pestle grating low against stone. The scent rose—sweet ache, sharp as pressing your forehead to a door you weren't ready to open.

When everything was in place—the salt ring, the powder, the half-finished notes Bailey had left—she and Wesley stood shoulder to shoulder before the cauldron-mixer abomination. Its gears ticked faintly in the hush, runes pulsing like an anxious heartbeat.

"Ready?" she asked.

His nod was curt. Serious.

Maude measured, every motion clipped as though the wrong breath might topple it all. A pinch of ironvine to bind intention. Shavings of blackthorn for teeth against undoing. Rosemary to cut through the muddle, to make clean paths. A smear of bloodroot to tie it to the living heart. Crumbled yarrow for purification. A careful drift of moondust caps to speak to tides and timing.

And finally, the shadowbell—ground to dark silk, petals dissolving into dust that smelled faintly of rain. Shadowbell was grief made tangible—loss distilled. It gave the spell memory, weight, the ache that made magic linger when it wanted to slip away.

Wesley poured water in a thin stream, and the salt-and-iron circle brightened under their feet. The runes on the iron casing woke, violet and low.

Bailey's lines came out of Maude's mouth like she'd been carrying them inside of her cheek the whole time, saving them for when they tasted right. His script had always been more music than instruction. She hummed the notes of it under her breath, then did the thing he'd taught her when magic refused to listen—she changed one thing.

Tiny. A twist in the last couplet turned inward instead of outward, not *"bind the breach"* but *"teach the blend to loosen."* Not an order. A suggestion.

The dough hook turned.

Slow, then faster, catching the petals, the powders, the shred of rosemary. The air thickened. The floorboards heaved under their boots. Somewhere, glass sang.

"Steady," Wesley murmured, and the word curled deep in her gut. It was the first time she'd heard him talk to magic like it could listen—like she did. Her fingers faltered for half a breath before she forced them to behave.

The runes flared sapphire. The mixer bucked once, hard enough to rattle the jars, and then the hook settled into a thick, rolling pull. Power climbed the air—damp, sweet, iron, smoke. Sugar and sage rose together, braid over braid. The floor shivered. The glass bell above the door trembled against its bracket with a delicate, maddening *tink*.

The walls tried to split—she felt it like a stubborn seam under her palms—and she pushed the cadence harder, urging the binding to change its mind about what binding meant. *Not you to me. Not thing to thing. Tie to breath. Tie to dawn.*

Rot pulled back like a tide. The damp tug in the boards dried to simple old wood. The garish confectionery sheen dimmed to an honest gloss. Shelves straightened. Jars shimmied back into their grooves. Sprinkles retreated from her apothecary scales; her labels unblistered, curling flat again.

The air cleared to something that still wasn't proper but was no longer a fight—lavender and cinnamon lacing instead of clawing. Even Grim's ears relaxed.

Maude didn't realize she'd been holding her breath until her lungs remembered themselves. She braced a hand on the counter. "Oh," she said stupidly.

Wesley's laugh broke out of him like relief does when you've had a hand around your throat for too long and it finally loosens. Warm. Unvarnished. It made space in the room. And, saints help her, she laughed too. It sagged with exhaustion, but it was real. A sound she'd lost somewhere in the last six months elbowed its way up and out and existed again. She clapped a hand to her mouth.

"Saints," Wesley said, staring at her like she'd grown a second head. "You laugh."

"Don't make it weird," she managed.

"Too late," he said, grinning in a way that erased ten years and three layers of armor.

She almost smiled again before the room tipped—no, not the room. Her vision. For a second, everything blurred and swam and—

Wesley vanished.

The space where his body had been went cold so fast that the blood under her skin tried to follow it out. Maude's stomach dropped to the floor.

"Wesley?" It came out as a bark, a stupid, desperate thing that bounced off glass.

Silence. The cauldron hummed on, very proud of itself.

"Wes—" Panic snapped a cord in her chest. Her mind flashed through all the ways magic ate: unraveling, unmaking, pinching the wrong thread and watching a person come apart like cheap knitting.

A shout cracked the night open across the street. "Maude!"

She pushed off the counter too fast and almost fell, but caught herself on a shelf and flung herself out the door with enough force to rattle the bells. Maude stumbled into the fog, breath tearing, and there—across Blightbend Way—his shop stood where the shell had been, pastel and ridiculous and whole. Light burned in the window like a smug sunrise.

Wesley leaned in the doorway, grinning like the cat that got the cream. His hair was a disaster. His shirt was torn at one sleeve. He looked like a painting of joy made by someone who'd sworn they didn't believe in it.

Maude's laugh—real this time, bright and wicked—ripped out of her so hard it bent her double.

Five strides across the narrow lane and Wesley was there, scooping her off her feet before she could pretend she didn't want that to happen. She went airborne—just a spin, the world a blur of crooked roofs and wet stars and the foolish, relief-drunk face of the man who'd helped her breathe tonight. He set her down before any part of her pride could file a complaint, but not before her hands had found his shoulders and held.

"You did it," he said, breathless, laughter threaded through his voice. "You brilliant witch."

The street tilted pleasantly. Her mouth hurt from smiling. She felt like she'd swallowed a spoonful of Shifter's Delight. For one slow, ringing heartbeat, it was just them and the fog and the empty street and the relief.

A bell in the distance tolled the hour.

Clarity cut through on the tail of it, sudden and uninvited. She knew he felt it too—could read it in the way his touch turned hesitant. He set her down as if she were glass and eased back a hand's width.

They looked at each other like the first inkling of a headache, like a good dream caught by daylight.

"Well," he said, mouth tipping crooked. "That's that, isn't it?"

"It is," she said. The words felt too tidy and not true enough. She lifted her hand between them anyway, palm open for a shake. "Terms of truce honored."

He looked at her hand, and a soft, incredulous snort escaped him. "A handshake? After all that? Saints, Harrow."

"Take the win, baker."

"Yes, ma'am." His palm met hers, warm and wide, callused in ways that made sense now. He squeezed once—proper, businesslike—and didn't let go for a beat beyond polite. His thumb twitched, as if he had to stop himself from doing something unwise—and then he released her.

She brushed a hand down her unruly curls. "Go to sleep, Wesley."

He studied her face. "Are you heading home?"

"Not yet." She forced her voice back into its old shape. "You go. I have a few things to wrap up."

He looked like he might argue. Then he didn't. "Don't explode the town while I'm gone." He tipped her a mock salute and jogged back across to his own door.

She watched him go, the swing of his shoulders unaccountably interesting. The Sugar High sign creaked, as if clearing its throat. He turned once at his threshold, caught her looking, and for one dizzy beat they just...smiled at each other like idiots.

Then he vanished inside.

The moment folded up and put itself away.

Maude breathed. In. Out. She turned, went back into her shop, and shut the door.

The room felt like itself again. The counter wore its scars without apology. The herbs on the wall hung with their old, ordinary gravity. The cauldron gave one last contented sigh and went quiet, runes dimming to a sleepy pulse.

Grim leapt onto her shoulder as if he'd always intended to, dug his claws in just enough to sting, then settled like an arrogant scarf.

"Yes," she told him. "I know. You did everything. Please accept this promotion."

He purred.

Maude returned to the counter, moving carefully, as if sudden motion might wake something. She tidied because she needed to put her hands on tasks that ended. Ironvine back into its jar, label facing front. Blackthorn wrapped in oiled paper. Rosemary bundled tight with twine. Bloodroot scraped, dried, stored. Yarrow's pale heads rubbed between her fingers until they surrendered to dust. The moondust caps tipped into their tin with reverence, making the faintest chiming sound as they settled.

Last: shadowbell.

There were a few blooms she hadn't needed to grind—a margin for error she'd refused to use. She lifted each with careful fingers, the petals cool and tender as night. Their scent rose—sorrow tempered, gentled by work done well. She slid them into a small glass bottle, stoppered it, pressed wax into the cork, and set it on the shelf where Bailey had kept rarities.

Her hand went to smooth the shelf and caught on a burr. No—paper. Something tucked between wood and the backboard, a corner curling like a beckoning finger. Maude frowned, slid her nails in, and worried the thing free.

Vellum. Bailey's, from the weight. The edges were singed as if he'd held it too close to a candle. Ink had bled in places where damp had found it. She knew his hand the way you know the inside of your house in the dark.

Her stomach made a slow, unpleasant turn.

She unfolded it.

Lines. A diagram she recognized and wanted to pretend she didn't. Couplets. A rune set.

The lamplight jittered. Or she did.

She read.

Not a sabotage. Not even close. The top line named the thing without flinching, and the name sat in her mouth like ice: *interlock.*

Her breath thinned to a thread.

Bailey had written like a man leaving a message under a floorboard for a future version of himself he didn't trust to remember. Notes in the margins:

Interlock, variant: for the holding of what strains to part. Temporary stabilizer only. Masks fracture, buys time. Must be severed. Left unchecked, bond will keep seeking more until all is drawn into one.

The room seemed to tilt and then tilt back. The words held steady.

He'd made the interlock as a stabilizer, something to hold fragile things together until they could be mended—a cracked wall until the mason arrived, a bridge until new timbers could be laid, a broken body held together until a surgeon could finish the work. Pragmatic, temporary, a way to buy time. His notes stressed it again and again: *must be severed. Left unchecked, bond will keep seeking more until all is drawn into one.* He assumed anyone using it would know how to unpick the seams.

Two spells not meant to touch had tangled—her spell meant to fracture, his meant to hold—and the result had been a runaway loop. Fracture, bind, fracture, bind. Over and over. Until it stopped being a patch and became a hunger.

That was why the street had blurred, softened, melted into nightmare. The combined spells were simultaneously trying to break Blightbend and make it one.

Her mouth went dry. She read the lines three times, then four, hoping they would rearrange themselves into a joke. A test. Anything but exactly what they were.

Maude put her hands flat on the counter because they were shaking. She shut her eyes and saw the street as it had looked an hour ago: marshmallow grass and sugared wheelbarrows, stone cracking to rot. She saw the line of shops as a mouth of crooked teeth, all of it softening under a tide.

Wesley's laugh echoed in her skull, warm, unguarded. *You did it.* Her own laugh answered it, like a fool.

The cauldron ticked once as the spell cooled. The lamp over the counter hummed. In the alley, something—crow, demon, wind—scratched stone.

Maude opened her eyes.

Bailey's hand waited on the page, neat as ever. She swallowed. Across the street, the light went out in the bakery. Wesley's silhouette passed the window and vanished.

"Of course," she said softly. It didn't sound like her voice. "Of course it isn't over."

Grim head-butted her jaw. She didn't swat him away.

She folded the parchment along its original crease, then folded it again because she couldn't bear to see the words. She slid it into a drawer and closed it gently, the touch of a priest at the altar.

The shop was quiet. The quiet had teeth.

Outside, Blightbend Way slept like a beast that had only rolled over, not settled.

Maude blew out the lamp. The dark came down all at once, clean and absolute. In it, she could hear her heart and the last, almost inaudible murmur of the runes in the cauldron—like a clock ticking toward a time she didn't like the sound of.

Not long at all.

Fourteen

Opaline light spilled through the shop windows, turning dust to glitter and cracks to character. Even Blightbend Way looked polished instead of crumbling. Maude stood at her counter, hands wrapped around a steaming mug, and tried not to think about how wrong the quiet felt.

The curse had lifted—but only the way a shadow lifts when a candle gutters. The shop sounded whole again: jars settling on their shelves, the faint chime of glass in the draft, wood groaning softly in reply. Across the street, Sugar High gleamed like fresh paint over a wound. No grotesque fusion. No marshmallow cobblestones. Just two shops, separate again, as they were meant to be.

She should've felt triumphant. Instead, her chest was a hollow drum.

The shadowbell petals she'd jarred sat on the shelf, deceptively still. Bailey's scrawled note gnawed at her thoughts. *Interlock.* The word branded itself on the inside of her skull.

When the first knock rattled the glass door, she nearly dropped her cup.

It wasn't the magistrates, or Wesley, or even Oli—worse. It was a customer.

Then another. And another. By midmorning, the Elixir Emporium sounded like festival day—murmurs, laughter, the scrape of boots across its uneven floorboards. Her newly found sanctuary was officially breached.

And they weren't here for what she actually made. No one asked for Bailey's calming tonics or the lung draught he'd perfected after weeks of testing on himself until he coughed blood. No, they came clutching Sugar High's greasy little paper bags, faces glowing with excitement, chirping requests that made her teeth grind. *Can you just sprinkle something on this? Make it sparkle? Maybe make it wiggle, like it's alive?*

At first she tried the death-glare-and-wave-off approach, perfected over years of discouraging the cheerful. But then came the sound—coins clinking against the counter, one after another, a metallic waterfall. Each drop felt like an accusation, like the stack of unpaid bills in her drawer whispering, *"Take it, you coward."*

Maude pinched the bridge of her nose, muttered a curse at the universe, and finally sighed. Against every better instinct she had, she agreed.

A charm of floating candles woven into a croissant. A sugared rune that made eclairs sing—off-key, but the crowd howled with laughter. Cupcakes that whispered compliments when bitten. The shop transformed into a theater of edible mayhem.

Every time someone clapped or gasped, Maude's stomach sank further. This wasn't Bailey's legacy. This wasn't what he'd built, what he'd taught her. He hadn't spent years turning weeds into salves and superstition into medicine just so she could enchant muffins to moo like cows.

But the coins piled high, glittering with promise.

By noon, Wesley appeared in her doorway, sleeves rolled to his elbows, flour still dusting his jaw. He took one look at the crowd, then at her, and had the audacity to grin. "So this is what success looks like."

"Careful; your smug is showing," she muttered, binding another eclair with a shimmer of sparkle-dust.

He leaned a shoulder against the doorframe, watching her work. After a beat, his brow furrowed. "Have you eaten lunch?"

"I'm busy," she said, not looking up.

"Well then," his tone turned infuriatingly light, "you won't be wanting this." He produced a small paper packet from behind his back, unfolded it, and revealed a still-warm cheese roll, crust blistered, edges flecked with rosemary.

Maude froze, gaze darting from the roll to his face. He raised an eyebrow, waiting. She snatched it, bit down, and nearly burned her tongue.

"When was the last time you ate, Harrow?"

She chewed, swallowed, ignored him. The bell above the door chimed again—loud enough to slice the air.

Town magistrates.

The crowd parted instinctively, murmurs swelling like storm clouds. Three officials swept inside, gray coats buttoned to the throat. At their head was Alderman Veyne—gaunt as a crow, with a nose too long for his face and eyes that seemed permanently damp.

His gaze moved like a blade over the shelves stacked with jars, over eclairs still faintly glowing from her last spell, over the children smiling with sugar and delight. Then, at last, to her.

"Curious," Veyne said, his voice soft but cutting, like the scrape of steel on stone. "Last week this street sagged under blight. Today it feasts."

Maude's fingers twitched toward the hem of her sleeve, nails worrying the seam.

"Excellent work, Rivers." Veyne clapped Wesley's shoulder. "The street hasn't looked this lively in years. A remarkable turnaround."

Another inspector scribbled in a ledger, his gaze flicking toward Maude. "This was nearly a disaster. You're fortunate no one ended up dead. Next time, we'll shutter these doors before you can light another candle."

Her teeth clicked together, biting down on words she wanted to hurl.

"We understand." Wesley's voice was smooth, too smooth, like a balm poured over boiling water. Then he turned, his eyes bright as sea-glass as he added, "But let's be clear—this wasn't my doing. You owe the stability of this street to her. I mixed what she told me to mix. Drew lines where she pointed. That's not a partnership—that's me following orders."

Veyne's quill stilled above the page. "The fact remains—the collapse began with your hex, Maude. Are we to praise the arsonist for dousing her own flames?"

He wasn't wrong. But Maude was feeling petty.

"Better an arsonist who puts out her own fire than a bureaucrat who starts one and leaves it to spread."

The room shifted. Murmurs rippled through the crowd still lingering near the door. Even Veyne's pinched expression faltered, his gaze burning. "Careful, *witch*. Insolence doesn't erase culpability."

Maude's jaw locked, but before she could spit something out, Wesley spoke—voice smooth as honey. "Then perhaps you'll judge us by outcomes. The street is standing. The people are safe. That's what matters."

The magistrates shifted, unsettled, but Wesley's calm was a current they couldn't quite fight. Veyne sniffed, scribbled something into his ledger, then snapped it shut. Without another word, the three swept out, robes trailing in their wake.

The crowd scattered, chatter filling the silence like bees stirred from a hive. Coins clinked, footsteps retreated, and soon only a few stragglers remained, reluctant to leave the spectacle.

Maude stayed rigid, every muscle coiled tight, her pulse refusing to slow. She should've been grateful—he'd deflected, shielded, drawn their righteous anger off of her. But instead it felt like he'd stripped her bare in front of half the town, her failures and triumphs paraded together under their judgmental stares.

Maude sighed. "You didn't have to do that."

"You did the work." Wesley shrugged. "Credit belongs where it belongs."

The words slipped under her defenses, unsettling in their simplicity. For a breath, she almost said thank you. The words hovered, fragile and feathered, aching to take flight. She swallowed them whole instead, the taste bitter.

The bell above the shop door rattled as the sun slid toward the horizon, its last light bleeding copper and red across the crooked glass panes. Maude nearly sloshed the simmering pot of Willow's Rest Draught—her own sleep elixir that slowed the pulse and coaxed even the most restless mind toward dreams—when Oli's voice came sweeping in before him, warm and unapologetically loud.

"Pack it in, darling witch. We're abducting you."

She arched a brow as she capped the jar on the counter. "Hard pass."

The door swung open, revealing Selene trailing Oli, cheeks pink from the cool evening. Maude hadn't seen her in days, and something uncoiled in her chest at the sight. Saints, she'd missed her.

One corner of Selene's smile quirked, like she already knew the protest by heart. "We're going out. Just one night. The Silver Thistle. There's food, and cider that's allegedly worth selling your soul for."

"I already have food." Maude gestured toward the shelf of powders that could kill or cure depending on her mood. "I already have a drink. And I already have you two."

"Exactly." Oli swooped closer, grin wide. "So why not combine all three into one glorious evening of my company in public?"

"Because that sounds like punishment."

Selene giggled behind her hand—warm, conspiratorial—and Maude's sulk cracked just a little. "We'll be back before midnight. Promise."

A sigh escaped her as she uncorked a bottle and sniffed the contents. "Fine. But if this involves dancing, I'm putting warts somewhere creative."

"Excellent." Oli clapped once, delighted. "Nothing says friendship like threats of bodily harm."

The Silver Thistle was older than half the town, built low and crooked into the roots of an ancient tree. Lanterns dangled like fruit from its branches, green flames guttering inside glass globes etched with runes. The door creaked like a coffin lid when Oli shoved it open.

Inside, the gloom gave way to warmth. A hearth blazed against one wall, its smoke curling through gaps in the stonework like lazy phantoms. Tables crowded close, each one scarred with old knife marks and burn rings, sticky with spilled cider, yet softened by sprigs of lavender tucked into jars at their centers. A fiddle played somewhere near the back, threadbare notes weaving around bursts of laughter.

At one table, a cluster of nixies played cards with a centaur whose hooves clicked irritably against the floorboards each time he lost. In another, a banshee hunched over a cup of black liquid that shimmered faintly while goblins heckled her hair.

It was dark in all the ways Maude preferred—shadowed,

strange, and thick with the sense that if you blinked wrong, you might catch a glimpse of something you'd regret.

"This," Oli said, sweeping his arms like a host unveiling a masterpiece, "is atmosphere. Drink it in."

They slipped into a booth, and Selene waved down a serving girl who looked mostly human if you ignored the small horns curling above her ears. Drinks and plates began to arrive with dizzying speed: mulled cider so spiced it steamed, dark bread slathered with honey, roasted pheasant that gleamed under candlelight.

Oli immediately lifted his mug. "To Maude! For finally prying that pastel nightmare off her shop and reclaiming her dignity!"

Maude huffed a laugh. "Don't start."

Selene lifted her mug anyway. "To Maude."

"Thanks, guys," she muttered, clinking hers against theirs.

The conversation spiraled fast. Selene, halfway through her second cup of buttered rum, launched into stories of healer training, punctuating each disaster with wild hand gestures that nearly smacked a passing goblin.

"So Lydia Dross storms into the hospital two weeks ago," Selene began, "claiming she's cursed. Says she can't stop hiccupping."

Oli raised a brow. "Hiccups? Hardly life-threatening."

Selene wagged a finger. "Oh no, not just any hiccups. Every time she hiccupped, she passed wind."

Maude nearly choked on her cider, coughing into her sleeve.

Selene smacked the table proudly. "Yes! Exactly! A full symphony. Like clockwork. Hic—fart, hic—fart. The whole street was howling before she even made it inside."

Oli gasped so loudly that the satyr at the next table turned. "Selene, you can't tell this story. Client confidentiality!"

"She forfeited confidentiality the moment she weaponized her digestive tract."

Maude snorted. "Please tell me you fixed it quickly."

Selene winced, sheepish. "Define quickly."

Oli clutched his heart. "No."

"Yes," Selene said grimly. "I tried a clearing draught. Thought it would purge the hiccups. It...amplified them. For two whole hours, Lydia Dross was a one-woman brass band."

Maude set down her drink. "You made her louder?"

Selene dropped her forehead to the table, muffling her laughter. "It echoed in the rafters, Maude. The rafters. I thought the quadrant was going to collapse."

Oli slapped both hands over his ears like he could hear it. "The scandal! The indignity! Poor Lydia—"

"Poor Lydia?" Maude said. "I'm surprised the magistrates haven't commissioned a statue of Selene. Finally gave the town something useful to laugh about."

Selene peeked up, grinning. "Thank you. Some recognition at last."

Oli looked between them in open horror. "This is corruption. Medical corruption! I thought healers swore an oath or something."

Selene lifted a brow. "We do. First, do no harm. Second, if Lydia Dross walks in, all bets are off."

Maude cackled, and Oli pressed a hand to his chest. "I weep for your moral compasses."

Selene was still giggling into her sleeve when Oli sat back in his chair, swirling the dregs of his cider like he was about to deliver a speech no one wanted.

"Inevitably," Maude muttered, stabbing her spoon into her stew, "here it comes."

"So," Oli said, lips curling slyly, "how's our sunshine baker?"

"Alive. Presumably."

Selene nudged her shoulder. "That's all?"

"That's *all*," Maude confirmed, taking a bite. It was spicy enough to make her eyes water, which worked well for disguising the spike of heat in her cheeks.

Selene leaned in until Maude could practically feel her breath. "You hesitated."

Maude slowly lowered her spoon, her gaze flat as stone. "I was deciding whether to say he's an idiot or an imbecile. But thank you for your forensic analysis."

Oli slapped the table. "Coward! You didn't say either."

"I said he's alive. Isn't that enough? For some people, that's already too much."

"Pathetic," Oli declared with mock solemnity. "We raised you better than this."

Selene grinned. "So if he's not an idiot, what is he?"

Maude swirled her spoon, watching potatoes sink. "He's...not brilliant."

The table went silent for a beat. Then Oli leaned forward, eyes wide. "*Not brilliant*? That's the best insult you could conjure? Saints help us all."

"I'm tired," Maude whined. "My creativity clocked out hours ago."

Oli patted her shoulder. "Tragic. The mighty witch of Blightbend felled by vocabulary."

Selene snorted, and Maude gave her a look.

"Wesley and I are not friends. We worked together. That's over."

"You know you can have more than one best friend," Oli said, lifting his mug.

Selene smacked his arm. "What about me?"

"Fine. More than two best friends," he corrected without missing a beat.

That earned him a genuine laugh from Maude. "You two are exhausting."

"Admit it," Oli said smugly. "You'd be bored without us."

"Wrong. I'd be thriving. My skin would glow. Flowers would bloom in my footsteps."

Selene threw her head back, giggling. "I'd pay to see that."

Maude stabbed another potato chunk. "Anyway. He doesn't want me as a friend. Trust me."

Oli's grin went sharklike. "I don't know. From the way he was looking at you last week…"

Her spoon clattered into the bowl. She nearly slammed her mug down for emphasis. "That's ridiculous. He's…I'm… We'd drive each other insane."

Selene leaned her chin on her hand, her smile soft. "Or maybe you'd balance each other. Light and dark aren't enemies, Maude. Sometimes they're just halves of the same day."

The words clung, stubborn as burrs, snagging places she didn't want to admit were tender. And then, mercifully, Oli ruined everything.

"Or," he said cheerfully, "you'd just have really enthusiastic hate sex and terrify the neighborhood."

Maude sputtered, cider spraying across the table. Selene shrieked, shoving her chair back as the splash hit her, then hurled a bread roll at Oli's head. "You're disgusting."

"I'm a visionary," Oli corrected, tearing the bread in half and eating it like he'd achieved victory.

"If I hex you right now, no jury would convict me."

Selene, still blotting cider off her sleeve, muttered, "Do it, Maude. Make it itch."

Oli only grinned wider, crumbs on his lips. "See? This is why I keep you both around—your dark, homicidal tendencies, my sparkling charm. Perfect harmony."

Maude rolled her eyes so hard it hurt. But under the table, her boot tapped against Selene's in silent agreement: someday, they really were going to hex him.

They staggered back through the streets later, Selene hiccupping with laughter every few steps, her braid coming loose and bouncing wildly against her shoulder. Oli had taken up humming a scandalous ballad about sailors and nymphs, his voice far too loud for the hour. A shutter cracked open above them, and a poor townsman shouted for quiet. Oli only blew him a kiss and kept singing scandalously louder.

"Do you know the second verse?" Selene giggled, tripping over the curb.

"Do I know it? Darling, I wrote the second verse. And possibly the third, depending on which edition you've heard."

"Tragic," Maude muttered, steadying Selene by the elbow as she tried to veer into a hedge. "Truly, your legacy will outlive us all."

"Yes, worship me appropriately."

Oli's manor rose ahead, bathed in moonlight, all ivy-draped stone and sweeping gables, every window glowing warm and golden like an invitation. A place that screamed *wealth* but also, annoyingly, *comfort*.

Maude had always hated how the two could coexist so easily here.

Inside, they clambered up the wide stairs, boots clunking, laughter bouncing off polished wood and oil paintings of solemn ancestors who would no doubt be appalled by what their descendant was doing with his fortune.

And then there it was: the bed. Oli's absurdly massive bed, sprawling across half the chamber like a ship at sea. The carved headboard was inlaid with silver leaves; the quilt was stitched in rich jewel tones. It looked like something stolen from a queen's summer palace.

Maude dropped onto it without hesitation. The mattress dipped beneath her with a luxurious sigh. "Tell me you changed the sheets since your last lover."

Oli, peeling off his jacket with exaggerated dignity, gasped like she'd accused him of murder. "Of course. I have standards."

"Barely," Selene snorted, crawling across the bed to burrow under the blankets.

"I'll have you know," Oli said, flopping down beside them, "these sheets are imported. Enchanted by elves to stay crisp *and* cool." He waggled his brows. "Perfect for company."

"Ew," Selene groaned, pulling the blanket over her head.

They collapsed together in a tangle, warm and heavy-limbed.

The chamber smelled faintly of amber and myrrh; the curtains were drawn back to let moonlight spill across the floor. Maude let herself sink into the mattress without thinking of bills, curses, or what she'd lost. Just warm cider, friends, and the blissful hum of exhaustion.

It couldn't last. Because, of course, Oli had to open his mouth.

He murmured something so indecent that Selene and Maude both shrieked and shoved him off the bed with their feet.

He hit the floor with a satisfying thud.

"Barbarians," he groaned. "Miscreants. Betrayers of hospitality."

Selene cackled, burying her face under Maude's arm. "Shut up and sleep on the floor like the scandalous dog you are."

"Careful," Maude murmured into her pillow, cider humming through her veins. "He'll take that as encouragement."

Selene wheezed laughter into Maude's sleeve while Oli sprawled on the floorboards with all the grace of a felled tree. "One day," he declared to the ceiling, "you'll both miss me when I'm gone."

"Out of spite, maybe," Maude muttered, eyes already slipping closed.

Fifteen

Mistwood Hills had always been a bit crooked, but now it was... *wrong*.

To everyone else, life went on. Vendors shouted about fresh pears and fish salted straight from the coast. A fiddler perched on the corner played something jaunty. Kids darted between carriages, shrieking with laughter.

But Maude saw the fractures. The world was wearing a cracked mask.

The cobbles outside Lydia Dross's florist stand crumbled when a cart rattled past, reforming themselves a shade darker, like mismatched teeth. Roses in the display bloomed bright and lush —then, as she passed, their petals flaked into paper, curling into the spines of little gilt romance novels. Customers barely blinked, more annoyed by the mess than the metamorphosis.

Across the square, the baker's rival bell clanged from inside the smithy. Not one, but two notes, like a duet between hammer and anvil. The smith swore, yanking off his gloves, muttering about "haunted steel."

Maude shoved her hands deeper into her coat pockets, shoulders hunched against the cold and against the looks. No one else seemed to notice the way the curse crawled, thin as veins under skin, threading through the mortar and stones. Not yet. But she felt it. Every step on Blightbend vibrated. Binding. Fusing.

Bailey's handwriting lingered in her mind worse than his absence. The interlock was a temporary stabilizer only. Masks fracture, buys time. *Must be severed.* His neat script burned behind her eyes. He'd meant it as a warning. But she wasn't him. She didn't have his reckless brilliance, his knack for pulling impossible solutions out of thin air. She was just...her. Capable, but not enough. Not him.

She'd flipped the sign on her shop to *Closed* long before sundown, ignoring the confused stares. It wasn't as though she'd been raking in business today, anyway. The thought of another customer asking for a glamour tonic while the street collapsed into a surreal nightmare made her want to hex someone into a toad. She didn't even have a destination—just walked fast, boots striking the stones like punctuation.

"Maude!"

The shout cracked across the square.

She winced. *Of course.*

Wesley stood across the way, light in human form, holding a tray of sample pastries, smile bright enough to make her teeth ache. He waved as if nothing in the world was wrong. Like the roses weren't busy turning into sultry fiction a few feet away.

She spun on her heel and strode off.

Boot steps caught up, quick and sure. "Hey—wait."

"I'm fine," she snapped, not slowing.

"Didn't say you weren't," he answered, slightly winded. "Just asking if you're—"

"All saints, baker," Maude snapped, whirling on him. "I said I'm fine."

His brows rose. "You just—"

"I just what?"

Wesley paused, choosing his words. "You look tired."

Maude's throat tightened. She wanted to double down, to lay another brick in the wall between them. But all she could do was stare—at the calm way he stood even after she'd snapped at him, at the flicker of hurt in his eyes he didn't bother to hide.

He let out a slow breath. "You don't have to keep swinging at me, Maude. I'm not your enemy."

Something twisted in her chest. She wanted to tell him he didn't understand—that *she* was the problem. The rot in the roots. The crack in the glass. The enemy of herself, of this town, of anyone foolish enough to stand too close. But the words jammed behind her teeth.

She turned and walked. Boots too loud on the cobbles, breath thin and sharp.

Samhain crept closer, tallying her failures in its dark little ledger.

Fine. Add another line.

Behind her: silence. No footsteps following this time.

And that was what hurt most.

Maude did not go home to wallow like a respectable disaster. She turned her boots toward the Lantern Ward—Mistwood's not-quite-hospital and very-much-haunted clinic stitched to the back of the healer's guild. The place sat in the crook of Brackenhall, where the streets narrowed and wild grapevine clung to the walls, its leaves turned red and gold, its withered clusters hanging like forgotten offerings. A slate roof sagged over arched windows clouded with age; lanterns burned with slow, bluish fire behind stained glass cut in moons and palms. Someone had carved a motto over the door in an ancient hand: *Suffer softly. Pay promptly.*

It always made Maude smile.

Inside, the Lantern Ward breathed in hush and tincture-sour. Iron bedframes lined the walls like polished skeletons. A briny steam rose off the covered baths where feverish men soaked their feet in kelp and hot stones. A nurse with raven feathers for hair glided past; a boy fidgeted on a cot, palms glittering with a glamour rash he was clearly pretending not to adore. The whole place smelled of alcohol, rosemary, and a hint of misery.

Selene spotted Maude near the front table and blinked like she'd seen a ghost. "You're here."

Maude shrugged out of her coat. "I needed to be somewhere I'm not a walking calamity. Thought I'd diversify my catastrophic portfolio."

Selene's mouth tilted. "We're very honored. Also, put this on." She tossed Maude a linen apron. "Try not to terrify the patients."

"I'll subdue the impulse."

Though Maude preferred the solitude of her own shop—or the comfort of her cluttered rooms—this wasn't the first time she'd come to lend a hand at the Lantern Ward. The place had its own rhythm: poultices to grind, herbs to sort, endless shelves of tinctures that needed labeling. Work so steady and simple that it hushed the noise in her head. It was the perfect environment to untangle her thoughts, to let them rise and settle while she moved through the rhythm of someone else's routine.

Selene handed her a slate of orders and a tray of dried comfrey, arnica, and willow bark. "We're low on bruise salve. And Captain Farrow has spectral frostbite again—refuses to stop night fishing. He'll need the ghost nettle tincture."

"Spectral frostbite from fishing? Sounds like natural selection at work," Maude said, tying the apron.

They fell into the rhythm of the ward. The good thing about healing rooms: they wanted hands, not feelings. Maude crushed comfrey into a paste with a mortar, folded in goose fat and a whisper of sun salt so bruises would fade quick as morning mist. She labeled jars with neat, sharp letters that looked nothing like

Bailey's, even when she tried. Across the aisle, Selene murmured to a child whose ear was sprouting a very small, very embarrassed mushroom—a side effect of a wish left too close to a damp pillow.

"Hold still, little barnacle," Selene soothed, dabbing. "It will fall off by supper."

The mushroom wobbled, offended. Maude handed Selene a strip of cloth. "Tie it snug. Tell him it adds character."

Selene bit back a smile. "We say '*texture*' in the ward."

A man limped in with a knee the size of a pumpkin. Sprain. Maude rolled up her sleeves and wrapped him—sage and vinegar compress, tight figure-eight band, four-beat knot. "Rest, elevate, repeat," she instructed, tugging the wrap tight. "You can manage that, can't you?"

He flushed. "Thank you, mistress."

She kept moving. She knew the ward's cadence the way she knew Blightbend's damp stones. Pinch of yarrow for bleeding, three drops of ghost nettle for cold that seeps from the inside.

Her mind was moving, too. It spun scenarios while her hands did the work. Bailey's handwriting scrolled behind her eyes. *Interlock, variant: for the holding of what strains to part. Must be severed.* Severed with what, exactly? She moved from bed to table to shelf, crushing, pouring, cutting gauze, while inside she was building an argument with the dark.

Maybe I can find every scattered contamination and stitch wards around them? No, too many, too far. Sever the curse at its source? Bailey never wrote what that source was... Helpful, Bailey. Very thorough of you. Or maybe...ground it. Redirect it. If interlock wanted to fuse, then maybe I could give it something else to fuse to. A decoy. A focus, something strong enough to drink the curse dry.

A Weftmark.

Her fingers smudged rosemary across the slate as she wrote the word without meaning to. Weftmark: a focus for warp-prone magic. Thread must meet anchor. Anchor must not break. Which meant iron and thorn. Which meant something living, something remembering, something that could sit at the crossroads and say *here* to every wayward stitch of the spell.

She bit her lip. The plan was a skeleton at best, more jumble than theory, but it was the first thing that didn't sound like *"lie down and die."*

"Maude?" Selene's voice dropped in. "You're grinding the slate."

She looked down. Her pestle was carving neat aggression into the tablet. She set it aside. "Oops. New texture."

Selene's eyes were a question. Maude ignored them. *You're helping,* she told herself. *You're not burning anything down. You're helping.* She moved to the tincture table and measured ghost nettle drops—two, not three, unless she wanted Captain Farrow to sleep 'til spring. She corked the bottle, tied a label with quick, ruthless bows that would never come undone.

Selene watched from across the aisle, suspicion and affection warring. Maude kept her face neutral: a hint of menace, *nothing to see here.* Inside, it felt like she was building a dam with matchsticks.

By late afternoon, the ward slowed. Selene finally cornered Maude at the jar shelf. "Do you want to tell me why you're here?" she asked lightly.

Maude tucked stray hair back with two fingers. "Enjoying the ambiance. Love what you've done with the foot baths."

"Uh-huh." Selene tilted her head. "You came to take care of people."

"Don't spread that rumor."

They just looked at one another for a beat. Selene, patient and luminous; Maude, dead-eyed and dug-in.

Eventually, Selene sighed. "Fine. Keep your secrets. But take a sandwich." She pushed a heel of honey loaf and ham into Maude's hands like it was a prescription. "Eat. Then go do whatever you came to do. Preferably without dying."

"Noted." Maude tucked the food under her arm like contraband and stripped off the apron. She paused at the door. "Selene?"

"Mm?"

"Thanks. For letting me...not break anything."

Selene's smile was quiet and warm. "You never break the things you decide to hold."

Sixteen

Her cottage met her with its usual mutter of charms. The runes Bailey had carved into the beams glowed their low, reassuring amber. On most nights, they felt like a hand at her back. Tonight, they felt like a row of tutors watching to see if she'd cheat.

She cleared the table of ordinary life—a teacup with a lipstick crescent, a spoon she didn't remember using, a single bobby pin she'd been pretending was a bookmark. She pulled the leather-bound spellbook with Bailey's margins into the lamplight, then set out the old, sensible scaffolding first because muscle memory insisted: ironvine, blackthorn bark, yarrow, rosemary, bloodroot, moondust caps, and shadowbell bloom.

A *Weftmark*—braided vine studded with thorns, parchment sigil sealed in beeswax, tuned to shadowbell. Not a charm so much as a siphon. Bailey's old stopgap, something he used when a hex outpaced him. Not a cure. A bleed-off. A way of tricking the curse into thinking it had somewhere better to be while you scrambled to fix the real damage.

She stood over the neat little list, hands braced on the table, and felt a lump rise in her throat. A simple drain wouldn't be enough. Not for this. Not with the changes slipping quietly through the village so quickly. What she needed was something she could build with her own hands that wasn't Bailey's, something as stubborn and ugly and unkillable as what lived in her ribs.

She closed his book.

"Fine," she told the lamp. "We do it my way."

She unlocked the bottom drawer of the apothecary cabinet—the one Grim never tried to pry because even he respected boundaries when they hummed—and brought out the rarities she saved for stubborn problems.

Ashen ivy, brittle and gray, cut from ruin-stone upriver where the water had long since given up.

Glasswort resin, a honeyed lump of sap bled from plants along a shattered ley line.

Heartmire salt, dull silver, scraped from the bed of a storm-cracked lake.

Wolfsbone, ground fine from grave-bone mineral.

Night-apple peel, ribbons that glimmered like bruises in the dark.

Together, they would bind and steady, draw old magic out, mute her power's glare, and hold what didn't belong anywhere else.

Maude laid the new bones of her spell beside Bailey's tried-and-true, a before-and-after she refused to apologize for.

The shape came to her hands first: a seam-loom, a narrow figure-eight woven from ashen ivy so the spell had to pass through one throat, then the other. She warmed the glasswort resin over a low blue flame until it went clear, then brushed it along the ivy to harden the braid without killing its mean little will. Wolfsbone crumbled to dust beneath the pestle, the rhythm a drumbeat under the cottage's runes. The dust met the heartmire salt in the bowl, shining together until it looked like crushed moonlight. Night-apple peel came last, pared into long, even ribbons that curled when the knife left them, slick with their own secret.

With a silver needle, she threaded peel through the figure-eight, cross-stitching it over the narrow throat where the two loops met. A muffler. A cover. So the spell wouldn't look directly at her when it snarled.

She chose three shadowbell petals and set them on her tongue one at a time to warm her voice, then laid four more along the seam-loom's center line, each one a soft, impossible note.

A knock hit the door like a dare. One, two, three—in Oli's exact rhythm: *I'm a nuisance; open up.*

She thought about hiding like a feral cat. Instead, she opened the door.

Oli filled the threshold, smelling like night air and too-expensive soap. A coat slung over one shoulder, collar loosened, his smile tempered by worry. "You've been ignoring me," he said, breezing past like the house belonged to him.

Maude rubbed at her temple. "I haven't had it in me to be social lately."

"Lucky for you, I *have*." His grin snapped back on, quick and bright as a lantern. "In fact, I've been hosting my ass off with the city magistrates." He paused, eyes glinting, letting the words hang like bait. "Because I'm maneuvering for an open seat."

She blinked. "You want to be a wolf?"

"I want to be the fox inside the henhouse with the blueprints," he said dryly. "They'll vote after Samhain. If I win, I can stall condemnations, pull inspections, funnel protection your way. Quietly. I don't even need the seat to gum up their gears—a tavern expansion's already crawling because I asked a few too many questions about the builder trying to push a widow off her lot. The magistrates don't like the smell of scandal, so the paperwork found its way to the bottom of the stack. She gets another month. If I lose, I still have leverage on three of them—debts, favors, little knots they don't want untangled. Enough to buy time when it matters."

"You've been...campaigning."

"Like hell," he said. "Not for the hat. For the door it opens. I didn't tell you because you'd make a face."

She made a face. "This face?"

"That face." He huffed a breath that wasn't quite a laugh. "I've made promises I don't love to people I don't trust so I can put my body between them and people I do. You can be furious later. Right now I came because—" he glanced at the loom, then back, "—because I—" The grin drained out of him. For the first time in forever, Oliver Hale looked not in control. Not composed. Human. "What's going on here, Maude? What are you making?"

"A mess," she said. "Hopefully a useful one."

"What kind of useful?"

"The stop-this-before-the-curse-swallows-everything kind." She didn't look up. "It didn't end with the shops."

He went still. That was the thing about Oli—under the silk, he was a wire you could pluck, and he'd sing.

"Tell me."

She did. Not the worst of it—she didn't need to hand him her panic—but enough. Roses turning into books. Duet bells. Cobbles wrong. The itch of something rooting beneath plaster and skin. Bailey's note about the interlock.

"I'm making a drain. A place the curse has to pass through, one throat then the other. I've braced it, muffled it, salted it down so it can't flash or wander. It'll cut if it tries to swell, but it'll catch, too—hold it, keep it from spilling into everything else."

He folded his arms. The careful smile didn't come back. "And you were going to do that alone because...?"

"Because people make things more complicated." She met his eyes. "And because if it goes sideways, I'd rather it burn me than anyone else."

He looked around as if he were searching for a second opinion. "Shouldn't we fetch the coven? The wizards? The druid-whatsits who charge triple on solstice?"

"No, they're all twits," she said, "and they'll crowd my home. And argue. And make a committee."

He pointed at his chest. "What about this twit?"

Her mouth tugged, but the retort lagged. For one unguarded

beat, her face slipped—eyes catching on him, touched with something bare. Worry.

Oli's grin faltered. "I can follow directions," he said. "I won't get clever. I'll grind, I'll stir, I'll keep my sleeves out of the fire. You don't have to do this alone."

She hesitated a second, then nodded once—briskly, like she was signing a death warrant. "Fine, but if I tell you to duck, you duck. If I tell you to run, I'd better see your ass hurling out my front door before the words finish leaving my mouth."

His grin crooked, warm as a lantern flaring back to life. "Deal. Though, for the record, my ass has *excellent* reaction time."

They moved like they'd practiced, even though they hadn't. Maude explained, and Oli didn't interrupt unless there was a reason to. He warmed the glasswort while she tested the ivy's give. He sifted wolfsbone and heartmire together carefully until the powders married and shone. He cupped his hands, and she shook a pinch of the blend across his palms so he could feel the weight.

He looked like a man being knighted by dust.

"What's this part do?" he asked, nodding to the bone-and-salt mixture.

"Draws out old magic," she said. "Interlock loves whatever's buried and afraid. This coaxes it above ground where I can make eye contact."

"How charming." He gestured to the night-apple peel. "And the ribbons?"

"Mask," she said. "Keeps the thing from seeing me seeing it. So it doesn't decide to graft onto my spine."

He winced.

She set a copper bowl at the seam where the figure-eight pinched and poured in warmed resin until it pooled like a melted window. The cottage smelled sweet and electric. While it cooled to tack, she dropped in the four shadowbell petals one by one. Oli didn't ask what it was. He just breathed with her. It helped, which made her nervous and grateful at the same time.

They chalked a circle on the floorboards. Her circles were always a little oval, a little mean—more ditch than lace. She set dishes at the cardinal marks: heartmire salt in the north, ash in the south, water in the west, and thistledown in the east to remind the spell that weightless things rise when you let them. Oli placed a single silver coin at the center of each dish—"For the ferryman," he said, and when she gave him a look, he amended, "For luck, then."

"Luck is for people who don't plan."

"Indulge me," he said, and she didn't argue because the coins gleamed like small promises.

She pricked her thumb and let a single drop fall onto the resin's cooling skin. It spread, red threading the clear. *Honesty clause*. The spell wouldn't hold a lie. She didn't look at Oli when she did it, but didn't explain. He said nothing, which was the right kind of mercy.

"Ready?" he asked, hands hovering.

"No...let's do it."

She set her palms over the seam and began. It wasn't Bailey's cadence. It wasn't neat. Her magic rose the way it always did since Bailey died—like ink spilling too fast across paper, tangled and uncontainable, the taste of storms that refused to be scheduled. She whispered the unbinding line she'd stitched from three different dead languages, laced with the memory of how Bailey had once said her name when she was small and mean.

Oli caught her rhythm fast, breathing in on her in-breath, out on her out. When she tipped her head, he poured a narrow trickle of wolfsbone salt into the pinch of the figure-eight—the tight throat where both loops met—so the spell would have grit enough to catch.

The air changed. It always did when big magic bent its head

to look at you. The runes in the beams ticked like a dozen clocks all deciding on one time. Somewhere outside, a nightjar called and then didn't. The cottage floor lifted half a hair, or maybe it was the skin on her arms.

She felt it come: not a thing, not a mind, just a pressure with intentions. Hungry to belong. Hungry to bind.

"Don't say hello to it," she muttered, eyes on the seam. "It gets attached."

"I hate that," Oli whispered.

The first nudge pressed along the figure-eight like a palm sliding across a banister. It found the throat, slipped, found it again. Maude pressed her hands inward, crimping the space just enough to force the current through the narrow. It pushed. The glasswort held. The night-apple muffler did its work, dampening the flash, funneling the pressure. Her jaw ached. Oli tipped in another pinch of bone and salt at her jerked nod. He didn't flinch when the resin hissed like a candle taking a breath.

The singing started then—a thin thread of sound not heard with ears. Bailey had called it the seam-note. Maude called it the warning. It meant the thing was choosing. She leaned closer, smelling heartmire and old rain, and said, "Here," to the spell in the voice she saved for cats on ledges.

It listened.

It flowed.

Not all of it—she didn't expect mercy—but enough. She felt the pull in the boards under her boots, in the chalk of the circle, in her spit and her spine. The cottage air cooled. Her scalp prickled. The runes went from ticking to a low, satisfied hum. The seam-loom's narrow throat brightened one breath and then settled to the dull glow of something that would work as long as it was fed.

Her knees trembled. Oli slid his hand closer—not touching, but close enough to catch her.

She did not fall. *Excellent*. Character growth.

The pressure eased by degrees. Maude waited until she could

taste her tongue again, then lifted her hands. The singing faded into the background. The coins in the dishes did not rattle. She looked at the loom until the room sharpened.

"It's grounded," she said, voice low.

"How grounded?"

"Enough to start drinking," she said. "Enough to keep the seams from wandering while I build bigger teeth."

Oli exhaled a breath that probably had five unprintable words braided into it. He rose stiffly, poured coffee that could have removed paint, and handed her a mug with both hands like she might refuse and bite him. She didn't. She sat and let the steam hit her face and tried to look like a person instead of a badly concealed runic fire.

"And after this?" he asked when the coffee was half gone. "When this holds?"

"I'll need to set three more," she said. "At Mistwood's cardinal edges. Weave them into Samhain's warding net." She watched him over the rim of her cup. "That night the veil thins, and magic moves like quicksilver. The only time the veil leans toward us instead of away." Her lips curved, not quite a smile. "Which means I fucked the town up at the most opportune time possible. We'll need bodies. People who won't faint and ruin my geometry."

"I can get you that," he said. "If the vote goes my way, I can get you the city watch to keep the curious off your chalk. If the vote doesn't go my way, I can get you Lydia as a brass band and a scandal—both distract nicely."

"And Wesley," she added before her brain could stop her mouth. "My magic runs cleaner through his process, and I hate it, and it's true."

Oli's mouth did the slow, feline thing again. "Noted." He paused. "But the magistrate's seat—there are promises attached. I'm not proud of all of them. Some are...less than noble."

"I assumed," she said, dry as bone. "You're you."

He huffed a laugh that was only one-third performative.

"And after Samhain?" she asked, because she liked to ruin conversations with reality.

"After Samhain," he said, looking at the seam-loom instead of her, "I find out if I became part of the machine I hate, or if the machine made the mistake of letting me in. Either way, I'll be loud about it."

She stared at him, cataloging the dust along his jaw like war paint, the neat bite at his thumb from where the thorn had caught, and the stubborn light in his eyes.

Irritatingly heroic. *Her best friend.*

The loom purred. Somewhere in the town, a single bell rang once. Not a duet. Clean.

Maude stood. The room wavered and then behaved. She picked up the seam-loom and felt the hum climb into her palms, travel her arms. Not cured; held. It would have to be enough for now.

"Congratulations," she told Oli, deadpan. "You're hired."

"For what?"

"Assistant. Bone-sifter. Political fox. Whatever. Don't die."

"I'll pencil that in between committee meetings."

She snorted—small, involuntary, almost a laugh. He looked like he'd frame it and hang it in the foyer.

"Go," she said, because the hour had gone cobalt at the edges of the window. "Sleep before you charm yourself into a stroke. I'll set this one in the foundation and watch it for an hour."

He hesitated at the door, one hand on the frame. "Maude."

"Yes?"

"If you need me before Samhain," he said, "need me. Don't decide I'm part of the problem because it satisfies your brand."

She made the face again. He grinned at having earned it, kissed the top of her head, and slipped into the dark.

Maude set the seam-loom into the shallow niche Bailey had carved under the hearthstone *"for later"* and warded it in with three slow words and a press of her palm. The cottage shivered like a dog settling into a new bed. The runes hummed. The air became easier to breathe. She leaned both hands on the mantel and let herself feel the smallest slice of relief a witch was legally allowed.

Then she straightened, pulled a clean sheet of paper toward her, and began writing the list for the other three looms. Names of corners. Names of volunteers she didn't want to ask and would anyway. A single word underlined twice: *Samhain*.

She blew the lamplight thinner, and the cottage watched her work like it had from the first night she slept within its walls. She pretended not to notice that it was proud.

Seventeen

The square was emptying fast.

Maude pushed through the thinning tide of merchants with the single-minded focus of someone who had already rehearsed the scene a hundred times in her head. Lanterns guttered out one by one, shutters clapped shut. The air carried its familiar tangle—fish brine and tar, the smoke of meat stalls, the crisp bite of river water cut with salt off the bay. This was the Driftmarket, Mistwood's sea-facing bazaar where ships docked low against stone steps slick with algae, where gulls wheeled lazy arcs overhead, calling for scraps.

It all felt ordinary, almost soothing—except for the rumble that thrummed under her boots.

She was too tired to be properly afraid.

The ley-point was here. Old as the town—older, maybe—vibrating at the bend where river met sea and trade had been struck for centuries. Bailey always said ley lines carried memory. Oaths, promises, bargains—you could hear the bones of them if you pressed your ear to the cobbles.

She stopped in the center of the wharf, shouldering off her satchel. Her body was still running on scraps after the night with Oli, the two of them bent over the first loom until dawn, his voice full of political promises and coffee-laced optimism, her hands blistered from weaving ironvine and blackthorn until they bit. When he'd finally left, she'd stripped down and scrubbed herself raw in the bath, then collapsed into bed and slept like she'd been struck with a mallet. The sun had moved across the sky and set again before she'd dragged herself upright.

A wasted day. But the sooner she set the three looms, the sooner this mess would be contained, and maybe—*maybe*—she could rest. Maybe even take a much-needed break from it all.

Oli's ambition flickered through her head as she dropped her satchel on the cobbles.

A seat in the court.

She huffed. It was a game only he could stomach—meeting hunger with charm until it thought itself fed. Though...if he pulled it off, everything in Mistwood Hills might shift. Maybe it would mean protection. Maybe it would mean more knives waiting in the dark.

Maude knelt and drew the salt circle, voice flat with exhaustion as she muttered the working lines. "Second loom," she said to the empty dock. *"Anchor. Drain. Hold."*

The pulse under her feet deepened. Dust skittered inward across the stones. And then, like a held breath snapping free, the pull began.

Crates groaned, splitting; the air bent sideways. A lantern snapped its hook and careened into the circle before crumpling to ash. The river's surface rippled, tugged as though invisible hands were dragging it up the bank.

Maude braced harder, pressing both palms into the ironvine ring. "Hold," she hissed, sweat burning her eyes. "Just *hold*—"

Her heart slammed. She didn't move. Couldn't.

The ring buckled, flexed, then locked with a low boom that rattled her ribs. The pull collapsed inward, the sucking wind cutting off so fast she nearly fell face-first into the dock.

Silence crashed down with such force it rang in her ears.

Maude dropped her arms, hands scraped raw against the

buckled wood. Her lungs burned, her body shaking with exhaustion.

"Maude?" Wesley's voice cut across the docks.

Through the haze of flour dust, he stumbled into view, a torn sack at his feet and white powder plastered over his coat like some ghostly disguise. All around them, crates had toppled, gulls shrieked overhead, and half the traders were coughing through the mess—one man wringing out his fishnets now powdered pale, another swearing as his apples rolled off the pier.

Maude stayed crouched in the center of the wharf, the ring still blazing hot beneath her palms. Wesley's eyes went wide as they locked on her. "I thought we fixed this."

"We patched it," she said, throat tight with strain. "That's all. The curse is still feeding. I had to cut it off before it spreads."

"You didn't tell me."

"Didn't matter if I told you. It still had to be done."

Wesley was breathing hard. His eyes searched hers, narrowing with worry. "Have you told anyone else about this?"

She swallowed. "Oli knows."

His shoulders loosened. "Good." He stood, wiped his hands against his trousers, then held one out to her. "Come on."

Maude only stared at it. Her own fingers shook faintly where they pressed into her knees, and she curled them into fists, willing the tremor still.

His gaze lingered—on the pallor of her face, the cracked press of her lips, the way her shoulders sagged. She felt him measure all of it.

"You need food," he said at last, firm but not unkind. "When did you last eat?"

Her silence was answer enough. His mouth set in a hard line.

"I don't know much about the craft, but I'm fairly certain spellwork and an empty stomach is a bad mix," he said. "Bad for your aim. Bad for my nerves."

Maude sighed long and thin, then placed her hand in his.

They walked together down the emptying square, boots scuffing in the flour dust.

Wesley glanced at her sidelong. "What are you craving?"

She opened her mouth, then closed it. *Craving?* She couldn't think of anything. Mostly, she craved sleep. But her stomach made a low, traitorous growl. Her mind scrambled. Something quick, easy, anything to stop him fussing.

"There's a stall near the edge of the wharf," she muttered. "Strings of fairy lights. *Char & Chime*—they do moon-crusted skewers."

He wrinkled his nose. "Moon-crusted...?"

"Charred meat with star-anise glaze. The fairies sprinkle it with powdered comet-tail."

"Sounds perfect."

It was more than perfect. The stall shimmered in the river breeze, fairy lights dancing in a shifting canopy overhead. The lights weren't bulbs—they were the fairies themselves, small as fists, wings glimmering like stained glass. They darted between the branches and the open grills, trailing sparks that rained down on skewers lined with jewel-bright cuts of meat and vegetables. Smoke curled fragrant and strange: sweet, metallic, threaded with something like lightning. It made her mouth water.

Wesley's eyes narrowed. "I've walked past this place a hundred times. Never stopped."

"Well, you're about to discover flavor. Big day for you."

Wesley nudged her shoulder, the kind of casual contact that felt both right and wrong all at once. She shook it off as they ordered two skewers each, the fairy vendor chittering in a language like bells dropped into water.

Maude sank her teeth into the meat. Comet dust burst across her tongue—sweet at first, then sharp, like biting into thunder. She hissed softly through her teeth.

Her body, stupid thing that it was, sighed in gratitude.

Beside her, Wesley groaned, head tipping back. "Saints. This is better than anything I've ever made."

"You said that out loud."

"I'll live with the shame." He licked honey from his thumb and went in for another bite.

Maude tried not to stare. Tried not to notice how the glittering light threaded through his hair, catching on strands of gold, or how the river wind tugged at his shirt. She told herself he was annoying. A nuisance. But for the first time, she also thought: *safe.*

Damn it all.

They sat on the low stone wall, steam curling from their food, the black water lapping below. Sparks drifted from the fairies overhead, making the river look star-pocked.

The words slipped out. "What brought you to Mistwood Hills?"

He blinked at her, then chewed slowly. "That's the first question you've ever asked me that wasn't an insult."

"Miracles are rare. Consider yourself blessed."

A laugh escaped him, fading into something quieter. He leaned his elbows on his knees, skewer balanced in one hand as he stared at the water. "I lived in Tarrowfast before this. Big place, all brickwork and smoke, streets so tight with people you could barely breathe. You'd think being packed in tight would make people closer, but it didn't. Everyone rushing, eyes down, no one knew anyone. I hated it. Felt invisible in a crowd moving too quickly to even look you in the eye. Kitchens there were the same —fast, loud, brutal. Work 'til your bones give, and still no one remembers your name. Everything was about profit margins and perfect plating, not people.

"I wanted...something closer to the earth. Something that mattered." His gaze slid toward her. "I heard people lived slower here. Thought maybe I could make something I was proud of. I wanted to build a place where the bread on someone's table wasn't just another transaction. So far...I think I was right." His gaze skimmed the square, the fairy lights, the river breathing steadily against the dock. "My mother used to say healing meant giving people back to themselves. Baking feels like that too. Just a sweeter way of doing it."

Maude tilted her head, studying him. Not mockingly—she didn't have the energy for it. Just a quiet filing-away of the fact that maybe, for once, he didn't seem like an idiot. "Sweet," she echoed. "Very on-brand."

He smiled, but his eyes stayed on the water.

Maude tilted her head again. "Tarrowfast...I know the one. Big merchant village across the marshlands? I've heard the witches there charge fortunes just to steep tea leaves."

That pulled a low, genuine sound from him, head shaking. "You're not wrong. Except it's worse. They'd sell you nettle soup as an elixir if you looked rich enough."

"So you won't be returning?"

"Not a chance. You're stuck with me, Harrow." His smile crooked.

Maude chewed, skeptical. "Sleepy villages come with slow-town gossip. Everyone knows everyone's business. You'll be watched twice as hard as you were ignored in Tarrowfast."

"I'm starting to realize that." He shrugged. "But even with the gossip, it feels more like a home than anything I've ever experienced." His smile tilted toward her. "I think I like it better this way."

Something in her chest gave a foolish little lurch at the certainty in his voice. She shoved a grape tomato into her mouth to cover it. "Family still there?"

"Mm." He shifted the skewer in his hands. "My little sister, Briony—sharp as a thorn, that one. She makes candles. Half of our house back home smelled like beeswax and lavender. And my father still runs a ferry across the Greywick inlet. Been doing it since before I was born." His expression softened, distant.

"Do you miss them?"

"All the time. But I write, and I'll visit in a few months once Sugar High is steady on its feet."

A hot twist of guilt caught Maude under the ribs. She

scratched her cheek, eyes darting away. "Yeah. Sorry about... y'know. The whole ruining-your-shop thing."

Wesley chuckled, low and warm. "It's fine. Honestly, it was a lot of fun. Met more people in those weeks than I would've in months otherwise." He tilted his head, eyes gleaming as they caught hers. "Some more interesting than others."

Her stomach went traitorously tight. She bit off another piece of meat to give herself something to do instead of reply.

After a moment, he nudged her knee lightly with his. "What about you? What do you do when you're not out being a naughty witch?"

She snorted. "*Naughty?*"

"Sabotaging bakeries, building illegal looms—"

"Illegal-ish."

"—definitely counts."

She rolled her eyes. "I garden."

"You garden."

"Specifically poisonous things."

"Of course you do."

"I also paint. Badly. Mostly skulls." She ticked off another finger. "And taxidermy."

He nearly choked. "You—taxidermy?"

"Don't look at me like that. It's a hobby. Better than knitting."

"I don't know," he said, amusement edging his words. "I think I'd like to knit."

The image of Wesley, flour-dusted and ridiculous, holding knitting needles almost made her snort. "I think you'd stab yourself before you managed a square."

"I'm a fast learner."

"I'll believe that when you're not singeing your eyebrows off with sugar fires."

He snorted, but let the jab pass.

When the last bite was gone, Maude carried a new kind of weight. Full, her limbs loose and heavy, her head a little light—but it wasn't exhaustion. It was something warmer, softer, curling through her.

They bought spiced apple cider from the next stall—hot, frothing, laced with cinnamon bark and charred orange. The cups steamed between their palms as they walked the wharf in comfortable silence. Somewhere down the quay, a musician plucked a fiddle, notes skating thin over the lapping tide. Maude blew across the cider, the steam curling into her hair. She took a sip—too hot, scalding her tongue—and muttered a curse into the rim of the cup. Wesley chuckled under his breath.

She wasn't used to silence being easy. Usually it pressed against her ribs, the kind of quiet that screamed *you're alone, you'll always be alone.* Tonight it pressed placidly instead, like a shawl draped over her shoulders without asking. Exasperatingly gentle.

By the time they reached her cottage door, she felt suddenly self-conscious. Too full. Too warm. Too...light. The cider sat in her belly like a coal, glowing. Wesley's steady presence at her side only made it worse. Was this what happy felt like? It had been so long, she'd almost forgotten the shape of it.

The words burst out before she could stop them, like steam from a cracked kettle.

"I don't know if I can do this without Bailey."

Silence. Then Wesley's head tilted, the shadows shifting across his face. "You can. You already are," he said simply. "You've been carrying more than you think, longer than you realize—and you haven't broken yet." He leaned closer. "I'm no wizard, but I'm a damn good ally. Next time you need help, ask. I'm only ever a couple of steps across the street."

Her back pressed against the door, cool wood grounding her as her breath caught. Something trembled under her ribs, harsh as grief, soft as relief. The part of her that always snapped back with barbs—*sarcasm as armor, cruelty as cover*—went mute.

"Thanks," she muttered.

His answering smile was soft, so unguarded it almost hurt to look at. Then he held out the parcel he'd been carrying—his extra skewer wrapped in parchment.

"Take it. You've been eyeing it the entire walk home."

Heat flared across her face. *Caught.* "I wasn't—"

"Maude."

Her name on his lips landed like a touch. She snatched the bundle from his hand, scowling, but the scowl cracked and—traitorous, unstoppable—she laughed.

The sound startled her first. Startled him, too. He looked at her as if the world had just been rewoven before his eyes, as if he had waited lifetimes for that single thread of joy.

Slowly, as if testing the air, his hand rose. Fingers brushed a curl from her cheek, the warmth of him lingering, seeping further than she dared allow. His face tilted close, the river wind weaving his hair into hers, binding them in a breath's span of silence.

Her pulse answered in thunder, a storm breaking in her chest.

And then Grim, promptly as ever, dropped squarely onto her shoulder from a window above.

Wesley startled, cider sloshing down his coat. "Shit!" he barked, jerking back.

Maude froze. Then— "Right. Bye."

She fumbled for the door handle and slammed it shut before she could see what expression he wore. Inside, her chest heaved, the cider still burning her throat. She pressed her forehead to the wood, eyes shut tight.

Grim purred, vibrating smug satisfaction into her collarbone.

"You little saboteur."

Eighteen

Morning made a show of itself—fog lifting off the river like a shrug, gulls heckling the rooftops, Mistwood Hills blinking awake one creaking shutter at a time. Lanterns were strung like pearls along the street; vendors were elbow-deep in cinnamon and gossip; children in antler headbands rehearsed Samhain lines at full volume—"FROM THE SHADOWS, WE—*no, Milo, louder*"—while parents pretended this wasn't their personal nightmare.

Everywhere Maude looked: ribbons, carved gourds, paper bats, and the kind of cheery industry that should've made her want to hex a scarecrow on principle. Instead, her mouth twitched like it hadn't gotten the memo.

She pushed through the bustle, letting the tide of festivity carry her down the lane until the familiar crooked sign of the Elixir Emporium came into view. There, perched primly on the little table by her door, sat a neat bundle—waiting for her with the air of something far too pleased with itself.

Brown paper. Twine. Steam curling out of the seams. Beside it, a lidded tin that smelled like caramelized promise, a small star carved into the metal lid.

Maude did not look across the street.

She absolutely did *not* clock the lack of smoke ghosting out of Sugar High's chimney, or the way the bakery windows were still dim, as if their sunny tyrant had not yet begun his day-long assault on teeth. She bent, eyeing the parcel as if it might sprout fangs, and pinched the twine with two fingers and maximum suspicion.

"I don't want you," she told the parcel.

Then her stomach groaned like a fiddle being strangled.

She cracked the lid of the tin. Coffee steam hit her in the face: smoky roast and clove, orange peel, a whisper of cardamom. The paper parcel yielded two shapes, unmistakably Wesley: one sweet, one savory. The savory was a hand pie glazed with rosemary-honey, the crimped edges browned perfectly, the scent of charred mushroom and leek sneaking out. The sweet was a pear tartlet under a glossy vanilla-bean lacquer, its crust so flaky her fingers picked up confetti.

There was no note. Just a small line inked on the parcel: *Eat me*.

Infuriating. Thoughtful. *Infuriating*.

Maude considered marching the lot straight back to his bakery and informing him she did not need his fussing, thanks; she was perfectly capable of starving herself like a responsible adult. Instead, she opened her door, shouldered in, and carried it to her counter.

Inside, the shop's runes hummed low—Bailey's old wards approving of the fresh coffee like they were in on the joke. Shelves of amber jars watched from the walls; the cauldron sat cold on its ring; the list she'd inked last night waited on the worktable, four corners under paperweights.

*Weftmark Looms: North Gate—***BOUND** (lucky her cottage sat beside it—handy geography for the most unhandy curse of her life). *River Quay—***BOUND**. *South Gate—Tonight? East Gate—Samhain.* Beside it: another list, the one that lived behind her ribs. Volunteers: names she didn't want to ask and would, anyway. And underlined twice: *Samhain.*

She ate the hand pie standing up, pretending her knees hadn't just sighed in relief. The pear tartlet she set aside because she had self-control. She poured coffee, took one scalding sip, and tried very hard not to think about last night: the almost-kiss, the way his fingers had pushed hair from her face, the way the world had narrowed to breath and river wind—

She set the mug down a little too hard, coffee sloshing over the rim.

He must regret it. She'd seen it before. Regret wasn't apologies or explanations—it was normalcy, perfectly performed. And, saints, wasn't she the expert at that game? Maude decided that was fine. Great. *Perfect*, actually.

Maude rolled her sleeves. The Lantern Ward would need more poultices before noon, and if she kept her hands busy she could pretend her heartbeat wasn't still echoing against her molars.

By midmorning she had three trays cooling: greenglass paste for burns, iron-spine salve for sprains, fever-break balm steeped with willow and moonleaf. She decanted into jars, wrote labels and sealed each with wax and a thumbprint. She worked the way she always had: methodically, sparingly, in a rhythm old enough to quiet ugly thoughts.

Outside, the town kept decorating itself like a very determined gallows.

When the sun stood high, the bell chimed. Maude blinked at the sound, frowning. No scrape. Her door usually dragged across the warped boards like an old man hacking up phlegm. She hadn't heard it this morning either. When did that happen? She'd been too tangled up in Wesley's care package to notice the absence.

The thought crawled in anyway: had he fixed it?

Absurd. Completely absurd. She shook her head, but then remembered the way he'd stared at the frame that last day their shops had been stuck together, like the hinge had personally insulted him.

Before she could chase the idea further, Selene breezed in with a wicker basket hooked over her arm and her hair in a braided crown. Her coat swung just a little too dramatically. She looked like a selkie princess on her way to steal the crown jewels—and probably succeed.

"What is this?" Maude asked.

"Lunch with my friend," Selene said, innocent as sin, already setting the basket on the counter.

"You don't have other friends?"

"Rude." Selene produced covered bowls and two spoons out of nowhere, as if she'd stashed the tableware up her sleeves. "Pumpkin-ginger stew from the wharf's cauldron kitchen. And these are sea-herb crisps from my people; try not to be a cultural disaster."

Maude eyed the stew. The steam carried nutmeg, pepper, roasted squash. Her stomach released the trumpet fanfare of betrayal. She sniffed. "Fine. But only because bribery is my love language."

They ate at the worktable. Selene kicked her boot against Maude's under the bench, smiling at nothing in particular. Outside, a troupe of children marched by, their papier mâché skull masks askew, a parent trailing them with costumes under one arm and a look of quiet despair.

"How's the Lantern Ward?" Maude asked, reaching for a crisp like she hadn't been trained to refuse help from birth.

"Chaotic," Selene said cheerfully. "Two festival-related sprains, one toddler who tried to swallow a torch charm, Mrs. Kettle came in because her cat keeps coughing up fortunes instead of fur, and she swears it's rigged because they're never good ones."

Maude snorted into her spoon. "Tell her to stop reading them. Problem solved."

Selene's mouth twitched, but her eyes were watchful. "You look less corpse-adjacent today."

"I hate that."

Selene smiled but didn't push. That was one of the reasons Maude loved her. They finished the stew; Selene slid two folded invoices toward her: one for hospital stock, one for the free stock

Maude insisted didn't exist. Maude signed both with a flick and nudged a crate of poultices across the floor with her heel.

"You're giving us the greenglass for free again," Selene said softly.

"Accounting error," Maude said.

"Right." Selene shrugged into her coat, lifted the crate with ease, and paused at the door. "You deserve it, you know."

Maude narrowed her eyes. Selene tipped her chin toward the Sugar High Bakery box—note still glaring up with its smug little *Eat me*, the pear tartlet she'd set aside sitting like evidence.

Shit. She'd forgotten about that.

Maude rolled her shoulders back, spine stiffening. "That's nothing."

"You ate contraband hand pies from the enemy."

"I confiscated them."

Selene's grin spread, sharp as a secret. "See you tonight?"

"Maybe," Maude lied.

When Selene left, the afternoon thinned into its usual slow stretch. She got some customers: Mrs. Haddingham stumped in, took her daily sprig of thyme with the gravity of a blood oath, and left without a word. Two teenagers in cloak-hair and terrible eyeliner came for "something that makes your eyes black," and left with charcoal salve and a lecture on avoiding organ failure. A young mother asked for a sleeping charm "for the baby, obviously," with haunted raccoon eyes that begged for a dose for herself; Maude tucked a quiet-breath sachet in the bag for free and pretended she hadn't.

Then the novelty crowd: a pair of sisters, hair braided with ribbons, a box of Wesley's sugar moons balanced between them like treasure.

"We heard you can make them...sing?" one ventured.

"Briefly," Maude said.

She laid a thread of runes across the pastries and the crescents hummed a four-note lullaby sweet enough to calm a banshee.

They clasped hands like she'd parted the clouds. When they left, the shop felt the tiniest bit warmer. She did not smile. (She did.)

By early evening, Maude had cleared the counter, relabeled three jars, and restocked cough elixirs. She flipped the sign to *Closed* and was reaching for her coat when the bell chimed again and Oliver Hale swept in like a wealthy storm, carrying a picnic.

The basket was ridiculous: braided willow, embroidered cloth, enough food for a rehearsal dinner. He dumped it on the counter. "Supper," he sang.

"You've mistaken me for someone who's fun."

"Never." He arched a brow, caught sight of the pear tartlet she had totally not been saving, and smirked. "Oh, good, dessert."

Maude stared at the basket, then at him, then back at it. The math did itself. "Wesley told you."

He had the grace to look sheepish for half a second, then decided against it. "He might have mentioned that you needed extra help. I might have mentioned to Selene that he mentioned it. Do not bite the courier's head off; it's very pretty."

"I don't need people looking after me," she said, folding her arms so tightly a rib complained.

"Right," Oli said brightly, "you're the only one allowed to look after people."

She bristled. "I—"

He ticked items off on elegant fingers. "Let's consult the record: Maude Harrow has quietly financed potion stock for the Lantern Ward for months. She repaired Old Rook's roof when it failed in a rainstorm at two a.m., because he was too proud to ask and too frail to fix it. She spent three nights on the stables floor weaning Pickles off a fever tonic, because the healers gave up and you did not. She slipped that scholar from the bookshop a tea so he'd stop dreaming himself mad. She stabilized a cursed street with her own hands and no sleep, and would absolutely do it again rather than ask for help."

He lifted his gaze. The teasing softened; the care didn't. "You like to act like you're heartless, Maude, but you're the one who keeps giving pieces of your heart away."

She stared at him. The shop, the lanterns outside, the hum of the runes—everything sharpened and blurred at once. She sat down hard on the stool and pressed her fingers to her forehead. "Saints, Oli. What am I going to do?"

"You're going to do whatever you're going to do," he said matter-of-factly, "because you're you. But you'll do the right thing. You always do." He let the beat sit, then added lightly, "And for the record, I vote we appoint Wesley as head of Maude Maintenance."

"No."

"Yes."

"Absolutely not."

"Democracy at work," Oli said, unbothered. He began unpacking the basket: roasted root vegetables shimmering with herb oil; a slab of butter bread; a wedge of sharp cheese; small hand pies that were definitely stolen from Wesley's production like a raccoon raid in human form.

He set a fork in front of her like a challenge. "Magistrates' patrol doubled today," Oli said, slicing the cheese. "They're sniffing for infractions like boarhounds. Lydia told one of them your sign was 'too pointed.'"

Maude snorted and pulled the butter bread apart. The heat steamed between her fingers. "How's your scheming?"

"*Thriving*. The Seat Gambit proceeds. I have a majority of endorsements, one bitter rival, and a wardrobe that could run for office without me. I just need to not commit homicide in front of witnesses for three days."

She swallowed a smile. "Manageable."

"Borderline." He studied her face for a long second. "You look like you slept a little."

"Four hours," she said. "Record-breaking."

"Then you'll do it again tonight after you set the South Gate."

She didn't ask how he knew. He knew because he paid attention; it was his entire job, and sometimes his gift. She nodded once.

He packed half the food back into the basket, thrust it at her, and kissed her forehead in that infuriating big-brother way he'd invented the day they met. "Eat. And if you won't appoint Wesley to Maude Maintenance, I'll unionize him and do it, anyway."

"*I'll* salt your bones."

"Hot," he said, and sauntered out, whistling.

When the door shut, the shop's quiet came back like a tide. Maude leaned her elbows on the counter and let her head drop to her hands for one long breath. Grim hopped onto the ledger and curled his warm, heavy body across her lists like a furry paperweight. His ears still held a faint pink glow at the tips—a reminder that containment wasn't a cure, that time was a thread she was burning on both ends.

Outside, laughter rose, and the brass trio slid deliciously off-key. A string of lanterns lit all at once, one-two-three, like a held breath exhaled.

She moved. Locked the till. Checked the wards. Blew out the front lamps one by one until the shop was an amber sigh. Then she shouldered the basket Oli had forced on her and tucked the pear tartlet into the top of it like a tiny bribe she'd earned.

On the worktable, the Weftmark list waited. *South Gate— Tonight? East Gate—Samhain.* Under it, in her own tight script, a note: *Ask for help (ugh).*

She stared at it until the letters swam, then drew her coat tight, stepped into the evening, and locked the door. The street glowed gold and violet, lanterns swaying, shadows long. Somewhere, a child shouted a line about ghosts with triumphant terror. Somewhere else, a magistrate sniffed at a sign.

Maude stood in the doorway for a heartbeat and listened to the town dress itself—ornamented and doomed in the same breath. Then she tucked the basket under her arm and stepped into the warm, strange night to save it.

Nineteen

The sign at Sugar High Bakery still smelled faintly of frosting, even at the late hour. Maude stood on the stoop, arms folded, cobblestones under her boots tacky with what looked like a toffee spill. She had brought a thank-you. If it could be called that.

Balanced in her hand: a paper cone stuffed with roasted chestnuts she'd hexed to squeak "*ow*" every time you bit one. Juvenile. Petty. Wesley would love it.

She knocked with her boot. The door swung open, steam curling out, and Wesley leaned against the frame, hair askew. He blinked at her, then at the cone.

One eyebrow climbed. "What...is that?"

"Chestnuts. Obviously." She thrust them at him like a weapon. "Eat one."

He plucked one free, popped it into his mouth, bit—

"OW!" the nut squealed in falsetto.

Wesley choked and nearly spat it back across the doorway, laughter folding him in half before it broke free.

Maude smirked, satisfied. "Thank-you gift. You're welcome."

He wiped at his eyes, still grinning. "You're ridiculous."

"Speaking of ridiculous," she said, folding her arms. "My door doesn't scrape anymore."

That grin faltered, hesitation flickering through. "Right. Uh. I may have...fixed it." He shrugged. "The hinge was driving me mad. Figured you'd rather hex me later than listen to it forever."

Maude blinked at him. He said it like a man confessing to a crime, waiting for judgment. Saints—what had she done to him, that fixing a hinge made him look ready for the gallows? Still, it was one less task off her endless list—handled without her asking, just because he'd noticed.

Her grip on her arms loosened. "Thank you."

The words felt strange on her tongue. His eyes flicked to hers, searching, and for a moment he looked almost disarmed.

She cleared her throat, brisk again. "Anyway. I'm taking you up on your offer. For help."

His grin returned. "Good. Give me ten minutes. I'll change, and then we'll head out."

His apartment above the bakery was smaller than she'd expected. Narrow stairs led up to a space that smelled faintly of soap, undercut by something spiced—cardamom, maybe, and lemon. A narrow bed pressed against the far wall, sheets askew. A desk cluttered with scraps of parchment, half-finished recipes, and a jar of fountain pens with teeth marks in the caps. And everywhere—books. Stacks of them teetered like precarious towers.

Charcoal sketches hung on the wall above his desk. Not professional, but careful. Pages pinned in a patchwork of recipes and the pictures that went with them—loaves swelling mid-rise, sugared tarts like small suns, the curve of a cat's tail curling across the margin.

Maude's chest tightened. It was nothing like her cottage, which always felt like it belonged to someone older and wiser from whom she was merely borrowing it. This was...Wesley.

"I'll be quick," he said, grabbing a shirt and vanishing into the bathroom.

The moment the door clicked, Maude drifted toward the shelves like a thief.

She scanned the spines: treatises on fermentation, tomes of

folklore, a stack of plays—and then she squinted. A pile of lurid romances with covers so garish she snorted. *The Duke and the Dough Boy? Really?*

She flipped it open. *A lonely duke, weary of court intrigue. A humble dough boy, risen from the flour bins of destiny.*

Maude laughed, her gaze snagging on the gift card lying beside it: *From Oli.*

Of course it was.

And then—her breath hitched.

There, nestled in the middle of the shelf: *The Verdant Trials.* Her favorite book series. She leaned closer. Not just one set. *Three.*

The first: battered paperbacks, spines cracked, pages underlined in pencil. The second: leather-bound, gilt-edged, collector's edition. The third—she reached out reverently—was the limited pressing, forest green with silver embossing. The one she'd tried, and failed, to win at auction.

Her fingers brushed the cover as if it might vanish.

Behind her came the faint scrape of fabric, the whisper of cloth sliding over skin. She glanced back—and instantly regretted it.

Wesley stepped out of the washroom, damp hair curling against his forehead as he tugged a clean shirt over his torso. The motion pulled long lines of muscle across his chest and arms— lean but solid from years of kneading, lifting, carrying. He wasn't bulky—no, worse. He was compact strength, shoulders broad enough to make the room feel smaller, jaw shadowed and severe in the lamplight. His forearms were bare, corded, veins running down to strong hands she suddenly couldn't stop imagining pressed against her.

One brow lifted, slow as a drawstring pulled taut, his grin tilting. "Find something interesting?"

Heat shot up her neck. She snapped her gaze back to the shelf. "You have three sets of *The Verdant Trials.*"

He rubbed the back of his neck, sheepish. "I...like them."

"You *hoard* them."

"I *appreciate* them." He moved closer, still damp, still warm, smelling of soap. "Let me guess—you're one of those book snobs who swear paperbacks are the only real editions because they smell like actual trees?"

"Coming from someone who looks like they read cookbooks for the plot."

He laughed, low and rich, and it did nothing to help her. Then he plucked the green edition from her hands. "Which one's your favorite?"

Her arms crossed tight over her chest, mostly to keep from wringing them. "The fifth. Mirror maze. When Branna betrays them."

He groaned, running a hand through damp hair. "Don't. I'm still convinced she'll redeem herself in the last book."

"You're delusional."

"Optimistic," he corrected. "Which, granted, might be the same thing."

"You probably cry when the talking owl gives speeches."

"Only twice," he said with mock offense. "And once was allergies."

She caught herself smiling before she could strangle it. His shirt clung damp at the collar, eyes bright with laughter.

Saints. He was pretty. There was no other word for it. Pretty and warm and standing too close, looking at her like she was the only thing in the room.

Her pulse tripped. She turned toward the door. "Come on. We've got work."

"Running away already?" His voice followed her, teasing, but when she risked a glance back, his eyes weren't mocking. They were steady. Warm. Curious. Like he saw more than she wanted him to.

Her chest tightened. She spun faster, muttering, "If you're not ready in thirty seconds, I'm leaving you here with your romance novels."

"They're not romances!" he called, laughing.

"Whatever helps you sleep at night."

She stalked out before he could see the flush blooming hot across her cheeks.

South Gate wasn't quiet. It never was—especially not the week before Samhain.

Lanterns strung from stall to stall burned in fat, honeyed orbs, glamour-flames flickering like fallen leaves caught in midair. A puppet stage clacked at the far end while a trio of teenagers practiced sword choreography near the fountain, their wooden blades colliding with the conviction of people who'd never actually been hit by anything sharp. The air smelled of roasted chestnuts, wet stone, cinnamon, damp wool, and the faint coppery thrum of the ley line that ran straight under the old bronze wyvern perched on the fountain's lip.

This spot had been Mistwood's first well. The bricks still showed where the mouth had been sealed and dressed as a fountain centuries ago—blue and amber tiles cracked into a star around the wyvern's clawed feet. The ley sang through it, soft and insistent, like a heartbeat under blankets.

"Here," Maude said, and knelt.

She unloaded the third loom's pieces: ironvine circlet; blackthorn shards cut thin as claws; the parchment sigil she'd inked with rosemary steep and yarrow ash; a wax-sealed shadowbell bloom; a vial of glasswort resin; a folded strip of night-apple peel still glimmering faintly in the shade; a measured scoop of heartmire salt; and, tucked in a cloth, a chalk of wolfsbone—petrified marrow that looked like a sliver of moon.

Wesley crouched beside her, one palm braced on a cobble, the other shading his eyes to watch the lanterns shiver. "So this is the one."

"This is the one," she said. "The fountain mouth sits dead center on the line. Everything feeds to it. If this holds, the rest of the street will stop...forgetting what it is."

He cut her a look. "You mean 'slowly merging into a patchwork nightmare'?"

"That, too."

She pretended she didn't feel the warmth of him at her side and bent to lay chalk: a clean circle around the star of cracked tile, four small dishes at the cardinal points—salt to the north, ash to the south, thistledown east, water west. A knot of kids drifted closer, then drifted back when Maude looked up. Her glance said, *Try me*. They tried her from a safe distance instead.

"You never actually told me," Wesley murmured, "why what we did the first time didn't work."

"The curse doesn't break—it moves," she murmured, ring finger steady as she finished the circle. "Bailey left a note: unspooled interlocks like to collect in a pool. The Weftmark at my cottage is a pool. But the pulse is bigger than one drain. We need three more to keep Mistwood from drowning." She slid the iron-vine ring into place and felt the hum rise through her palm. "Congratulations. You're standing at drain number three."

He went quiet—watching, weighing. He did it the way he baked: measuring time, gauging heat, knowing when something was ready without checking twice. Always waiting for the exact moment things turned.

"What do you need?"

"Resin," she said, handing him the vial of glasswort. "A thin line along the inner rim—clockwise, slow. Count with the ley. Don't rush. It steadies volatility like a truce: both sides stand down, no one wins, no one loses. It only holds so long as nobody breaks it."

He nodded, head tipped as if he could hear the beat she meant. After two careful breaths, he poured. The resin ran thin and clear, catching light like water over glass, and for a moment Maude's throat hurt with something like relief.

She set the blackthorn teeth at quarter points, pressed wolfsbone dust into each thorn's base to give the ward some bite, then laid the night-apple peel like a ribbon shield over the ring's heart. "*Mask*," she told it, because if the interlock couldn't smell them, it might not charge them like a bull. "This is to keep the pull from grabbing everything else."

He didn't answer. He was laser-focused on the pour. When he reached the end, the resin line connected—one clean loop—and the ring gave a small, satisfied *tick*.

Maude wiped her palms, ignoring the thin burn of nerves in her wrists. "All right." She set the parchment sigil in the ring and pricked her thumb. One drop of blood sank into the ink, and the lines darkened, as if the sigil had been waiting to wake up. "Honesty clause," she muttered.

"Because spells that lie don't work," Wesley said, soft, repeating her lesson back to her.

"Exactly." She breathed in, breathed out. "Hold the ring. Both hands, outer rim. If it flexes, give it back. Do not muscle it."

"I can not-muscle with the best of them," he said, but there was no smirk in it. He set his hands where she'd shown him, fingers splayed, forearms tense. He didn't look away from her.

Maude touched the shadowbell wax with a warmed pin. The seal gave. Scent rose: grief dressed in cool water and moonlight. The ley line under the fountain answered, a low chord deep in her bones.

"Okay. On my mark."

She spoke the weave and pulled. Her will coaxed the interlock's hungry, misguided binding to recognize the ring as the safest, most delicious place to go, to curl into, to sleep inside. Wesley's grip flexed when the ring arched—just enough give to keep it from cracking, just enough resistance to keep it taut. He didn't hum. He timed his breath to hers instead: three counts in, three out. It steadied the draw. The resin held. The blackthorn clicked, tiny locks catching. The night-apple peel dulled the pull. The ring warmed in their hands; the chalk circle lifted gooseflesh up Maude's arms.

Around them, the square…adjusted.

It didn't warp or howl this time. It exhaled.

The cracked star-tile under the wyvern brightened, blue and amber sharpening at the edges as if someone had just wiped them clean. The string of lanterns above them stopped their uneasy flicker and settled into a calm, regular glow. The bobbing apples at a nearby stall, which had been floating two inches above the water, dropped back in with a pleasing *plunk*. A stack of woven baskets that had insisted on nesting themselves into a single wicker serpent split neatly back into separate baskets.

No fireworks. No drama. Just a hundred tiny alignments slipping into place.

Maude could hear the moment the crowd caught it. Conversations faltered. Someone whispered, "Did you feel that?" Another: "The fountain's singing differently." The teenagers with swords lowered their props and stared. The fiddler's tune slid from jittery to something steady enough to dance to.

Wesley didn't look up. He held the ring until Maude touched his wrist—a small nod—and only then did he ease the ironvine onto the chalk, the resin seam settled, the glow banked to a quiet purr.

Maude's mouth tasted like copper. She let her hands fall, knees rubbery with relief. "It's grounded," she said, mostly to the ring, partly to Wesley.

She should have known the quiet wouldn't last.

A citrus-slick voice cut the air: "Well, isn't that convenient."

Alderman Veyne, who had never met a ledger he didn't love, arrived with two inspectors in tow. He smelled faintly of lemon oil and success someone else paid for. His smile to the crowd was for show; the one he aimed at Maude had teeth. "The same witch who created a spectacle on Blightbend now appears at the very heart of Market Square, performing an unsanctioned ritual."

Maude stared him down, deadpan as a gravestone. "Good evening to you, too, Alderman."

Veyne sniffed. "People have been...concerned," he said, smoothing his tone. "Strange phenomena. Merging. Malfunctions. It would be a terrible shame if the source of those disturbances turned out to be the very same person who has already brought this town so much grief."

The words slid slick as eels into the space between the crowd and Maude. She could feel the crowd straining, ready to be told who the monster was so they could rehearse their courage.

Maude's jaw ticked. "The 'source' was a miscast I already contained," she said, flat. "Now I'm cleaning what bled out."

Veyne tutted. "More trouble, then." He spread his hands, palms open, as though addressing a court instead of a crowded square. His voice carried with practiced poise. "I ask only what any reasonable magistrate would: how very convenient that the one who births the malady also profits from its cure."

Heat climbed Maude's neck. "I'm not profiting."

"Are you not?" He stepped closer, the sour tang of bitter wine and stale breath rolling over her. As he advanced, the crowd shifted with him, a restless rustling through the square. "I hear of your unsanctioned singing loaves at the west market. Of custard buns that glow faintly in the dark, wanted or not. Of pear tarts laced with petals that compel confessions after the third bite. Entire trays of honey-cakes sprouting tiny, grasping arms the moment a child cries. And who, pray, brewed those? Who reaps the coin when half this town cannot stop whispering of them? You have made yourself the talk of every corner and every hearth. Do not insult me by pretending otherwise."

He smoothed his sleeve, his voice lowering to silk. "Let me remind you, *witch*: there was a time when your kind were not permitted such liberties. When strictures bound every working, and no charm, no tincture, no careless whisper of magic escaped regulation. Those were safer years. If it were left to me, they would return. And though I stand outnumbered in vote, I do not doubt their hearts will turn—after all of this. This—"

"Enough." Wesley's voice cut across the square, firm. His hand clamped down on Veyne's shoulder and all but shoved him back, away from Maude. "Tell me, Magistrate, is it illegal to create things that make people happy? Things they ask for by name? Show me in your statutes where it's written that a loaf that sings, or a tart that glows, or a sweet that makes a child laugh, is a crime."

Veyne sputtered, face mottling, but Wesley pressed on. "Yes, Maude cast a spell that misfired. A single mistake, quickly mended. No shops ruined—no harm that lasted longer than a week's gossip. And since then? She's turned a mishap into something good. I'll ask again—slowly, so you can answer this time. Is happiness illegal? Is joy? Show me the line, the clause where kindness requires a permit."

Veyne shoved himself free of Wesley's grip, robes snapping like sails in a sudden gust. "That is hardly a kindness, Mr. Rivers. She is collecting coins for her unsanctioned concoctions!"

Wesley's eyes rolled heavenward. "So this is about her character, then? Because I'll tell you now—you don't want to drag Maude Harrow's name into question. Not with me standing here." His gaze cut narrow. "I don't see you stocking the healers' shelves when they run dry. She's the one handing blister balm to carpenters who forget to pay. She's the one letting the widow by the weir trade in buttons—and still sending her home with what she needs. She has done more for this town than any of you, clutching ledgers tight and pointing fingers."

If Maude's face burned any hotter, she'd combust right there in the square. Saints save her—Oli had to have told Wesley. That infuriating, ridiculous, wonderful menace of a friend.

"You all tell stories about Bailey Harrow," Wesley said then, and the square went still. Even Veyne's mouth snapped shut with a click. "You say he kept this street stitched together. You say he saved your sons from fevers, your fields from blight. Revered him." His gaze swept over the faces gathered. "But when he died—tell me—how many of you walked across Blightbend to check on his daughter?"

The word *daughter* struck Maude like a hammer to the chest. It always did. She never traded on it; she kept it hidden the way you keep a bruise covered. Hearing it spoken aloud—something that belonged only to her—made her vision wobble. Her knuckles whitened around the night-apple ribbon.

The crowd shifted. Nobody spoke. Even Veyne's ledger drooped like it was embarrassed to be seen. Eventually, he managed, voice brittle, "Be that as it may—"

"It may," Maude snapped. "And while you're reviewing, keep your hands off the ring. Anyone touches it, I'll hex their eyebrows so they migrate south and never return."

A child snorted with laughter so loud it became contagious. Somewhere behind them, a vendor muttered, *"Leave the girl be."*

Veyne, sensing his audience thinning, snapped his book shut. "Very well. We will...review." He aimed a last brittle smile at Maude. "Do keep it safe, Ms. Harrow. Another incident—"

"Then don't cause an incident," she said sweetly.

Veyne stalked off, the inspectors trailing behind with the careful faces of men trying not to look like cowards.

The tension bled out of the square by degrees. And then, as if a spell broke, life restarted: the fiddler picked up a tune; the teenagers resumed hitting each other; a pair of elderly women argued about whether the wyvern statue had always had that expression (it had).

Wesley stayed where he was, shoulders squared, gaze steady on Maude. Watching like she was something he'd set in the oven and couldn't afford to take his eyes off in case it burned.

"You okay?" he asked at last. Not soft. Not pitying. Just there.

Her throat felt raw. "No," she admitted, the truth scraping on the way out. "But the third loom is set."

He nodded once. "It is."

She could feel it now: a low, contented purr under the fountain, the way a cat hums in a room where it isn't being observed. The square had steadied. The tiny wrongnesses had un-wronged themselves.

Wesley angled his body slightly, shoulder brushing hers—barely a touch, easily misinterpreted as crowd mechanics—and lowered his voice. "I'm going to hang a sign near the ring. Polite, firm. '*Do not touch. If you value your eyebrows.*'" A beat. Then, "I'll also post myself here for a while. Make it look official."

"You have a business to run," she said, eyes on the chalk line. "Go bake something, smug."

"I did. At dawn." He tilted his head toward the chimney in the distance. "Sourdough boules the size of your ego."

She almost smiled. "Must be enormous."

"Colossal."

Silence stretched, weighted. He didn't move. She didn't either.

Finally, she muttered, "Thanks. For what you said."

"It was true," he said simply.

She kept her eyes on the chalk ring, unwilling to let him see her face. But low in her gut, ache and warmth folded into one another, a knot of feeling so tightly drawn she could no longer name its strands.

Twenty

Fog hung low over Mistwood Hills, slow and hazed, the air thick with the char of woodfires and the copper bite of spent offerings burned on doorsteps. Samhain always smelled like endings and beginnings tangled together—sweet rot from carved gourds left overnight, wax from guttering candles, the faint tang of mulled wine spilled sticky across the cobblestones.

Light pried through the crooked panes of Maude's bedroom, catching the chalk of her runes and tugging their metallic scent into the air. Her quilt had long since migrated to the floor. So had she. Now she lay sprawled across the boards, cheek pressed into their ridges, hair a halo of strawberry-blonde curls fanned unevenly on the rug. The floor and she were on speaking terms— it didn't mind her company.

Selene knocked once and then didn't bother with a second, because boundaries were for people without ward-defying key-shaped hairpins. She breezed in wearing a sweater the color of storm-light and carrying a basket that steamed in three distinct directions.

"Breakfast," Selene sang, kicking the door shut with her heel. "And before you ask—no, I didn't bring a lecture on joy. I brought carbs."

Maude pushed up on her elbows. "Those are the same thing."

Selene set the basket on the trunk at the foot of the bed and untied the twine. Not just any twine—bakery twine. Pastel colors, all smug about it. Inside: a garlic-salted croissant still warm enough to fog the lid, a savory hand pie that smelled like caramelized onions and thyme, a little jar of lemon curd with a ribbon (kill it with fire), and two paper cups of coffee, one marked with a tiny ink star.

Maude stared at the star until it felt like it was staring back.

Selene coughed into her fist in the world's least innocent way. "I passed a place on my way here."

"Oh? Which place would that be," Maude said, "the one that knows I hate rosewater but will accept clove in small, weaponized doses, that a croissant without salt is a cry for help, and that I drink coffee like it owes me money?"

"Yes, that...very specific place."

Maude plucked the star-marked cup like it might bite her. It didn't. It breathed steam into her face that smelled like a better mood. She tried not to look pleased and failed a little.

"The Samhain festival starts basically now and goes all day and all night," Selene went on, tipping the contents of the basket into gentle little stacks like a priestess arranging offerings. "You promised to do fun things and not work until your eyes bleed, remember."

"I promised under duress."

"Like all the best promises."

Maude took a bite of the hand pie because she was a coward in only one way and it involved onion. The pastry shattered in perfect flakes and the thyme hit her tongue. She made a noise that was not a compliment and not *not* a compliment either.

Selene's eyes sharpened, unfairly knowing. "Good?"

"It's food."

"Uh-huh."

They ate at the foot of the bed like teenagers planning a curse. Outside, Mistwood Hills stretched awake—bells testing their throats, distant laughter already leaking into the lanes. The second loom thrummed somewhere under the cobbles, far away and close as skin, both—the way a cat who lives in your house also lives a little in your lungs.

Selene dusted nonexistent crumbs off her skirt. "Oli says to meet at the square at noon. We'll wander, buy ridiculous things, you'll insult vendors in a way that somehow makes them love you. Then dancing tonight. Speaking of—what are you going as?"

"Home."

"No."

"Fine." Maude sipped coffee. It hit like salvation. "I'm going as something festive and true to the spirit of the season."

Selene narrowed her eyes. "Define *festive*."

"Alderman Veyne's conscience."

Selene choked so hard on a croissant flake that Maude had to thump her between the shoulder blades. "You cannot," Selene wheezed, delighted and horrified.

"Why? It's extremely rare. No one will have the same costume." Maude sipped again, thinking. "I'll make a sash that says *VIOLATION*, carry a ledger, and a brass stamp that reads *DENIED*. Maybe a little bell I can ring when people make bad choices."

"Maude, that's not a costume. That's psychological warfare."

"Potayto, potahto."

Selene rifled through the garment bag she'd brought like she was possessed. "Okay, fine, if you're going as Veyne's non-existent soul, I'm going as the concept of informed consent."

"Timely."

Selene's grin softened. "Also, you invited Wesley."

"I mentioned there would be dancing."

"You *invited* Wesley," Selene singsonged, feral joy returning. "What's he going as? Sunshine? Manners?"

"I told him costumes were not mandatory. He said he'd come as '*better company*.'" Maude twisted a ring she didn't remember putting on.

Selene leaned in. "And what about you?"

"I said I'd go as myself. Terrifying enough."

"And he said?"

"That I should at least warn people in advance." Maude stared at the wall like it had personally offended her. "Rude."

Selene made the kind of face people made when they were restraining themselves from squealing. "You like him."

"I like my cat."

"You don't have a cat. Grim owns *you*."

"Semantics."

Selene glanced at the basket again, at the little star on the lid of the finished coffee. "So, he knows your order."

Maude picked up the lemon curd and turned it so the ribbon faced the wall. "He knows I eat food, yes."

"And that you like curd."

"I like that it makes people pucker."

"Sour on the outside, gold in the middle," Selene murmured reverently. "Maude, distilled."

They slipped into an easy rhythm that had, somehow, crawled back into Maude's life: Selene combing out the fuzzed ends of her curls, fingers deft as she teased them into shape. She tucked sprigs of rosemary at her temple, murmuring something about adornment while Maude muttered about fortification.

"Corset," Selene ordered, pulling the fitted bodice tighter than Maude would've dared on her own. It cinched clean lines through her waist, lifted her chest just enough that Maude shot her a glare. Selene only smirked and reached for the pot of rouge, pressing a red stain over Maude's lips until her reflection looked like someone who knew how to flirt with murder.

Maude reached for the black skirt that swished like whispering when she moved and added a narrow leather belt for her pouches. Alderman Veyne's "conscience" required props: a strip of cream linen she'd inked into a sash—*VIOLATION*—and a little steel stamp with a skull carved into the handle.

"You're dangerous," Maude said, half-impressed, half-accusing.

"I listen when you monologue," Selene said smugly, tilting her head to admire her handiwork.

Maude slid the sash over her shoulder. The beams hummed, runes glowing faintly, approving.

Selene watched her with that look again—the one that said *I see you, even when you try very hard not to be seen.* "You look like yourself."

"Tragic."

Selene leaned a hip against the trunk. "And you look...not murderous about today. Which is new."

Maude considered the floorboards. The lines cut by Bailey's hand, the small shine of the old polish, the way the house settled around her like a cloak. "I'm tired," she admitted. "There's that. And there's a festival, which is basically sanctioned chaos. My natural habitat."

"And there's Wesley."

Maude didn't look at her. "He's...helpful."

"Uh-huh."

"And infuriating."

"Keep going."

"And—" she grimaced, then surrendered, "—not entirely awful to be near."

"I am so happy I lived to see this day."

Maude sighed, then stood, testing the fall of the skirt, the set of the sash. She reached under the bed and dragged out a battered wooden box. Inside: a ledger with crisp blank pages and a brass inking pad, both of which she set neatly into her satchel beside her vials. "If anyone tries to touch the looms, I'll cite them."

"For what? Crimes against peace and quiet?"

"For disorderly existence."

Selene laughed, bright and ringing, then softened again. "We'll make it a good day, okay? Eat stupid things. Win a rigged game. Put a hex on a pumpkin. Maybe kiss someone under lanterns."

"I'll kiss your forehead if you stop talking."

"It'll have to do," Selene said. She scooped Grim—who had slunk in at some point to supervise breakfast—off the windowsill and deposited him in Maude's arms for precisely three seconds of enforced affection.

Grim tolerated it like a monarch permitting taxes. His nose was less pink now. It still glowed faintly in certain light. Maude set him down, and he trotted to the bed, climbed onto her pillow, and began kneading like he was trying to pummel tenderness into the linen. The room felt—dangerously, treacherously—good.

Selene gathered the detritus of the morning. "Oli says noon at the square, but I want to go out sooner. The charm-casters sell out of their best nonsense before midday."

"And by 'best nonsense' you mean…?"

"Glow-thread for braids, nipple tassels that spin on their own, liar's dice, and a teapot that screams when the water's ready."

Maude closed her eyes and laughed. "So…essentials, then. I was worried you'd say something impractical." She checked her buckles before standing. "We're meeting Oli at noon?"

"We are," Selene agreed, and then, because she couldn't resist, "And Wesley sooner?"

Maude opened the star-marked lid and took a long, long drink of coffee. "If he knows what's good for him, he'll arrive late and at a safe angle."

Selene grinned. "I'll leave you to brood. Don't be late." She disappeared down the hall.

Silence rolled back in, warm rather than harsh. Maude looked at herself in the scratched mirror: black skirt, fitted bodice, the rosemary at her temple, the sash slashed across her like a dare. She looked like a woman who had made choices and was going to keep making them even if the town's favorite hobby was narrating her wrongdoings.

She picked up the lemon curd and tucked it into her satchel—

because somehow he knew she loved it. Then she slid her ledger in beside it, pressed *DENIED* into a fresh page just to feel the satisfying thunk, and snorted despite herself.

Happy Samhain, Alderman. I brought your conscience.

The festival bells started in earnest outside, notes stacking like ladders into the sky. Maude squared her shoulders, checked the weight of her pocket vials, and headed out of the room—the house's amber runes warming in her wake like the place was exhaling, *There she is. Go start trouble.*

Twenty-One

Against all odds, Maude didn't feel like an abnormal shard jammed into a puzzle. Begrudgingly, it was as if she'd finally stepped into a picture everyone else had been painting without her.

The midday sun spilled over the square, catching on banners and streamers strung high across the lanes—paper moons, glass stars, pumpkins carved into wicked grins that squinted in the glare.

Stalls crowded shoulder to shoulder, every surface dripping with ribbon, laurel, and charm gone a little overboard. Steam curled from cauldrons of cider, sweet and spiced, while the air tangled with roasted chestnuts, candied pears, and woodsmoke laced with sage. Children darted through the press in masks like nightmares, laughter clattering like bells.

A fiddler played fast enough to start a fight. A drummer answered, low and steady. The whole square moved to it—feet stamping, skirts flaring, mugs clinking. Fire-dancers spun near the fountain, sparks streaking upward like meteors.

Her sash read *VIOLATION* in stark black letters. The rosemary Selene had braided into her curls scratched faintly at her temple. Each time a gaze snagged on her, she pretended not to notice.

"Maude!"

Selene tore through the crowd like a comet, skirts hitched in one hand, nipple tassels attached and spinning wildly of their own accord.

Laughter rippled; applause broke out. Someone nearly dropped a mug. Selene didn't care. She went straight for Maude, eyes bright with feral delight.

"What is that?" she demanded, breathless, pointing at the box Maude clutched tight.

Maude smirked—slow, dangerous—and flipped open the battered wooden box. The lid bore her runes, faint heat pulsing through the grain. "Something better than tassels," she said. "Fireworks."

Selene's grin went wicked. "You're going to blow the pants off Alderman Veyne."

"Off him," Maude said, hefting the box, "and every sanctimonious crony he's got lined up beside him."

Selene whooped so loud—her tassels spinning into such a frenzy that they nearly lifted her off the ground—that the fiddler lost his place.

Maude threw her head back and cackled, helpless against it.

"Give me that," Selene said, snatching the box before Maude could pull it away. She flipped the latch with all the reverence of a thief mid-heist. "Oh, saints' teeth—what have you done?"

Maude only waggled her eyebrows. "You'll have to wait and see."

With a flick, she shrank the box to a manageable size and tucked it into her satchel. That was when Wesley appeared.

He wove through the midday crowd with infuriating ease— like the press of bodies simply parted for him. Sunlight struck off him as if he'd stolen it: gold bright in his hair, bronze along the cut of his jaw. He wasn't in costume. Just a dark shirt with the sleeves rolled, trousers neat, boots scuffed.

But when he saw her, he smiled. And the world tilted a fraction.

"Witch," he said by way of greeting, voice warm.

"Baker," she shot back, deadpan.

His eyes swept over her cloak, her sash, the rosemary tucked. "You clean up terrifying."

Heat crept up her neck. *Treacherous.* She turned to Selene as if glaring could redirect blood flow. "Why did I invite him again?"

Selene only smirked, which was a *crime*.

Then Oli crashed into them—literally, sequins and glitter flying like confetti—already holding four mugs of spiced cider. "My favorite people!" he sang. "And Wesley."

"Charmed," Wesley said dryly, taking a mug.

They fell into step like a troupe: Oli leading with scandalous commentary, Selene laughing at every outrageous thing, and Wesley—of course—at Maude's side. Close enough that his sleeve brushed hers once, twice. Close enough that the scent of him— yeast, cardamom, clean soap—cut through cider and smoke. She told herself she didn't notice.

As they wandered the Samhain festival, Oli heckled the fire-eaters until one threatened to set his hair alight. Selene dragged them to a mask stall where enchanted visages whispered ghost-echoes with every word. Maude let herself be bullied into trying one. She spoke three words—"*Get bent, Oli*"—and nearly collapsed laughing when Wesley doubled over at the sound.

"Beautiful," Wesley wheezed, bracing a hand on his knee. "Say it again."

"Die," Maude intoned, the mask echoing like cathedral bells.

She ripped the mask off and shoved it at Selene, but Wesley was still looking at her like she'd turned the world sideways for a second.

They ate their way down the square: roasted squash stuffed with sage and cheese; skewers of charmed apples that sparked cinnamon when bitten; hand-pies filled with spiced meat and fig. Wesley kept handing her things without asking. She kept eating them without complaint. This should have concerned her. It didn't.

It was…easy. Easier than she had any right to let it be.

When the crowd pressed too close, his hand lingered at the small of her back. Warm. Steady. *Maddening*. When smudges of ash from a roasting pit clung to her sleeve, he brushed them away with infuriating care. Each touch was nothing. Each touch was *everything*.

She didn't stop him. That shocked her most of all. Because usually? She bit. Or hexed. Or both. Instead, she found herself watching him. The way his mouth curved easily when he laughed. The way he carried himself—easy, unbothered—even while Oli tried to scandalize a fiddler by demanding a ballad about goats at full volume.

She'd called Wesley an idiot so often, it had become doctrine. But he wasn't. Not tonight. Maybe he had never been.

He was…a friend.

Maybe—*terrifyingly*—something more.

Her fingers curled into her skirt.

Grief had taught her that need was weakness—that it gutted you clean when it left. She had promised herself never again. But Wesley wasn't asking her to need. He was just there. Hand at her back. Brush of ash from her sleeve. Food passed without words. And she let him. *She let him.*

Maude was not careless. She was catastrophically careful—and also, apparently, doomed.

The music shifted, and the square opened like a mouth; the crowd flowed toward the fountain for the next set. Fiddles sawed, pipes trilled, the drum grinned. Someone whooped.

Oli grabbed Selene's hand with a flourish.

Wesley offered his to Maude.

She stared at it as if it were a suspicious mushroom.

"Truce," he said, soft, as if the word might spook.

Her fingers slid into his, warm against his calluses. "Under the original terms of truce," she said dryly, "this gesture qualifies as a renewal. Limited duration. Subject to breach without notice."

A smile ghosted across his mouth as he tugged her toward the square. "Then consider this a clause you forgot to write down: when music plays, the witch is obligated to dance."

Her eyes narrowed. "That was never in the contract."

"It is now," Wesley said, drawing her into the rhythm anyway. "Section Eight, Subpart B: *all smoldering glares must be performed in time to the music.*"

Wesley tugged her into the circle as Oli sang and spun Selene until her braids whipped like comets. The wyvern fountain spat silver arcs that misted their faces when they passed too close. Someone pressed a cup into Maude's free hand; she drank without looking—spiced, hot, perfect—and told herself the warmth in her chest was the cider, nothing more.

"You're terrible at this," Wesley said cheerfully over the music, executing a smug little step that had no business being that light on a man his size.

"Thank you," she said. "I was trying to radiate menace."

"It's working." He grinned—the kind of smile that made the lantern light show off for him.

Her body did the traitorous thing of remembering: the shape of his palm from earlier, the weight at the small of her back. She scowled at her own feet and let the reel yank her two steps right, one left.

They lasted three rounds before the music turned, the crowd folding inward like a current. Fiddles slipped into something low, vowels drawn out like wind through a hollow reed. The drum fell to a heartbeat. Couples drew together, palms and shoulders and breath.

Before Maude could bolt, Wesley's palm slid along her spine.

"Stay with me," he said.

"No. I don't do slow."

"Come on, *menace.* One song."

She folded her arms. "I bite."

"I'm vaccinated." He offered his hand again, palm up. "Please?"

It was ridiculous how loudly the word *Please* landed. She searched for an excuse and found only Oli, already draped around Selene like a scarf, whispering something into her ear. Selene laughed so hard she nearly toppled. Useless. Both of them.

Wesley's hand was warm where it settled at her waist. Up close, he was broader than she ever let herself acknowledge—baker's arms, a heartbeat steady as a drum beneath his shirt. She stepped into him because the alternative was letting the awkwardness hang forever. Her forehead brushed the center of his chest.

"You're so short," he murmured, amusement in his low tone.

"And you're obvious."

He laughed, then—carefully—set his boots wide and lifted her by the waist the smallest fraction and set her on his shoes.

She made a sound she would later deny on penalty of murder.

"It's practical," he said, solemn. "I don't want my spine to seize from leaning."

She grinned into his shirt. Heat climbed up her neck. Her laugh got lost in the fabric and came back gentler than she meant for it to.

They moved. Not gracefully—she would never give him that—but in time. His stride shortened; her chin found the hollow near his collarbone; the thrum of the band threaded through him into her. The square pulsed around them: cider steam, pumpkin glow, fire-dancer sparks catching the air and winking out like tiny meteors. Selene's laugh cut bright as a bell; Oli shouted something obscene about hips that Maude refused to process.

She slid off his boots after a bar or two, dignity reasserting itself, and put her palms flat against his chest where his shirt was soft and heat lived. "Don't you dare try to spin me."

"Oh? What would you do if I did?"

He dipped his head a fraction, close enough that she could count the blue flecks in his eyes, close enough that she felt the shape of the kiss he hadn't taken last time like a heat map on her mouth. For half a second, the square, the town, the curse—every-thing—thinned to the ache of *maybe*.

Until something shifted in the air.

The fountain hiccupped. Once. Then again—deeper, wrong, like a heartbeat skipping a step. Lanterns overhead flared too bright and began to drip, glass stretching into hot teardrops that hardened midair and shattered like frost. Stalls shuddered; canvas warped into timber, then back again, grotesque in-between. The square's hum bent off-key.

A chord plucked too hard beneath the skin.

The third loom.

Maude felt it flare across the ley—bright, hungry. Not break-ing. Not yet. But reaching with sticky, greedy fingers past the boundaries she'd given it.

Her stomach plunged. Salt crawled down her spine.

She tilted her head as if angling to hear the Weftmark more clearly and did the math that had been running in the back of her skull since dawn: Samhain's tide rising, the whole town's atten-tion braided tight, magistrates meddling at the net, the first loom holding steady at the North Gate—until the third tried to carry more than it was built to hold. *Of course it did.*

The music faltered. Children froze mid-dance, wooden swords lifted in question.

Her stomach dropped again.

"Mau—" Wesley started.

"I know." She was already moving. "I know."

A murmur sharpened to a point. Someone shouted, "The witch!"—because of course they did. Nothing delights a crowd like blaming a woman.

Heads snapped toward them as they bolted for the wyvern. A row of carved pumpkins warped—faces stretching, grins sagging —before snapping back into place. A chair split into two, then collapsed back into one, ugly and indecisive. The wyvern foun-tain's eyes flashed lacquer-bright, then dulled; water hiccupped in the basin like it was trying not to retch.

"Selene!" Maude shouted, because she needed the only competent person besides herself—and Selene was already running.

Oli skidded in beside them, glitter looking suddenly absurd in the bad light. He gripped Maude's elbows, eyes gone flat. "What do you need?"

Her hands were already in her satchel. "The fountain. She's pulling too hard. Selene—second loom. Rosemary on the northern quadrant, yarrow ash on the southwest seam, heartmire salt across the sigil. Light touch. Don't let the bind choke."

Selene didn't argue. Healer eyes, sharp and calm. "On it."

"Oli—distract them." Maude drew out the fireworks box, enlarging it. "Light the sky. Keep their eyes up and their feet back."

"Are you sure you don't need me?" Oli's jaw was set.

"Don't worry," Wesley answered, steady. "I've got her."

No theater in it. Just truth. Oli searched his face, found whatever he needed, kissed Maude's forehead, and sprinted after Selene—already shouting about fireworks to a boy with the look of someone who'd just been given his first quest.

The square was tipping toward panic. Magistrates' ledgers snapped open like jaws. Veyne's voice carried, oily and righteous—"Stand back! Stand back! Witchcraft!"

Maude seized Wesley's wrist. They ran. The crowd peeled back the way people do for calamity, for authority, for women who look ready to bowl you over with a jug if you don't move.

They reached the wyvern in a handful of strides that felt like a thousand. The fountain's water sloshed wrong, spilling in thick, syrupy ropes that clung where they landed, then snapped back like elastic. The Weftmark beneath the basin—ironvine ring, blackthorn teeth, waxed shadowbell heart—glowed too bright, the hum pitched high enough to make her skull ring.

All around, Market Square was forgetting itself. A baker's stall and a cooper's bench had leaned too close and gotten ideas, reshaping into an ungainly creature with flour drawers where hoops should be. Two neighbors who'd been arguing over goblin-made spoons a moment ago now found their coats fused at the shoulder—threads knitting fast, deciding they were married. Maude flicked her hand, muttered a quick word, and the fibers snapped apart. The men stumbled, looking at her as if she'd both slapped and saved them, before scuttling back into the crowd.

"Okay," Wesley said, low, both to her and to the fountain and to the part of himself that counted by intuition. "Talk me through it."

Her hands shook. She hated that they shook. "We re-anchor, slow the draw, give her something sweeter to drink." She dumped her satchel at the fountain's edge. "Night-apple peel—covering agent. Glasswort resin—stabilizer, three drops only. Heartmire salt to tune the balance. If I overdo it, she'll eat us."

He reached without hesitation. "Night-apple."

She slapped the dark ribbon of peel into his palm. "Wrap the ironvine clockwise. Don't cross the ends."

"Yes, chef," he said, then grimaced. "Sorry. Habit."

She flung a line of salt in a thin, exact curve, feeling for the place the ley bucked hardest. "When I say breathe, you breathe with me."

"Copy."

A firework hammered the sky into gold. The crowd *ooh*ed like the world wasn't lurching under their boots. Good. Oli doing what he was made to do.

Maude's pulse tried to gallop away without her. It wasn't the panic that got her—it was the memory braided into it, the way the wrongness in the hum wore Bailey's absence like a face. The spell was a hunger for belonging. She knew that hunger. She'd fed it all summer on anger until it grew teeth.

"Hey." Wesley's voice cut clean. He had the night-apple peel already looped around the ironvine, his fingers moving with that maddening baker's precision. "Look at me."

She kept working.

"Look," he said, "count with me. Four in. Hold two. Six out."

"I don't—"

"Maude."

She looked. He didn't smile—he grounded. One, two, three, four in; hold; six out. His chest rose and fell like a metronome for a nervous system. Her own breath caught it without permission, matched, steadied. Rage moved to a back burner. Not gone— never gone—but tamed enough to wield.

"Glasswort," she said, voice lower now, hands sure. "Three drops. Not four. If you give her four she'll glass the whole square."

"Three." He uncorked the little vial with big, careful hands and let the resin fall exactly where she pointed—lemniscate over the waxed heart. The Weftmark shivered and then moaned as if somebody had rubbed the edge of a wineglass. Good. Not catastrophic. Yet.

"Heartmire," she said. "Pinch only. We want her listening, not lashing out."

He arched a brow. "You're talking to a spell like it's sentient."

"It is." She flung him the salt. "Every spell has a will. You just hope it agrees with yours."

He didn't argue. He pinched and scattered, his rhythm matching hers. He touched the ring with his fingertips—not timid, but respectful—the way a man might touch proved dough he could ruin if he forgot it was alive.

"Now," she breathed, and set her palms down on the basin stone. "Breathe with me."

They did. Together. Her words found the old track Bailey had cut for her when she was a girl—how to ask a thing to hold. She altered a line without thinking, made it blunter, and felt Wesley catch the shift and steady it like a second pair of hands on her magic.

The hum dropped half a tone. The water lost its syrupy thickness and went back to being water. Lanterns stopped dripping and started behaving. The distorted stalls sighed, canvas forgetting it ever flirted with wood. The ring under the fountain dimmed from fever to warm.

It took two minutes. It took a year.

When the Weftmark settled into that low, contented purr she recognized, Maude let herself sag back on her heels. Her hands trembled so hard she had to curl them into fists to get them to stop.

"It's done."

Wesley didn't touch her. He only tilted his head—first toward the sky, where Oli punished the night with fireworks, then toward the far end of the square, where a slim figure knelt by the northeast corner, holding it steady with healer's hands. Selene had the second loom singing like a wineglass too.

Around them, shouting tilted from fear to curiosity. People are simple: if a thing looks like it is going to eat them, they panic. If it looks like it is someone else's problem, they gossip. Veyne hovered with his ledger as if it might block a hex on contact. A few brave idiots stepped closer.

Wesley didn't even look up. "Back," he snapped, voice pure command. "Unless you want your buttons fused to your shirt and your eyebrows in your shoes."

They backed up. He didn't even have to shout.

Maude's heart skipped as the ring's glow eased to a low murmur. "You're useful."

"Be still my heart," he said. "Where to next?"

"The Bonebridge. The last loom."

The bridge arched black over the river, an iron spine crossing white water. Ley lines braided there with currents and old stories. She'd saved it for last because it would be worst.

He rose and offered a hand without thinking. She ignored it and stood on her own, then took it anyway when her legs swayed. His fingers closed around hers like a promise.

She grabbed her kit. He shouldered the rest before she could argue. And they ran.

Twenty-Two

Behind them, light cracked the sky.

Maude's fireworks burst into wyverns, crowns, and one very questionable shape that made three grannies gasp before laughing behind their hands. The crowd *ooh*ed at just the right volume for a town being neatly distracted. *Bless you, Oli.*

As they cut through an alley and over the weir, Maude's mind tried to cram panic, calculation, and the stray flicker of joy into the same corner. She shoved the happiness into a pocket. Later. Maybe. If they lived.

The river wind hit like a slap. The Bonebridge rose ahead: old iron gone black with weather and stories, its arches spanning white water that hurled itself at stone like it bore a grudge. Paper lanterns dangled from the rails, small moons shivering in the gusts. The air quivered. At the bridge's center, the Weftmark pulsed faintly where she'd chalked sigils into the pitted iron earlier and wedged the ring into a cradle of stone.

She dropped to her knees and opened the satchel. Ashen ivy shimmered in her fingers; she wound it through the ironvine band, whispering the unbinding's exact opposite, a promise that the ring would hold what didn't belong anywhere else. Heartmire salt—three lines, then three more, then the little crosshatch Bailey had taught her. Glasswort resin, one bead on each cardinal tooth of blackthorn. Night-apple peel braided through the copper chain with hands that refused to tremble because she told them not to. Wolfsbone dust along the rivet line.

Wesley had already set the quadrants: salt, ash, water, thistledown. He poured the moondust oil in a slow figure-eight over the ring, and when the wind tried to take the shimmer, he cupped his hand and blocked it like he'd been born with the instinct.

"All right?" he said.

Her throat locked. She forced a nod. "Now."

They spoke together. Words layered, tangled, caught in the river's roar. For a heartbeat Maude faltered—surprised he knew them. She shouldn't have been; he'd done this with her twice already. But the fact that he was paying this close attention, that he'd memorized them down to the syllable...

The bridge shuddered beneath them, iron drawn taut as a bowstring stretched too far. Lanterns above snapped against their strings, light jerking wild across black water.

The ring answered, its glow climbing sharp and ravenous, singing high and thin as glass about to crack. It wanted more.

The first interlock snapped wrong. Bolts split their seams, and the bridge rolled under their knees. Maude pitched sideways, breath torn out of her throat—but Wesley caught her, his arm clamping around her waist, hauling her upright as the whole span lurched like a beast trying to buck them off. They slammed against the railing. Rusted iron bit her palms as she clung. The spell stayed rooted, tethered to the bridge's bones, and the structure groaned under the weight.

"Merging!" Wesley shouted over the roar. She followed his gaze: a cart piled with gourds and candied pears had collapsed into itself, wheels and fruit fused in a sticky, rolling mass. Nearby, a string of festival lanterns had fused into one long, wavering spine of glass, their flames trapped inside, flaring in unison. A dog yelped, half-swallowed by its owner's coat until the cloth spat it out again. Reality itself was mis-threading, knotting tighter with each beat of the spell.

And then the bell tower struck midnight.

The sound didn't just ring—it shook. One toll, then another, each strike reverberating down her spine. The air snapped taut. *Samhain.*

The veil was not a curtain drawing back. Not something gentle. It was a tear in the weave of the world, sudden and bright, as though someone had split the sky with a knife.

Light bled through first, faint and silvery, but wrong—too pale. The lanterns on the bridge guttered, and every shadow stretched long and unfamiliar, bending toward that seam. The air grew heavy, copper-sweet, metallic like blood in the mouth. Maude's skin prickled as if thousands of tiny hands brushed against her arms, curious. The smell changed: smoke, old incense, something damp and grave-cold threading beneath it all.

And the sound. *Saints*, the sound. The veil sang low, a deep current threading her bones, a cadence like a second heartbeat. Voices drifted through it, not whispers but impressions: laughter that was not laughter, crying that was not grief, names half-remembered. Bailey's voice, clear as bells, *Let go*—or maybe it was only the sound of her needing someone to say it. *Magic is meant to bind so it can loosen. Stop trying to hold the whole world by yourself, Maudie girl. You'll break your fingers.*

The veil didn't just open outward; it pressed inward—like standing at the mouth of a storm and feeling it reaching for you: your breath, your bones, the small spark that kept you tethered. Her vision blurred as the fabric of things rippled. The river split into two currents at once, one flowing white, the other black, as though every possibility of it existed together.

The bridge rails wavered, half iron, half bone. Her own hands flickered in and out of themselves. She tried to seize it, to force that flood into her lines, to drive it through the Weftmark's throat. It screamed back, ravenous. It wanted everything she had —and still clawed for more.

Heartache surged through Maude, stronger than the magic, teeth at her throat. The urge to step back nearly broke her—not from the spell, but from the ache that never left.

She clenched her jaw and shoved it down into the pocket where she'd already buried her joy. No room for either. Only the spell. Only the line.

The bridge bucked. Lanterns snapped free, spinning into the dark. Water below rose in fists of foam, slamming stone with the sound of applause turned violent.

Her knees wavered. Her voice cracked. She was slipping.

And then Wesley's hand closed over hers. Heat poured through her knuckles, a current steady enough to tell her body what to do when her mind locked.

"*Trust me*," he shouted over the veil's howl, voice hoarse and unflinching.

Grief wants rules, she remembered. *Give it rails and it will carry itself.*

So, Maude did the worst, bravest thing: she let Wesley in. She opened the channel they'd stumbled on before—between her magic and his craft, first discovered at the counter when grief and anger had nearly chewed her to paste. Sorrow bled into warmth like water into flour. It didn't vanish; it folded, stretched, turned malleable. His strength caught her fury and gave it shape.

The Weftmark drank. And this time, it drank true.

She felt the interlock's hunger meet the softness she'd braided into the ring—the promise of a place safe to be contained. The pull redirected. The lanterns stopped crying glass. Across town, canvas decided to be canvas. Wood decided to be wood. Two men who'd been stuck hip-to-hip in a macabre almost-embrace shuddered and stepped apart, blinking like they'd forgotten their own names.

On the bridge, the iron shuddered and then settled. The chalk line under their hands cooled. The moondust sheen sank like stars drowned in cloud. The river kept hurling itself at stone in that belligerent way rivers do when they love something enough to try to break it; the stone loved it back by not moving.

Maude's breath hitched. The quiet that followed wasn't empty. It was full.

"It listened."

She didn't say it for drama. She said it because the words arrived and deserved air.

Wesley looked at her the way people look at sunrise when they've been convinced the night is permanent. "You made it listen," he said, voice rough, reverent in a way that made her skin prickle.

Then he did something reckless, and also entirely obvious.

His hand found her waist, tugged her close—and before her brain could protest, his mouth was on hers.

Bright, fragile, firework mid-burst—she went still. The world stilled with her: river hushed, iron low, the veil sharp on her tongue.

Then the dam broke.

Her mouth met his, fierce, aching, like she'd been starving without knowing. Like she'd held her breath for months and only now remembered air lived here—in him, in this impossible closeness. Her hands fisted in his shirt, not to pull away, but to keep from falling.

Wesley stumbled with her, backing them into the rail, iron biting through her coat. The world tilted, steadied only by the desperate knot of their bodies.

It wasn't pretty. Pretty was for ballads. This was crushing, exhausted, startled—his hands sliding to her jaw, her mouth opening on a gasp that wasn't permission so much as recognition. He tasted of sugar and smoke and the warmth she'd been refusing since spring. Tears came the moment relief cracked her open. She hated that. She let them anyway.

"I've got you," he said against her mouth, against her cheek, into the place under her ear that heard truth first. He didn't loosen his hold when she shook. "You don't have to keep carrying everything by yourself."

It was as if he knew the words weren't only his—like he'd caught them drifting through the veil, whispered once by Bailey and now returned, full circle, to her.

"Let me hold some of it. Maude. Let me stay."

Her name in his mouth did something stupid to her lungs. The words stampeding in her chest jammed against her throat until it was a fist. The future loomed like an animal at the clearing's edge—wild, skittish, ready to bolt if she so much as looked at it.

So Maude did the only thing she trusted herself to do: she nodded—one small, furious, grateful dip—and leaned an inch closer. Just enough to admit she liked the way the world felt when he was holding it beside her.

Behind them, the square roared a different sound—cheers and shaky laughter, the sputter of one last firework drawing a pumpkin that arced and bowed across the sky.

Across the way Maude could see the magistrates fidgeting, caught between rage and a public they suddenly couldn't lead with a pitchfork. Veyne clutched his ledger like a life raft and looked personally offended by miracles.

Maude turned away, swiped her cheeks with the heel of her hand, and sat back. Wesley's thumb lingered at the edge of her jaw. He looked like he wanted to say more. She looked like she might allow it later.

They crossed the Bonebridge side by side—a little too close, a little too careful, as if one sudden move might startle the night back into chaos. Below, the river hurled itself at stone and survived. Lanterns swung. The town exhaled, something it hadn't known it was holding finally loosening, sliding back into place.

Maude didn't say thank you. Not because she wasn't grateful, but because if she opened that door, the flood would take them both. She did, however, let their fingers brush once. Twice. Then tangled for three heartbeats before she pretended she needed both hands for her satchel. *Growth*.

In the square, the wyvern fountain purred. The Weftmark held, content. Children restarted their stupid sword fights. Oli, predictably, found a drum and declared ownership. Selene leaned against a post with her arms folded and her smile quiet, watching Maude like she'd just witnessed a feral cat decide a human hand was a good place to sleep.

The night wasn't done with them. The town would still talk. Veyne would still scheme. There were ledgers to terrify and looms to tend and a hundred ways for everything to go crooked again. But the ground under Maude's boots was balanced. The pull in her chest had somewhere to go that wasn't an open wound. And when the music tilted toward another slow song—because the musicians had a sense of narrative—Wesley's hand found the small of her back like it had a homing rune inked into the skin.

She didn't say yes. She didn't say no.

She stepped forward.

That counted.

Twenty-Three

By the time the Samhain fires guttered out, Mistwood Hills had already spun the night into half a dozen contradictory tales.

Depending on whom you asked, Maude Harrow was either the savior of their sleepy village or its favorite villain finally caught mid-curse. The blame shifted: lanterns, magistrates, or—absurdly —flour. (She suspected Wesley planted that rumor just to keep people talking about something edible instead of her.)

Naturally, her brain clawed at her completed spell like a raccoon with a lockbox. Did she do it right? Did she actually? Or had she built the prettiest coffin anyone had ever seen?

She would find out eventually. *Maybe*. If the town didn't burn her first.

The veil closed just after midnight. Maude felt it—the moment the world whispered back to itself. Her looms purred under the cobbles, braiding calm into Mistwood's bones. The air prickled against her skin. And somewhere deep, she swore she heard Bailey's laugh cut through the dark, brief as a spark. She didn't look too hard. The veil always took as much as it gave.

Selene, of course, had no patience for existential dread. She'd insisted on buying every dessert they passed on the walk back from the square. "*For research*," she declared, cramming a honey-glazed fig into her mouth before Maude could point out that research usually didn't end with vomiting in an alley.

Wesley had kissed Maude's cheek good-night before vanishing back toward Sugar High. Selene and Oli squealed like children watching their first spell. Maude hexed their shoelaces together, sending them both sprawling across the cobbles, still shrieking with laughter.

Oli—glitter still shedding off him like dandruff—tried to drag her toward his manor afterward, promising "*post-festival debauchery.*" Maude declined with the sharpest smile she could muster. She broke off from them halfway down the lane, warm cider and too many fried pears heavy in her stomach, her chest heavier still.

She should've floated. Instead, she felt like she was wearing a borrowed coat that didn't fit. Her mind did what it always did when something good happened—*her specialty*: take a moment that felt almost like happiness, hold it to the light, then chip away until nothing remained but flaws, cracks, and the aftertaste of her own foolishness.

By the time she reached her cottage, she'd convinced herself of four things:

Wesley left early → obviously meant he regretted the kiss.

He'd smiled too much → definitely mocking her.

He'd danced with her → charity, clearly.

He hadn't come after her → proof, absolute proof, that he wanted nothing to do with her.

By the time Maude crawled into bed, she was convinced she'd hallucinated half of it. By the time she tossed through dawn, she was certain he'd only ever look at her with pity.

Which was why, when sleep gave up on her, she drew a ritual bath for clarity. Rosemary for focus, lavender for calm, mugwort to stir intuition, verbena for protection. The steam rose clean and green, the air thick with midnight and memory. *Clarity*, she told herself. *Or punishment.* She wasn't sure which she was better at.

By dawn, Maude had scrubbed her emotions raw and padded across the floor in her linen robe, hair dripping onto her collarbone, when the knock came.

Three raps. Not Selene's impatient fist. Not Oli's theatrical cadence.

Her stomach went cold anyway.

She opened the door.

And there he was.

Wesley Rivers, leaning on her threshold like he'd argued with himself the whole walk over. His shirt was rumpled, his jaw tense, his eyes—saints, his eyes—lined with exhaustion. He looked like he hadn't slept either.

Maude's heart slammed. She braced for impact.

"Sorry for leaving early," he said, hesitant. "I shouldn't have—"

Here it was. The speech. The tidy undoing. The confirmation her mind had gnawed on all night.

She cut him off. "It's fine." She stepped back, already closing the door. "You don't need to explain."

His hand caught the wood before it shut.

"Don't do this," she said. "Whatever that was at the festival—it doesn't matter."

"It does." His voice cut harder than she expected. "It matters."

She gave a brittle laugh, shaking her head. "You're wrong. I know what I am. And it's not something people keep."

His brows drew tight, frustration flickering under the exhaustion. "Don't tell me what I want."

"Then don't pretend you know what I am." The words spilled fast, a shield she couldn't stop raising. "I'm not soft. I'm not easy. I've never been good at—" she gestured, robe sleeve flaring like a wing, "—any of this. I don't work with people. I don't bend. I don't fit. Every time I've forgotten that, I've regretted it."

"Maude—"

"*No*, hear me. You'll grow to hate me. You'll want someone pliable. Someone who doesn't bite when cornered. Someone who doesn't burn everything she touches. That's not me. It's never been me."

Wesley stepped closer, heartbreak raw in his eyes, enough to make her stomach lurch. He cupped her face, palms rough and warm. "I don't need you soft and easy, Maude. I need you exactly as you are. Fierce. Stubborn. Brilliant. The cracks you think make you broken—the edges you think cut too deep—they're beautiful. Every piece of you is."

She stared at him, heart in freefall. Her robe belt cinched too tight. Her fingers itched to break something, anything, to release the pressure. A tear slid down her cheek, hot, traitorous. His thumb brushed it away as if it were holy.

Her heart stuttered. "You're wrong," she said again, softer this time.

The corner of his mouth ticked up. He leaned forward, bit her bottom lip—gently. His breath ghosted against her mouth. "Liar."

Her knees nearly buckled.

"Say what you know is true."

Her pulse pounded everywhere at once. She pulled back just enough to see his eyes, and there it was—clearer than daylight, truer than any spell she'd ever cast. The look he'd been giving her for weeks. Maybe longer. Maybe since the start.

"You want me," she breathed.

He smiled, soft and devastating, and pressed his lips to the spot he'd just nicked. "*So badly*, witch."

Her breathing turned shaky. They shared the same air, every inhale and exhale tangled. His hands shook against her skin—not hesitation, but restraint. He was waiting. For her. Always waiting.

"Wesley," she sighed—half a moan, half a warning.

They came together all at once, hungry and graceless. His fingers tangled in her hair, tugging just enough to pull a gasp from her. She clutched his shoulders, then his back, arms locking tight before thought could catch up to her body.

He stepped forward, crowding her into the frame, and kicked the door shut. The slam rattled the beams, a shudder that seemed to run through both of them.

Her robe loosened under his grip, slipping off one shoulder, fabric sighing against her skin. She bunched his shirt in both fists, yanking hard enough to feel the buttons strain. He only laughed into her mouth—low, breathless, wicked—and the sound melted her bones, sent heat sparking everywhere his body pressed against hers.

Maude exhaled, eyes dragging over him—the strength she'd always known was there, the clean lines of muscle tapering to his tight stomach. Her fingers found the ties at his pants just as his slipped to the sash at her waist. He tugged it loose, slow, reverent, until the robe slid from her shoulders and pooled at her feet. She stood bare before him, trembling breath catching in her throat.

His chest rose once, stalled. The air left him as if he'd been struck. "Beautiful," he whispered.

Maude rose on her toes and brushed her lips against his. "You already said that."

His mouth curved before he crushed her against him, kissing her hard. His tongue tangled with hers, heat sparking as his hands slid down to grip her backside, dragging her flush against him until she felt him hard—pressed against her.

Wesley groaned, thrusting forward as he broke from her lips to trail down her throat. Slow. Worshipful. His mouth found her breast, closing over her with a hunger that was aching, inexorable —as if he'd been waiting forever and refused to be gentle about it.

Maude panted against him, fingers tangled in his hair.

And then the growl came.

Shit.

Grim sat in the hallway like a king catching his subjects in scandal, tail curled, eyes glowing with judgment.

"Sorry, Grim," Wesley muttered, not sounding sorry at all.

Then he glanced back at Maude, breathless in his arms. "Where's your room?"

Still dazed, she managed to point a shaky finger upstairs.

In the next breath, Wesley scooped her up—cradled her like she was some tragic fair maiden—and took the stairs two at a time.

She hated how much she didn't hate it.

In the room, he lowered her onto the bed and just looked. His gaze moved slow, as though he meant to memorize her piece by piece. Heat climbed her cheeks, and for the first time in longer than she wanted to admit, she fought the urge to hide.

Her eyes slipped downward, catching the way he undid the ties of his pants. Her breath caught; her mouth went dry. She bit her lip without thinking—and the sound that broke from him, low and ragged, cut through her like heat. A sound she knew she'd chase again and again, if only to feel this impossibly, terrifyingly alive.

He moved toward her carefully, every shift across the mattress measured, as though approaching a spell that might bolt if handled wrong. His eyes burned when he reached her—so much want, so much patience—that she hooked her leg around his and rolled them.

In a beat, he was flat on his back, breath knocked out of him, staring up at her with startled eyes before laughter burst free.

She leaned back, smug, hair falling like a curtain between them.

"I knew it," he said, grin crooked, gaze burning. "Knew you'd be bossy in bed, too."

Maude tried to suppress the smile tugging at her lips. Impossible. It broke free anyway, and in his gaze—shining, open, undoing her at the seams—she let it stay.

Then his hand slid up, firm at the back of her neck, guiding her down until their mouths met again. The pressure of him left her panting, every breath caught between protest and need.

She pushed back, fumbling only a moment before tugging off

his pants. When she freed him, her breath stuttered, heat pooling low in her belly.

Her hand worked over him—up, down—greedy for every velvet-hard inch. She didn't linger. She wanted more, wanted all of him, so she took him into her mouth. His taste flooded her senses: salt, heat, and something entirely his. She moaned around him, the sound vibrating down his length.

Wesley's voice broke. He gasped her name as if it had been punched out of him, raw enough to brand her.

She dragged her lips from him slowly, savoring the wrecked look on his face, then crawled higher. Her knees bracketed his hips, body trembling with urgency as she sank down onto him.

It was slow—*agonizingly* so. Every inch claimed had her chest hammering harder, her breath catching in small bursts. Their eyes locked, and the world narrowed to the space between them, to the stretch and the heat and the way he gripped her like he might drown without the anchor of her body.

His hands roamed as if he couldn't decide where to venerate first—her thighs, her waist, the swell of her breasts, the curve of her face—before circling back, restless with awe. Everywhere, all at once.

They moved together, and fire curled through her core, wild and consuming—and for once Maude didn't feel jagged or wrong. She felt wanted. Warm. Cherished. And lov—

She cut the thought off before it could take flight, shoved it into the locked box where dangerous things belonged, and kissed him instead, whimpering when he caught her tongue between his lips like he meant to keep it.

Wesley's hand clamped at the base of her neck, firm, possessive, the other gripping her waist hard enough to brand before driving upward—a brutal snap of his hips that punched the air from her lungs.

She broke with it, a cry ripped from her throat as he surged inside her again and again, faster, harder, the bedframe rattling to the rhythm of his body against hers. Every thrust stole her breath, bent her spine, tipped her head back until her voice shattered on every exhale.

Lights detonated behind her eyes, white-hot and merciless, as release tore through her. Her toes curled, nails scraping across his shoulders, and she screamed into the night as if the spell itself had claimed her. Wesley never faltered. He worked her through it, drawing every last cry until her voice broke into soft mewls, her body trembling.

Only then—when she was wrecked and pliant, chest heaving—did he shift. With a low groan, Wesley flipped her onto her back, pinning her to the mattress in one smooth motion.

"I could spend a year learning every sound you make," he murmured against her skin, voice rough as gravel. His mouth trailed down the inside of her thigh, lips brushing sensitive flesh before he sucked hard enough to leave a mark. His hands slid higher, fingers urging her knees apart.

And then—*saints*—his mouth was on her. No hesitation, no mercy. The first stroke of his tongue had her jolting, too tender, too sensitive, but he only sighed against her, like her shaking was the only language he wanted. He licked into her slowly at first, a lazy tease that had her fists clenching the sheets, before his tongue flattened and dragged, before his lips sealed around her and sucked until she was arching off the bed.

She was undone in seconds, broken apart with his name caught between her teeth. He drank every bit of her down with a hunger that felt endless until she went slack beneath him, boneless and floating.

Only then did he crawl back up the length of her body, breath ragged in her ear as he disappeared inside her again.

He cursed—low, vicious, a word she'd never heard from his mouth before—and it made her clench around him, made her shiver. His mouth found hers, slower now, deep and unhurried. His kisses tasted of her, of devotion, of something that made her chest ache. One hand cradled her neck, thumb stroking the frantic pulse there; the other tangled tight in her hair.

They moved differently this time—languid, deep, each thrust a conversation she didn't dare translate. Tears burned at the back of her eyes, temper rising that something so wrecking could feel so close to absolution.

Still, the tide built. Release coiled low, tightening with every thrust, every ragged sound in his throat. Wesley shook above her, cursing into her mouth—half-broken, half-pleading. She sobbed against him as it tore through her, the world blurring white. He followed with a guttural sound, dragging her down into the wreckage with him.

Neither of them moved for a long moment. Their breaths tangled, hot and uneven, his forehead pressed to hers. His weight pinned her—not suffocating, but grounding. Safe.

When she finally managed a breath that wasn't shattered, Wesley shifted carefully, easing out of her with a low groan. His hands stayed steady as he reached for the blanket at the foot of the bed, pulling it over them with a gentleness that made Maude's throat ache. He brushed damp curls from her cheek, his thumb lingering.

"You're trembling," he murmured, tucking her closer, guiding her to his chest. His hand swept down her back slowly, until her muscles stopped twitching. His lips pressed against her temple.

The quiet grew between them, shaped into something almost sacred by the even thrum of his heart under her ear. "You're a human furnace," Maude said at last, because if she didn't say something she'd drown in it.

"That's my best quality."

"Don't get cocky."

"Never," he whispered, his smile curving into her hair like a secret.

He kissed her lips, feather-light, lingering as though pressing his promise into her skin. His hand smoothed over her arm, down her side, centering her bit by bit back into herself. Every motion devoted, as if he believed she was worth memorizing.

Finally, she let herself believe it, too.

Maude's breath steadied. Her eyelids grew heavy. She tried to resist—stubborn as ever—but his warmth, his steadiness, the way his hand kept tracing quiet shapes against her skin...it was too much.

So she let go. Curled into him. Let herself be held. And slipped under.

Twenty-Four

A week vanished. Not in the way time usually dragged—barbed and heavy—but in a blur of warmth, limbs, and far too much bread.

For the first time in her life, Maude closed her shop without guilt, flipped the sign with a kind of feral delight. She let Wesley tug her across the street to his apartment above the bakery—a space warmed by ovens, layered with clutter and comfort, his presence in every corner. And she stayed.

They made love in the mornings, sunlight crawling across the low rafters. They ate until they were stuffed, Wesley pulling dish after dish from his oven like a sorcerer showing off—flatbreads dripping with honey and herbs, spiced stews that stained their mouths red, little cream-stuffed cakes that made Maude groan indecently enough to make him smirk and start kissing the sugar from her lips.

Afternoons vanished under quilts, pressed together as they read *The Verdant Trials* aloud. He took the heroic voices, overdramatic and booming, while she deadpanned through the rest until they were both laughing so hard they had to stop. When the plot turned devastating—as the series always did—they read quieter, their shoulders pressed tight together, her chest aching in a way that had nothing to do with fiction.

Then, inevitably, he'd set the book aside and touch her like she was a page he couldn't stop rereading.

Halfway through the week, Grim found them, yowling at the window as if to remind Maude she had responsibilities beyond being scandalously adored. Wesley muttered about *"privacy contracts"* with cats but opened the window anyway. The beast sauntered in, curled on Maude's chest like a stone idol, and refused to leave. When Wesley tried to evict him—*twice*—he retaliated by ripping his claws into a pillow. They reached an uneasy truce.

Oli and Selene checked in once, peering through the bakery like nosy parents. Selene left a basket of fruit on the step. Oli winked so hard Maude considered cursing him with permanent eyelid spasms. Then, mercifully, they vanished again. By the seventh day, even Maude had to admit civilization probably required their reentry before their shops crumbled. They lay tangled, the room hot with candlelight and breath, bodies slick with sweat from the latest round of trying to undo each other in increasingly inventive ways.

That was when Wesley whispered it.

"I—*fuck*, Maude—I love you."

It slipped out between one breathless motion and another, his cheek pressed to her shoulder, voice cracked with effort and heat.

She froze.

He froze.

His face went scarlet, red climbing his neck so fast that Maude half-wondered if she'd accidentally cursed him.

"It's okay," she said quickly, swiping a hand over his burning cheek. "That happens sometimes during sex. I know you didn't mean it."

He dropped his forehead to hers, eyes squeezed shut. Then, with a gentleness that made her throat close, he said, "No. I meant it. I'm in love with you, Maude."

The world narrowed.

He kissed her nose, her temple, her jaw—punctuation marks to every memory. "Since the moment you called me a bakery bastard. Since you scowled at me across that cursed counter and refused to let me charm you. Since you stood in the square with everyone against you and didn't bend. Every minute I've spent with you, it's only gotten worse—or better. Both. I don't care how short it's been. I don't care if it's mad. I'm crazy about you."

Her eyes burned. Tears slid hot and unstoppable, cutting down her cheeks.

"I love you," he whispered again, forehead pressed to hers. "And don't you dare try to convince me otherwise."

Her heart felt too big for her ribs. Words scattered like leaves in a storm. All Maude managed was "*Okay.*"

Not a declaration. Not a promise. But maybe the bravest word she'd ever said.

He laughed, breath shaking. "*Okay.*"

By the time they stepped back into town, the world had adjusted the way Mistwood Hills always did: with gossip, exaggeration, and, eventually, begrudging acceptance.

Maude reopened the Emporium after her week of exile and found the line curling out the door. Not for healing tonics. Not for poultices. For *pastries*.

"Not mine," she snapped at the first woman who asked. "Do I look like I bake?"

But Wesley—traitor—had already thought ahead. He pitched the idea like it was simple: spell-touched sweets, pre-made batches they could churn out in bulk so people wouldn't bother her during the day. His dough, her herbs. Pastries that eased headaches. Tarts that sharpened focus. Breads that let the over-worked sleep like the dead.

He insisted their creations needed a name. After days of pestering, bribes of frosted cakes, and kisses that left her dizzy, she finally caved. On the little parchment labels, in her grim scrawl, it read: **Sugar Spells.**

Each box bore her warning: *One per day. Don't be greedy. Side effects may include feeling less insufferable.*

Naturally, they sold out within hours.

The oddity shop became legend—a bakery-apothecary hybrid no one had asked for, and which everyone bragged about visiting.

Oli, meanwhile, made good on his schemes. Promises turned into votes, the votes into a magistrate's seat. He celebrated by throwing a party so lavish half the city came just to gawk.

"Now I can actually keep you from getting executed," Oli told Maude proudly, crown of ivy slipping sideways on his head.

"Touching," she said. "Remind me to embroider *Not Dead Because of Oli* on a pillow when I get home."

But she was proud of him. And then—she didn't know what possessed her—she admitted it out loud.

Oli looked beside himself, like he'd been handed a medal, a kingdom, and permission to never shut up about it again.

Selene thrived at the Lantern Ward, carrying Maude's tinc-tures with her and pretending she'd brewed them herself. And Maude...she walked lighter. She still scowled, still snapped, still hexed Veyne's ledger once for daring to lean too close to her shelves. But she wasn't walking alone anymore. Wesley was always a few steps across the street—or right beside her—brushing ash from her sleeve like it was his right.

One evening, when the shop was shuttered and the lanterns swayed low, she climbed the hill to Bailey's grave. She carried no herbs, no offerings. Just herself—and the battered wooden box she'd kept hidden under her bed.

The runes carved into the headstone glowed a faint amber, as if waiting.

Maude sat in the grass, knees drawn up, and rested the box between them. Her hand lingered on the scarred lid. "You didn't get to finish it," she said softly. "So I did. The interlock. Just a fragment, that's all you left me—half a thought scribbled down before the ink dried. But I carried it forward. Line by line, rune by rune, I finished it for you." Her throat tightened, but she pressed on. "It felt like sitting beside you again. Like hearing you mutter through the ink. Every mark, every stitch of it...it was you. And now it's whole." She let out a shaky laugh. "It's clumsy in places, probably not how you would've done it. But it's done, Bailey. And it's ours."

She pressed the box to the base of the stone, leaving it there like an offering.

"I don't know how to do this," she admitted. Her voice felt too loud out here, even though it was only a murmur swallowed by the grass. The graveyard held sound differently. Words clung to leaning stones and ivy-choked fences, caught in the damp air. "Letting go. Not blaming you. Not...carrying you around like proof I didn't dream the good parts."

Her hand scraped across her face, rough, furious at the wet there. "You were brilliant," she said, the word dragged out like a splinter. "And impossible. And sometimes I hated you—hated you for leaving me with nothing but a half-finished spell and a shop drowning in bills. But saints, Bailey...you gave me everything too."

Her words drifted into the wind, and it answered softly, brushing her hair across her face.

"I'm still angry," she confessed, fingers clawing at the dirt until it lodged under her nails. "But I'm alive. I'm fighting. And I think—I think I might even be happy. Which is disgusting—and, if I'm right, entirely your fault."

The grass bent under her grip. Her tears fell hot, streaking the earth.

"I'll never stop missing you," she whispered. "But I can't carry you like a chain anymore."

The wind stirred, soft as breath, lifting the hair at her temple. She pressed her palm flat to the stone, the cool runes humming faintly against her skin. "I love you," she said. Then, with more weight, more marrow: "And—thank you. For all of it."

She let him go that night. Not forgotten. Never forgotten. But the chain was no longer locked around her ribs.

When she turned, Wesley was waiting at the edge of the graveyard path. He hadn't followed her in, hadn't intruded. He simply stood among the leaning stones, steady as the old oaks that ringed the place, moonlight catching on his ashy blond hair. Shadows draped his shoulders, but his face was lit clean by the pale wash of the night sky, eyes fixed only on her.

He didn't speak. Didn't push. Just lifted his hand when she reached him, palm open, waiting.

This time, she didn't hesitate before taking it.

Market Square looked different now that Maude wasn't bracing for pitchforks. Lanterns from the festival still hung above, but instead of dripping molten glass, they only swayed in the morning breeze, faded streamers fluttering like shed skins. The stalls glittered with sugared fruit and polished trinkets, vendors hawking the last of their autumn charms and spiced brews before the town turned its face toward the winter rites. It happened every year—one final frenzy, a chance to wring the dregs of the harvest into coin before the holly and frost took over.

The air was thick with honeyed nuts, mulled wine gone sour at the rim, woodsmoke laced with pine. Merchants shouted their specials over one another like it was a blood sport. Children tore past shrieking, rolling dramatically across the cobbles in some invented game about demon hunters.

And at the center, beneath the wyvern fountain, the Weftmark ring glowed faintly—a reminder that things could break and still be held together.

People glanced at Maude as she passed. Not all friendly. Not all kind. But no longer with that sharp suspicion. They were... curious. Uneasy, yes, but no longer ready to shove her into the river. It was, she thought, exactly the kind of scene that used to make her scowl until her jaw ached. The kind that smelled too much like hope and humanity and all the things she'd once sworn didn't fit her bones.

But today, she walked through it. Coffee in hand. Grim perched imperiously on her shoulder, tail curled around her neck like a furry necklace. And *still*—most shocking of all—Wesley at her side, matching her stride so easily it looked rehearsed.

He handed her a pastry, like he'd somehow known she wanted it. She pretended at innocence after snatching it out of his hand.

"Breakfast number two," he said mildly.

"Your concern for my blood sugar is touching," she replied around a bite.

Oli swept toward them in a coat that looked like it had devoured three others just to achieve maximum drama, a magistrate's sash slung across his chest.

"My constituents!" he cried. "Rejoice, for I have graced you with my presence."

A child immediately hurled a half-eaten roll at him.

Oli caught it midair and took a bite. "*Delicious*. See? Democracy works."

"Saints help us," Maude muttered.

"My favorite witch and her besotted baker," he sang, sweeping into an extravagant bow. "And Grim, of course—our true ruler."

"Bow lower," Maude said without missing a beat. "Maybe you'll reach your humility."

Selene appeared behind him, hair mussed from the morning rush at the Lantern Ward, an armful of jars balanced precariously. "Don't encourage him, Maude. He hasn't stopped talking about his magistrate's seat since sunrise. I had to pretend a patient was vomiting blood just to get him to leave."

"I saw through it," Oli said smugly.

Selene rolled her eyes.

"Next time, fake your own death," Maude said, not looking up from her coffee. "More convincing."

"Careful, witch," Oli said, sweeping into their path. "You're positively radiant this morning. A week in bed with a baker will do that, won't it?"

Wesley choked on his coffee, but Maude didn't miss a step. "At least mine delivers more than breadcrumbs."

Oli clutched his chest like he'd been fatally wounded. "I'm under appreciated in this friend group," he declared. "History will remember me as the glue."

"Glue that never shuts up," Maude muttered.

Wesley pinched her arm. "Rude."

"Please," Selene laughed. "The only thing worse than his monologues is his...wheezing."

"Excuse me," Oli said, "I am a delight."

"You snore."

"I *purr*."

"You *howl*."

Wesley cleared his throat, cheeks still faintly pink. "Can we not?"

"No," all three of them said at once.

They wove together through the bustle, their odd little quartet slipping in and out of stalls. Oli couldn't walk ten steps without someone congratulating him on his "*victory for progress*," which he accepted as if he'd just slain a dragon instead of bribed three aldermen with coin and flattery. Selene bartered with every herb vendor they passed, muttering about Lydia Dross under her breath. Grim leapt from Maude's shoulder to Wesley's arm and back again like a tiny, furry diplomat.

Maude pretended to be annoyed. Secretly, she loved it.

At the edge of the square, children were rehearsing the next festival's play. A tiny girl in a witch's hat swung a wooden sword nearly her own height and shouted, "Back, foul baker!" at a boy in a flour-streaked apron costume.

Wesley froze, staring. Maude nearly choked on her coffee.

Oli doubled over. "Oh, this is art. This is social commentary."

"Shut up," Wesley said without heat, but his ears went pink.

Selene leaned in, stage-whispering, "You should ask them for pointers."

Maude smirked up at him. *"Foul baker."*

His eyes cut to hers, dark and heady. He leaned close enough that only she could hear. "Say it again, and I'll show you just how wicked I can be."

Heat curled through her. She shoved another bite of pastry into her mouth before her face could give her away.

At one stall, they bought honeycomb wrapped in paper, the sweetness sticking to their fingers. At another, Selene insisted on candied apples and Oli purchased a bag of roasted nuts and scattered them in Grim's path, declaring him *"the god of crunch."*

Grim accepted the offering with regal disdain.

It was warm. It was ridiculous. It was the kind of day Maude had convinced herself she wasn't allowed to have.

By noon, they collapsed on the fountain steps, stomachs heavy with food, cider steam curling through the air, the four of them piled together in an arrangement that made no sense and somehow worked. Selene leaned against Oli, who insisted he didn't mind her drooling on his sash. Grim stretched luxuriously across Maude's lap, tail twitching every time Wesley's hand strayed close.

The square buzzed around them—music, laughter, the smell of frying dough. And for once, Maude didn't feel like the dark cloud hovering above it all. She felt...part of it.

Wesley caught her watching him. Not just looking—studying, like she couldn't stop. His mouth curved, that quiet smile that undid her every time.

She looked away fast. "Your hair's stupid."

"Thank you," he said gravely.

"Don't agree with me."

"Wouldn't dream of it."

Oli groaned. "Gods, you both are nauseating already."

Selene smacked him with her apple stick. "Shut up. They're cute."

Maude flipped her hood up to hide the color in her cheeks. Wesley's fingers brushed hers where their hands rested on the stone.

For a long moment, she let it sink in—Oli, smirking like he owned the entire village. Selene, laughing as she poked holes in his arrogance. Wesley, steadying the coffee in her hand before it tipped. Grim, grooming himself with indifference for the entire human race.

Her people. Somehow.

It wasn't the picture she'd imagined. But it was the one she had. And, for once, she didn't want to trade it.

Oli raised his cider in a mock toast. "To survival. To power. To scandal."

"To not hexing you in public," Maude said, raising her coffee.

"To Bailey," Selene said softly, her eyes flicking toward Maude.

The name hit her chest like it always did—but it didn't hollow her out this time. It filled her, steady as the loom's hum beneath the cobbles.

"To Bailey," Maude echoed. Her voice didn't break.

Wesley's hand found hers on the bench, warm and sure. She let him keep it.

The day rolled on—merchants shouting, Grim stealing, Oli preening, Selene teasing.

Normal. Alive.

When they finally rose to leave, the square was bathed in late light, lanterns glowing like constellations overhead. Wesley handed her a fresh cup of coffee, because of course he had thought ahead. Grim hopped back onto her shoulder like he owned the world.

They walked out of Market Square side by side, still bickering, still themselves. Only now, Maude was smiling.

Epilogue

Wesley's bakery was bright because he'd made it that way—liked it that way.

He polished every pane of glass himself until the morning light spilled through like honey. Pastel boxes stood in neat rows, ribbons tied straight enough to satisfy even the fussiest aunt in Mistwood.

He wanted it to feel warm when people walked in. Easy. Which was why he burned the first tray of scones every week— *"insurance against getting too full of himself,"* he claimed—and whistled so loudly in the mornings that the neighbors complained. He made the shop smile for him, even if it meant scrubbing counters with too much elbow grease or slipping an extra dusting of sugar where only the light would notice.

Because to Wesley Rivers, a bakery should do more than feed people. It should trick them, if only for a moment, into believing the world wasn't quite as cruel as it liked to be.

He checked the ovens twice before dawn. Lined the counters with flatbreads that still sighed steam when torn. He sang while he worked, and when the words slipped his mind, he invented new ones that rhymed badly.

Because Wesley liked bright. He wanted bright.

And yet, his favorite corner in Sugar High Bakery wasn't bright at all.

He'd carved it out for her—the shadow in the back where the windows didn't quite reach. A wrought-iron table, black cushions instead of pink, a crooked little shelf of books leaning like conspirators against the wall. A pot of rosemary in place of roses. A candle that burned green instead of gold.

Her place. His witch's nest, tucked in among all the sugar and cream.

Maude sat there now—hood tipped low, curls spilling loose, a book balanced on her lap while Grim draped himself around the rosemary pot like poured ink. She looked utterly at ease, utterly out of place, and impossibly his.

Wesley's chest ached with it—this quiet vision of her. He drank her in as though her presence alone might sustain him. Every glance was a feast. Every scowl a prayer. Saints, she didn't even know.

Maude lifted her head when he laughed, as if the sound tugged her by some invisible thread. Her eyes caught his across the bakery. Green. Striking. And then she glanced away like she hadn't looked at all.

When she closed her book and rose, his pulse leapt. He tried for neutral, casual, the same face he wore for customers. But this wasn't a customer. This was Maude Harrow—witch, curse-breaker, sharp-tongued, impossible—the woman who had wound through him like breath, unnoticed until the thought of losing it left him gasping.

"Need a hand?"

He blinked once, certain he'd misheard, then again, because his heart had the audacity to leap. "You—" he said, unable to mask the shock. "You want to help."

"Yes. Don't make it a thing." She crossed her arms, a smile tugging at her mouth. "I've spent weeks mocking this place. Might as well see what all the fuss is about before I die."

His throat worked before he managed, low, "Come on, then,"

sweeping the counter clear like he hadn't been waiting weeks for her to want this.

She stepped up, and the air shifted. The counter glowed faintly in the firelight, dusted with sugar instead of flour. He set a bowl before her: dark chocolate, chopped fine, every shard gleaming like a heap of black jewels in the low light.

"Tempering," he said. "We're making truffles."

Her brow arched. "Sounds violent."

"Don't worry, the casualties are mostly spoons."

He showed her—the melting over low heat, the steady stir, the pour onto the marble slab. The rhythm of scrape and fold, dragging the shine back into the chocolate before it dulled. She didn't scoff. She watched, lips pressed, eyes intent. Her attempt was clumsy. Too much wrist, not enough patience—the chocolate streaked and refused to gloss. She swore under her breath, and he bit back a grin that threatened to give him away.

"Not bad," he said, gently.

"Don't patronize me."

"Wouldn't dare."

The next fold came smoother, less fight in her wrist, more focus in her hand. She caught the rhythm faster than he expected —scrape, lift, fold, the sheen returning under her stubborn persistence. He slowed his own pace until it matched hers, steady beside fierce, the sound of metal on marble finding a cadence that belonged to them both.

She muttered every time the chocolate resisted. He hummed absently, as he always did when baking. And somehow, the two sounds twined together, rough and soft, until the air in the bakery felt charged with more than just the scent of cocoa.

And then Maude did the last thing he ever expected—she sang.

Not words; just a melody, low and unguarded, spilling out of her as her eyes burned and the sound threaded through the warm kitchen air.

Wesley's hands went still. The tune was simple, lilting, *old*. It slid beneath his skin, hooking deep, tugging at nerves long gone numb. His chest tightened, breath catching wrong in his lungs. He didn't know the melody—couldn't place it—yet some part of him leaned toward it with the certainty that he'd once known every note. It felt like home, like warmth, like safety—like something he'd lost and only now remembered to miss.

His head tilted, eyes narrowing. "I've heard this before," he said, searching her face. "Haven't I?"

Maude's smile trembled, brittle with sorrow. She let the melody slip from her lips, quiet as a secret, until the last note faded.

Silence lingered, broken only by the hearth's crackle and Grim's low, contented purr.

"What was that?" His voice was careful. "A spell?"

"No." Her throat worked. "Not a spell. A memory. A... feeling."

"Yours?"

She shook her head, whispering, "No. Yours."

Wesley's brow furrowed. "Maude, I—"

"When you hummed it," she said quickly, eyes fixed on the chocolate as if it might save her, "back when we first met—I hated it. I thought you were just trying to get under my skin. And then I realized...it wasn't for me at all. It was for you. For *her*."

Wesley froze. Something flickered through him—grief? Wonder? Both, knotted so tightly he couldn't pull them apart.

Her. She meant...

His chest drew taut, ribs straining against a memory that wasn't there. No matter how hard he reached, he couldn't find it. He couldn't remember his mother's face—not the way he once had. But the song—*saints*, the song...it was hers.

Maude's voice shook, but she pressed on. "I kept it. Because you gave it up. Somebody had to hold it. Somebody had to remember."

His head shook before he realized he was moving. "Maude, I don't—" His voice cracked. He tried again, hoarse. "I don't understand."

Her chin lifted, color flaring high across her cheeks. Her green eyes burned—wet, furious, unguarded—and in them lived every sleepless night, every wall she'd built brick by brick, now splitting all at once.

"It means I love you, idiot."

The words struck like a blow, then unfurled like wings. He swayed with them, drunk, undone. His mouth went dry. He tried to laugh, to breathe, to move, but all he could do was stare—at her, at those verdant eyes burning into him as though she'd branded truth across his heart.

He felt it—her love—imprinted upon him as though the very fibers of his being had been stitched with it, indelible and irrevocable. And for once, Wesley Rivers, the man who always had a quip, a grin, an easy way out, found himself speechless.

"Say it again," he managed at last, the plea ripping out before he could stop it. He needed to hear it—needed it the way the tide needs moon, the way hands reach for warmth in winter.

"I love you." Tears clung to her lashes. "Fiercely. Stubbornly. Like a curse I can't undo."

His laugh broke, raw, almost a sob. He cupped her face in chocolate-sticky hands. Salt streaked his lips as he kissed her tears away. "I love you too," he whispered against her mouth. "So much it's absurd."

"Absurd suits us."

It did. Absurd. Perfect. Them.

Her smile outshone every corner of his laughably bright bakery. Every time, it unmade him. He thought he'd be ready for it by now. He never was.

The chocolate lay forgotten. Grim leapt onto the counter, tail flicking as he settled in to watch them with glowing eyes, the picture of feline judgment. Maude laughed against Wesley's mouth, tears still shining, and he thought he could live a thousand lifetimes and never have enough of her.

He was hers. Entirely.

Always.

Acknowledgments

To my husband, Michael—thank you for always believing in me, for holding space for my dreams, and for standing beside me with unwavering love. You are my anchor, my safe place, and my loudest cheer. None of this would exist without you, and every page is touched by your faith in me.

To my editor, Allison—your vision, guidance, and wisdom shaped this story into its strongest form. I am deeply grateful for your encouragement, insight, and steady hand throughout the journey. And to my proofreader, Erin—your careful eye, precision, and dedication brought clarity and polish, helping this book shine.

To my alpha readers, Sahra and Gloria—your generosity, honesty, and encouragement strengthened this tale in ways I never could have achieved alone. Thank you for giving so freely of your time, thoughts, and hearts.

To my children, Davey, Charlie, and Thomas—you bring laughter and light into every day. Your silliness, and the way you believe in me make me want to keep going, to keep writing, and to keep chasing these dreams. I hope you always know how much of my heart is written with you in mind.

And to Jessica—always.

About the Author

J.M. Grosvalet is an author based in the Washington, D.C. area. When she isn't lost in her stories, she can usually be found in her garden tending herbs and wildflowers, a mug of tea cooling beside her and paint smudges on her hands. She has a soft spot for rainy days, old books, and anything that smells like lavender.

At home, she shares life with her husband and best friend, their three wild boys who keep her laughing (and a little grey-haired), two loyal dogs, and a very opinionated cat.

Her stories are woven with myth, magic, and melancholy, exploring the strength it takes to hold onto hope and the beauty found in even the darkest places.